THE RIVERRUN
TRILOGY

VOLUME THREE

YESTERN

S.P. SOMTOW
THE RIVERRUN TRILOGY
CHRONICLES OF THE HOUSE OF DARKLING

VOLUME III

yestern

DIPLODOCUS PRESS
BANGKOK · LOS ANGELES

yestern

originally published in an omnibus
edition by White Wolf Publishing, 1996
This Edition Diplodocus Press 2013

published by Diplodocus Press
Bangkok • Los Angeles
Main Office • 48 Sukhumvit Soi 33
Bangkok 10110, Thailand

for information about the author:
www.somtow.com
about this publisher
www.diplodocuspress.com

ISBN
Trade Paper 978-0-9860533-9-9
Hardcover 978-0-9900142-2-5

0 9 8 7 6 5 4 3 2 1

dedicated with love to

Judy,

from me and Johnny,

in memory of your last July Fourth,
when we gave you the opals, and
you told us we were the two most
important men in your life.

Contents

Book Four: Recapitulation
Howl, Howl, Howl

Book Five: Coda
Fadograph

Row, row, row your boat
Up, against the stream;
If you fail you'll drown, and life
Will just have been a dream.

Book One:

Exposition: First Subject
The Etchisons

"I breathe the air from another planet...."
—Arnold Schoenberg

from a Sotheby's Catalogue:

On Truth
by
Philip Etchison

My writing block, it seems, is permanent. As a result, I find my annual address from the poetry chair of this august institution to be more and more of a joke, year after year. What can one talk about, when one has been struck dumb? What eternal verities may I discourse on? Do I have a right to discourse at all?

I have decided to venture into the treacherous shoals of ontology....

The greatest minds of all time have striven to answer the great question once posed by Pontius Pilate. Well, not all. Jesus Christ, to whom that question was addressed, managed to avoid answering it. And the Lord Buddha managed to skirt the issue by telling us that Truth does not exist.

I had more or less reached the same conclusion when, one morning, I heard a sound which I knew, instinctively and unquestioningly, to be an Absolute Truth. The sound came from my seven-year-old son Chris, who has been diagnosed by some as autistic, and who cannot, or does not choose to, speak....

— *coffee-stained ms. found in a shredder at Blair House, Washington, DC , along with a prescription for Prozac. Believed to be in the handwriting of Philip Etchison. (Analysis available for viewing one week before the auction, 9 a.m. through 4:30 p.m.)*

— *offered by an Anonymous Source.*

— *reserve $15,000*

One
Christmas in the White House

Serena Somers:

It was the 90s, the time before the mad millennium. But a dollar could no longer buy a Coke and a candy bar; indeed, the 90s had only a few more days to run. Indeed, some people would have said they were over, but the man I worked for was quite particular about how the first year of the new millennium was not 2000, but 2001.

"It's simple math," he would tell me, staring at me with those wide, ingenuous eyes, "because there is no year zero. If we were computers then I'd say yes, the first millennium goes from zero to nine nine nine, the second from one thousand to one nine nine nine. But it ain't so. Ask Arthur C. Clarke — he wrote the book on it." And did not chuckle, of course, at his own joke, for he was a man who expected others to provide the laugh track, the punditry, the musical accompaniment to his every sound bite.

"Yes, Mr. President," I said.

It was the 90s, the time before the mad millennium, and during the brief span of those 90s I had gone from a gung-ho student activist with shining ideals to the live-in lover of the president of the United States of Armorica. Everybody knew, and nobody minded anymore, because the millennium was upon us, and for all we knew, the end of the world was nigh. A man with a placard to that effect walked daily back and forth in front of the White House, and no one had the heart to send him packing, because this man, you know, knew things; he had been on Letterman once, and he thinks that the world we live in is only a shadow of a real world, a world in which our country is called America.

"Are they here yet? Jesus, I hate Christmas," said the president.

"We still have fifteen minutes, Mr. President," I said. I called him Mr. President because you never knew who might be listening.

America, said the man with the placard on Letterman, was vastly different from our own world, yet strangely the same; in America, there was no Letterman per se, Letterman having been superseded by some other late-night talk-show host whose name, said the man with the placard, he could never quite recall when he awoke from those troublesome dreams wherein this true world showed forth images of itself, images as evanescent and can't-quite-put-your-finger-on-able as a Zelazny fantasy novel, such novels being yet another figment of the man with the placard's dream-reality.

Okay, so I was thinking in twisted sentences that never seemed to quite gel into cogent utterances. That wasn't surprising.

You can easily get tongue-tied when you're about to be in the presence of one of the other guests at this very private dinner on Christmas Eve — Phil Etchison, P.P.P. (Pulitzer Prize for Poetry), the man who read the poem at President Karpovsky's inauguration, the poem that says everything about the 90s, and nothing —

(the time before the mad millennium)

These were the people, then, who were going to be sitting around the fireside: me, Phil, Mary Etchison, their son Chris, the autistic (or was he?) child prodigy; and a few assorted secret servicepersons, maids, butlers, and other staff-members, but they would all be off at midnight.

I'd known the Etchisons since I was a kid. Or had I? It's true, you see, what the man with the placard said. There were great gaps in the world's collective memory. Everyone knew this even though no one could put their finger on what it was that had been forgotten. Sometimes before I went to sleep I could catch glimpses into those other universes. Other Serenas lay down beside me in the same bed ... more than beside me ... in the very same space I occupied. Only some of them were not sleeping with the President of the United States of Armorica, and some of them were fat and some of then were anorexic, and some of them had known the Etchisons since they were kids, and some of them were dead; and others still were barely human at all.

I didn't remember ever meeting the Etchisons before. But soon, perhaps, I was going to remember it all. Perhaps too soon. I spent the afternoon anticipating and dreading, and listening to classic alternative rock on a battered old portable DAT, while my husband-in-all-but-name sat in the oval office pondering the treaty for the secession of the Lakota Nation.

Dinner, then, was a little awkward, though delicious; they were all of President Karpovsky's favorite dishes, and the man, though I'm probably biased, has taste. Nobody spoke at all. At last, all the way through the Sevruga on wafer-thin toast points, the lobster bisque, the medallions of beef (the same variety that had caused one of Oren's predecessors to barf into the lap of the prime minister of Japan) dinner was silent. All but for the footsteps of the staff as they changed the dishes in between courses.

It did give me a good chance to study the Etchisons, though, whom I was supposedly on such good terms with. Philip Etchison wore the distinguished-author persona like an ill-fitting toupée, and I could see that underneath it all was a kind of perpetual embarrassment. He smiled a few times — four string players from the Washington Symphony were playing Mozart's *Dissonance Quartet* in the background, and each little wincing discord made him smile more broadly. He dressed the part of the great poet, you know, the battered tweed jacket and unkempt hair and even the nervous twitch. But somehow it wasn't him.

Mary Etchison was different. She was totally serene. It didn't unnerve her a bit that no one was saying anything. They were almost a parody of an archetypal coupling: he the wind and she the mountain, he the turbulent sea and she the firm earth, or perhaps she the placid sea and he the fire that burns on the water ... what I'm trying to say is that they didn't seem quite human.

Then again, it was only days until the mad millennium. None of us were human. And Chris, their kid, was the least human of all, although he was the key to all our humanness.

Chris, too, was a celebrity. He was a kid who never spoke — well, he had been known to speak, so it wasn't that he had a congenital defect or anything like that — but at the age of four, he had wandered onto the stage at the Kennedy Center, where Emil Gilels was supposed to be giving a piano recital that night. He had climbed onto the nine-foot Bösendorfer in the empty auditorium, and he had begun to play. By dinner time, the concert hall was full. Gilels did not play. He was weeping in the wings. He came out to proclaim the kid the genius of the age, but the boy had vanished. It was on CNN. The oddest thing about it all was that everyone recognized the music, but no one could remember its name.

The next day, Philip Etchison encountered a writing block from which he had never recovered. Paradoxically, he became rich, a grand old man — except that I guess he wasn't really old — a laconic and soundbiteful lecturer commanding huge fees. That, I supposed, was the source of the terrible sense of loss I could see in his eyes.

You could see all sorts of emotions flitting through the Etchisons' eyes. All except Chris's, that is. You and I might see a few fish heads in the bouillabaisse, but Chris Etchison saw a world.

Dessert was a sort of a *crêpes suzette* thing, swimming in alcohol and whipped cream. Because we weren't talking, I was feeling this great big *thing* welling up inside me ... you know, like that feeling you get when you're watching a musical at the movie theater, and the lovers are looking into each other's eyes and romantic music is welling up around them, surging, soaring, until at last the dammed-up emotions burst out in an uncontrollable outpouring of melody ... well, it happened. I got up from my seat, flung my arms with such expressive energy that I thought I was going to turn into the Venus de Milo for a moment ... and I began singing, lustily and passionately. Which was amazing, because I can't sing.

What did I sing? That was the strangest thing of all. I can't remember a note of it. But it was a complex music, a strange keening punctuated with profound rumblings; it was definitely moving, because no one else at the table said a word.

Mr. Etchison, the great poet, sat there with his jaw dropping in slow motion, frame by frame; his wife Mary just beamed; my significant other sort of rocked back and forth and seemed to fall into a sort of postcoital serenity, except that he and I weren't hadn't done it in months ... and then there was the kid, Chris. I don't know. I mean, he looked right through me. Like he totally knew me, even more than sexually; and he couldn't have been more than eight years old. He just penetrated me with that gaze. He had the most amazing eyes, hazel with a hint of purple.

Like he understood every word of what I was singing.

As though the song was meant for him alone, as though I was just a kind of conduit or prism that the song passed through on its way from high up there in the sky where songs come from.

Mary Etchison wept.

To say that this was weird doesn't begin to describe how I was feeling. Because, you see, conscious as I was that Chris was looking at me, I also started looking at him, I mean really focusing. And what I saw wasn't just some angelic little kid with big soft teddy bear eyes, but myself. I mean pieces of myself that were missing, though I had never known I was missing them.

There had been another Etchison, a boy named Joshua. Joshua was inside Chris, somehow. I had been his lover. But how, and where?

And there was yet another missing Etchison: Theo. The Truthsayer. The boy who held the universe in the palm of his hand as though it were a marble. In fact, to him, it *was* a marble.

There had been adventures. Other worlds. Mad kings and dragon ladies and a vampire princeling. And more mundane adventures too. Losing one's way in the basement of a Chinese restaurant. Kidnapping Mrs. E. from the top floor of a lunatic asylum. Watching Mrs. E. turn to stone and turn back into flesh.

Were these all rabid fantasies, these vivid pictures that my singing seemed to conjure up? What images were the others seeing?

Mary Etchison was a goddess; in fact, she was the Great Goddess herself, who had fashioned the universe from her own flesh and fertilized it with her tears.

And now she was weeping again, which meant, perhaps, that the world was about to be renewed once more.

My lover, the president, said, "That was lovely, Serena. A lot more succinct than my Christmas address to the nation."

"Funny, Serena," said Phil Etchison. "I never knew you could sing."

"I can't," I said. "In fact, I'm not sure that it *was* me singing just now. It seemed to be coming from outside myself somehow. Or beyond myself. Or beside myself. Am I sounding like a schizophrenic?"

We retired to a little sitting room — not one of the rooms ever seen in any official tour of the White House — where the walls are covered in a velvety red wallpaper — a small, round room, not unlike a womb, in fact. A butler-type gentleman wheeled out the after-dinner liqueurs. The room contained a baby grand piano, and Chris immediately gravitated toward it. There were no servants. I myself poured Mr. E. a Cointreau, Oren a Remy Martin, and myself a guava juice. A tray of joints and a snuff-box of cocaine were proferred, in token deference to the new permissive drug laws, but we all ignored the drugs, being good clean children of the New Age.

Chris began to play a Mozart sonata.

Mrs. E. sat in a corner by herself, wiping at her eyes with a silk handkerchief.

"Sometimes," Mr. Etchison mused, "I wish my life were more like a Mozart sonata."

"In what way, Mr. E.?" I asked him.

"Well, you know, the wildness of it is so organized. Exposition, Development, Recapitulation, Coda; yet within this rigidity there's so much elasticity; you could fit a whole universe into a sonata movement, if only a universe was something you could listen to."

"But why restrict it to just listening?" I said.

"Listening," said Mr. Etchison, "is a metaphor. Music is a metaphor. But since our very existence is a metaphor, it follows, that it is all just metaphors within metaphors, and there is no point to the universe."

"Come on," said President Karpovsky, "you don't really believe that."

I said, "Who is Theo Truthsayer?"

Mr. E. said, "I don't know." But he shifted uncomfortably, and downed a second shot of Cointreau.

"And Josh? He dove into the sea once, and we spent an eternity — felt that way, felt at the very least like the middle volume of a trilogy — searching for him through a myriad universes."

"Never heard of him," said Mr. E., and looked furtively for the liqueur trolly, which a lackey had wheeled away for fear that he might become to inebriated. "Or have I? It does sound kind of familiar. Theo — there's a *theo*logical kind of name. And Joshua was the Hebrew name of Jesus, was it not?"

"Don't be pretentious," said Mrs. E.

"It's all I have left, dear," he said, "now that I'm permanently blocked as a poet."

The Mozart was getting to him. And to tell you the truth it was more than just Mozart. Chris's playing had begun as a well-known piece — I think it was the C minor, the one that begins like a tragic hero leaping into space and time and is answered by the delicate call of some unattainable grail. But somewhere before the end of the exposition, around half-way through the second subject of the sonata movement, Chris had veered into parts unknown. That was something that happened frequently with his playing.

Far up in the treble, there was a weird, tinkling counterpoint with a mind of its own. Booming in the bass, another voice, strident and dissonant. I wondered how little Chris could be playing all those things at one time, unless he had at least four hands.

He did.

You didn't notice this right away, mind you. I t wasn't anything so blatant as those Hindu god statues you see sitting up on the shelf in an Indian grocery store. But if you looked at him for a while, you became aware, as the nimble fingers ricocheted over the ivories, of other fingers, other wrists ... other selves, in fact, and you also became aware of Chris's profound, absolute concentration ... the ethereal tranquillity that seemed to radiate from his face, and I do mean radiate, because it was almost as though there were indeed beams of light darting about his eyes ... or was it just the music, easing slowly away from Western harmony now, into some darkly hypnotic Eastern algorithm?

"It's true," Mr. E. said. "When he plays, he becomes a god."

He was trying to sound playful, but I knew that he meant it literally.

"Which god?" said Oren. "A music god, I suppose. Apollo, maybe."

"Truer than you think," said Mr. E. "Apollo's also the god of truth."

For me, though, one of the Hindu deities was closer to the mark. The many arms, for one thing. The pale blue radiance. Krishna, perhaps. The glorious child, the vessel of absolute truth. That was what this music was saying to me.

I was starting to remember more and more pieces. The music was truth, a deeper truth than can be said with words.

"Mr. E.," I said, "just how much *do* you remember?"

Mrs. E continued to weep. In fact, her tears were gushing improbably, as though she were more fountain than woman. In fact, her complexion was becoming a little marmoreal. In fact, she *was* a statue — had, perhaps, always been a statue. She was a marble goddess sprouting up from the middle of the floor, her tears cascading down on the delicate patterns of a great Persian rug.

More pieces. I babysat little Theo once. He was a brat. He always blurted out the truth. He said, "You're just saying that because you're fat." Saying what? I don't remember. Suddenly though, there was this adjective. *Sluglike. Sluglike Serena.* They used to call me that. I loved my Joshua from behind folds of fat, knowing that such a love would always be safe.

Many-handed, radiant, the infant Chris-Krishna went on playing. Notes were spinning from the keys — I mean literally, little flurries of them with coruscating wings, here an eighth-note, here a school of thirty-seconds whirling around the boy's head, and finally, all at once, a storm of them, like stars, billowing.

What did it all mean?

Behind it all, dimly, I could hear a heartbeat.

Okay so you remember that we were in a sitting room. All very cosy. Christmas tree and little choo-choo train. American colonial furniture, all sorts of oaken eagles and fading maroon leather. But the room itself was metamorphosing. Or was it merely becoming more itself? The neo-classical mock-Ionic wall mouldings were stretching into stalactites and stalagmites. The divan I had been sitting on was softening into a bed of moss on a ledge of limestone. The walls were moist and breathing, and the tinkling piano blended with the sighing of a subterranean wind. In the whisper of the wind were angel voices, and I could almost understand the words of their song.

The heartbeat was a drumbeat now, deep, solemn, resonant.

The cavern walls were shimmering ... some kind of phosphorescence ... or was it starlight, and was the wind that whipped our faces some galactic storm?

The drumbeat-heartbeat came, still louder, bone-chilling now.

"Oren," I said. He put his arms around me, but seemed strangely far away.

We were in the eye of a dust storm, and the dust was the stars. And when the drumbeats suddenly ceased, and the dust abruptly settled, there was another man there with us.

A street person. Native American. He shook the stars out of his hair. In one hand he held a placard that read, **The End of the World Is Nigh,** and in the other a flute made from the thighbone of some animal. Or human, maybe.

The music came to a stop, too.

The churning world began to resolve itself. We were still in the little colonial sitting-room somewhere in the bowels of the White House.

"Thank you, Chris," said the man. His face was scarred and furrowed. He put the placard down on an empty fauteuil, the one with the golden lion paws, and looked at all of us, slowly, one at a time.

"Congressman Karpovsky," he said to Oren, "somehow I didn't expect you to be one of the pilgrims; I had you figured for a day player, not a principal."

"I'm the President now," said Oren. "Where've you been all this while?" He didn't sound all that confident.

"Phil," he said to Mr. Etchison. "The river has been dammed up these seven years. No poetry, just chunks of awful verse, scraps of paper fit for the shredder. It's time for the juice to flow again! Look up, man, see what's right in front of your nose! The dam has a chink, and soon the waters will come tumbling!"

Mr. Etchison was shaking.

The Indian turned to Mrs. E., who was still a statue. "Great Goddess," he said to her, and made a quick genuflection, "mother of us all, you honor us and bless us with your presence." And kissed her marble hand.

"Chris," he said, turning to the boy, who had climbed off the piano bench and was coming toward him shyly, wide-eyed, "you are the greatest Truthsayer who ever lived. But when you have said the greatest truth that can be said, will you be able to bear to say yourself out of existence?"

The boy seemed unsure of himself. He was sad. He stared like a bashful moppet. The Indian patted him on the head. "I feel for you," he said. "Yours is the greatest burden of them all."

And then he turned to me. "Serena," he said.

"Do I know you?"

"Yes."

"You're ..." And suddenly I remembered his name. "Milt. Milt Stone."

"Thank God! For a moment I thought you were going to say Santa Claus."

"You're ... a tribal policeman in Arizona, something like that. And ... some kind of magician."

"Yes, I suppose you could say I am. I am a *nadlé*, a sacred man-woman, one who bridges the unbridgeable. I can step from one river-bank to the other without passing through the river. What else do yo remember?"

"Not much," I said. "The Etchisons were driving through the desert. They fell into another universe. The Darklings were at war."

He smiled. "Not bad," he said. He touched my lips with the flute.

My lips smarted.

"You're the man with the placard who paces up and down in front of the White House every day," I said. "The madman. I wonder why the guards never —"

"I wonder too," he said. And laughed. Very softly. Like a creaky door. "All right," he said. "The fat lady has begun to sing —"

"I'm *not* fat!"

"But once," he said, "you were, Sluglike Serena."

I knew then with an absolute certainty that the images I had glimpsed when the music began were the One True Past, and that the reality in which we were now stranded was unraveling.

"This room and all its contents," said Milt Stone, "this country, this universe, and every event that the five of you have lived through for the last seven years, has been a dream. It has been only the blink of an eye. This whole illusory spacetime you've constructed around yourselves is a self-replicating tesseract, and only the power of Chris's Truthsaying can break you free of it."

He paused, perhaps to give us time to become adequately overwhelmed by the immensity of that statement. Then he went on: "There are pieces to picked up, lies to be untangled, wounds to be healed. There's no time, either. You think all this time has elapsed, but you've just been running in place. Wake up. Snap out of it. Trust me."

"Trust you?" said Oren. "But you don't even exist, according to what you've just told us."

Milt merely laughed.

"Peyote!" said Mr. E. "I remember now. You rammed it up our asses."

"No need for peyote now," said Milt. "Chris is our direct hypertext link to the Ultimate Truth. But we're burning daylight. Let's get going. We've only a few days left in which to save the universe. Chris, oh Chris, show us the way."

He handed Chris the bone flute, and Chris began to play.

Two
The Recombinant Yellow Brick Road

Chris Etchison:

why can't I speak
why can't I just come out and say
father
father
is it because
to say it would make it true

Phil Etchison:

Forget about growing old.   Forget about rolling up the bottoms of my trousers.

A hundred hours till the end of the world, and counting.

Forget about the tract house in Bethesda where I, a poet without poetry, had been living with my beautiful, stony wife and my child who spoke only in music.   Apparently it never happened.

Forget it all.

Forget mowing the lawn, kissing Mary on the forehead goodbye on the way to catch the Metro into Washington to give the weekly poetry lecture at the Corcoran that was only attended by half a dozen people, two of them vagrants fleeing the icy sidewalk. Never happened. Forget making love in the morning, trying to pull Mary back inside me when all she wanted was to turn back into the pillow, turn back into stone; forget, forget, never happened.

Forget picking Chris up to comfort him at three in the morning. Forget the dirty Pampers. Forget the way he looked at you, in his mother's arms, a few moments after he was born, staring right into your eyes and sucking the truth right out of your mind, when you know that a baby's eyes aren't supposed to even focus yet; forget that *have-I-created-a-monster* shudder that I tried so hard to repress but never quite had, not now, not seven years later ... forget even that? Never happened. Dreamt it all.

Why should I believe the rantings of some homeless wino? Liberal guilt, because he's an Indian? Some kind of New Age *frisson,* because ... he's an Indian? Or because I know it's true?

Or because of what I was remembering?

The images that were flooding back, flattening those other memories like sandcastles before a tsunami?

For example:

Christmas Eve's Eve. I'm shoveling the snow from the driveway. From somewhere inside the house I can hear Chris humming. It makes the shoveling go easier, somehow; the crunch of hard snow, the flop as it lands in the slush where the sidewalk begins, these sounds become the rhythm section for Chris's eerie, sidewinding melody.

Mailman shows up with half a dozen Christmas cards and a golden enveloped with 1600 Pennsylvania Avenue return address. Probably wants a contribution to some charity, I thought, and took the bundle inside, where Mary was gift-wrapping a little something for Chris, a box of marbles, ironic, perhaps, since some would say that Chris had none of his own. Chris watching her, still humming. The melody lingering in the air — literally lingering that is — you can see the rainbow-fringed sparks, slowly dying, slowly, slowly, slowly — there's always a kind of synaesthesia around Chris, you know.

"Mary," I said, "there's a letter from the President."

"Of the college, or of the United States?"

I showed her.

"Probably wants a contribution. Is he running for reelection, yet?"

I opened it.

Phil, it said, it's just an informal little thing, don't bother to dress up. "Mary," I said, "do we know the President of the United States?"

"We shook hands with him once, that big photo-op for the faculty, you know, the grant from the NEA."

I said, "He wants us to have dinner with him tomorrow night."

Bring Chris. This is really important. Okay, maybe you don't remember a thing, but you will once you get here.

"I don't get it," I said. "Some drunken orgy back in our college days, maybe? Oren Karpovsky is my closest friend, and somehow I've forgotten?"

"We all have big holes in our memories these days, dear," Mary said, putting the finishing touches on the gift wrap, sliding it under the Christmas tree, narrowly avoiding a collision with the O-gauge Southern Pacific locomotive that chugged around the landscape of Christmas presents. She looked at me, and I remember thinking, *She knows something.*

"Oren Karpovsky," she said, "he was so charming down in Mexico."

"We've never been to Mexico."

"Right. I forgot."

In my mind, I've been rehearsing the big speech I'm going to give on New Year's Day, to welcome the new millennium, it's my annual Address from the Poetry Chair, only since I can no longer write poetry, it's going to be a speech about the nature of truth.

Phil, Phil, don't sweat it, all will be made clear. A limo will pick up you, your wife, and your son at six o'clock sharp, and you'll get a police escort. Don't worry, this is not a hoax. it's a fork in the Yellow Brick Road.

"It appears that we've been invited to Oz. Or, perhaps, one of many Ozzes, since he speaks of a fork in the road."

"What do you give a man like that for Christmas? He probably has everything."

Do you remember Serena? the note said. She'll be there.

"Serena Somers? Didn't she babysit our children?" Mary said.

"We only have one child," I reminded her. Because Mary had never been firmly anchored in the real world. You could tell that she thought our entire existence was a dream. She was struggling right now ... struggling to wake up. If only....

I kissed her gently on the cheek.

"If I'm crazy," Mary said, "why do little things keep happening that confirm *my* truth?"

"What is truth?" I asked her.

We decided to give the president a frayed first edition of my first book of poems, *The Embrasure of Parched Lips.*

Crossing the Potomac, I experienced a wrenching reality shift. The borderline between the two parallel worlds ran right along the length of the river. Of course I knew President Karpovsky. I'd written his inauguration poem. We met in the lobby bar of a hotel in Mexico, where he'd gone to address a rally and I'd gone to take my wife to a laetrile clinic, in a last-ditch effort to patch together my gloriously dysfunctional family. My surly son Joshua, my dreamy son Theo. Serena was Josh's girlfriend, wasn't she? Or the babysitter.

No sooner did I know these things than I forgot them all over again, because, somewhere around Eighteenth

Street, there was another fault line in the fabric of the universe.

It wasn't so bad sitting around in the small reception hall. There had only been pleasantries to exchange, and my wife and the president greeted each other warmly, so I knew the insanity was mutual. Then, when Serena came in, wearing jeans and a teeshirt and hippie beads yet, things started to look a little odd.

"We're very informal around here," she said defiantly. "There's no press around. We'll do whatever we want."

Then not a word was said during the entire meal, until Serena started to sing. You couldn't call it singing exactly. It was a shrilling, thrilling sound, bloodcurdling, really. It was Chris-like in its apocalyptic splendor. I thought, in fact, that it must be the Last Trump, though heaven knows I'm no fundamentalist.

The first notes sent my mind reeling and I could see the road stretch on and on through the Arizona desert and feel the refractory choke of the airconditioner and hear my two sons quarreling and —

The next thing we knew, a withered old homeless Indian was expounding ontological niceties to us in the sitting-room, and handing my son a magic flute, and Chris was beginning to play, and the room, the White House, the entire city of Washington D.C. was folding in on itself like a Chinese puzzle.

A snowstorm was raging, and we were at a fork in a road. Definitely yellow brick. Little stretches of it were glinting through the blanket of white.

My wife, whiter than the snow itself, stood like a madonna at the cross-piece of the T, one hand pointing in each direction of the fork. I squeezed her hand but my flesh encountered only the cold hard stone. She wore the flowing robes appropriate to her godly status. You could not tell where the cloth ended and the snow began, for her vestments folded right into the landscape.

My son put away the flute. He looked frail and awkward in the dark jacket, shorts and little blue bow tie that we'd thought appropriate for dining at the White House — thank god we had such an outlandish costume in the house, but our son had played a concert or two, and even been on Letterman — but the flute slid right into the pants pocket with the ease of a gun into its holster. The music didn't stop, though.

The music was in the howling wind.

Milt Stone had changed, too. He was tall, his face more like a raven than a man; and I knew that in this world he had another name: Corvus, the navigator. "I was beginning to think," said this Corvus, "that none of you was ever going to come to his senses."

Only Mary's eyes seemed alive; and her left eye wept, slowly but continuously, a glistening glacier that ran down her cheek, down the snow-powdered folds of her robe, onto the ground, that was melting the snow about her feet so that we could see more and more of the road, glittering beneath the slush.

In this universe, my wife is a goddess, and my son is a seer. I, on the other hand, am nothing special. I didn't think I would ever get to be anything special, not in a thousand universes; did that, in itself, make me special, make me into a kind of archetype of Everyman?

"What are the plans?" I said to our guide.

"Hell if I know," said Milt. "This isn't Inferno, and I'm not Dante. Can't expect me to lead the way. I've brought you here — that's it. Didn't even bring you here, really; just sat around at the gateway, waiting until the moment that brought all of you together, then opened the door. Up to you people now."

"Where are we?" I said.

"Dunno," said Milt. "Chris would know."

"But he isn't talking," Serena said.

"No," I said, "he isn't."

"Should we split up?" said President Karpovsky. "I mean, there *are* two directions indicated ... three, if you include turning back."

Turning back, it seems, was not in the cards. As I turned to look at the road which snaked behind for quite a distance until it was lost behind a towering embankment, I saw that the road itself was eroding. A brick here, a brick there, the road was rearranging itself, tying itself in knots, all in slow motion, that is. It was then that I realized what was most different about my life, or rather about the mythic adventure that happened to be my life.

Normally, when you tell a story, you start off with one brick, you lay it, you move onto the next brick ... piece by painful piece you construct the unique path through the cosmos that is the tale. At any moment, you can look back and assess all that has gone by. The point you stand at is the sum total of all that has transpired. Stories are cumulative — like music, like sex, lumbering inexorably toward a climax.

Well, but you see, that is not *our* story. In our story, you may look back at any time, and the view will always have changed. It is a story that writes itself in both directions of time simultaneously. It is a story in which you anticipate the past with as little foreknowledge as the future.

What a journey! Or, as I would have said in the 60s, in at least one of my many pasts, what a trip!

Chris kissed his mother's cheek and turned to the right.

"Our mission," I said, trying to avoid portentousness (but not quite succeeding) "is to find ourselves."

"And to find the truth," Serena said.

"And to heal the world's pain," said Milt Stone.

"Tough missions," said the president. "Bullshit is more my line of work. Am I the scarecrow, the lion, or the tin man?"

There was more snow. I couldn't tell where the sky ended and the land began. Chris started to walk. He held the flute aloft, like a lantern. The flute played itself. The snow was thick and fast, but where Chris stepped, it parted for him, so I guess the flute was sort of like the machete in the jungle. I followed. We were all numb, I think, especially our feet; none of us had come dressed for inclement weather.

"You know what?" said President Karpovsky after only a few steps. Shouted, actually, because the roar of the wind was crescendoing. "I just don't feel right going this way. I mean, a shift to the right, on the eve of the millennium ... it just doesn't seem politically correct to me."

He looked back. We all did. The statue that was my wife gave no reply.

"Anyone coming?" he said, but it was mostly directed at Serena. "What, no one loves me? Ah, the lonely lot of the politician."

Serena seemed very confused. She looked at Milt for a moment, then back at Oren. Oren began to stride away. I suddenly knew why. In that direction, you could sense an easing of the storm. There was a feeling that the sun was there somewhere, hiding behind an arras of mist and cloud. A true politician, Oren had figured out the path of least resistance.

Corvus said to Serena, "All quests are, in the end, the same quest. But that doesn't mean that the grail can't be reached by more than one road."

"Are you saying I should go?"

"Do you love him?"

Amazing how far away he seemed now. Trick of perspective, I guess. In a minute, he was halfway to the horizon.

"Wait up!" Serena shouted. She began running after him, kicking up clouds of snow. In another minute, she too was just a tiny figure. So there was just me, my son, and our guide.

And my son, holding the flute above his head like a banner, was resolutely making his way down the right-ward path, toward a smudge of darkness on the horizon

that could have been smoke, or a thundercloud, or an
ocean of black ink.

"We'd better hurry," said Corvus.

Everyone was always in such a hurry around here.

Three
Absolute Power

Serena Somers:

The odd thing was, in no time at all the road led us through one of those weird fractures in causality or whatever it is, and we were no longer walking (him walking, me running to catch up) because we suddenly found ourselves in the back seat of some massive convertible limo and we were driving (being driven) down an avenue (still yellow brick) but widening and widening, though the snow was still falling, slowing a little, slowing and softening to an icy drizzle, snow falling at our feet, on the black leather upholstery, everywhere. Even our clothes were different now, a kind of cross between New Wave and Victorian, shaggy mink things with sci-fi collars. There were human skulls littering the plush carpeting, though. Other kinds of skulls, too. Couldn't figure out the species. Alien creatures of some kind.

The driver was dark and tall, and he never looked back at us, and he wore dark glasses. Next to him there was one of those tall Chinese guys. He wore a sort of Mandarin's costume, the kind you see in historical epics. He held a trumpet in one hand. Now and then, he did turn to glance at us. He wasn't like any Chinese guy you've ever met; he was like a cliché of a Chinaman, like

Christopher Lee playing Fu Manchu, stroking his straggly wisp of a beard and peering through exaggerated epicanthic eyes, and his accent came from a bad movie, too, when he finally started to speak.

"Cornelius Huang," he said, "always and forever at your service, esteemed sir and madam; might one proffer refreshment?"

The limo then seemed to be a little bit like a Chinese restaurant. Hovering before us was a lazy susan jammed with delicacies — braised sea cucumber stuffed with minced pork, abalone with bok choi, goose feet in red wine sauce — we'd had this kind of stuff at the Chinese ambassador's, never in a restaurant — and women in shimmering cheongsams bobbed up and down, translucent, ghostlike, pouring plum wine into golden goblets.

"You will, of course, eat," said Cornelius Huang.

"Sure thing," Oren said, and a pair of silver chopsticks appeared in his hand.

"Wait a minute," I said. "We just ate."

I ribbed him.

"Come on, honey, we don't know where our next meal may be coming from," said Oren.

I ribbed him harder. "Oren!" I whispered. "I think this is one of those Persephone deals. You eat the food of the underworld, you stay here."

Oren gulped. "I already swallowed," he said. He tried discreetly to spit out pieces of goose bone. "What am I supposed to do, starve?"

"Perhaps you'd prefer some wine?" said Cornelius Huang. "It's not bad — in a sanguinary sort of way." Yeah, he was solicitous all right. But there was a kind of disdain in him, too.

"He needs us," I said to Oren. "But he doesn't like us."

"How do those little old Chinese ladies manage to do it?" said Oren. "You see them popping their goose feet into their mouths, and then, rat-tat-tat, the bones come flying out as though from an AK-47. I've never been able to figure it out."

"Years of practice," Huang said. "Allow me to demonstrate."

He leaned over, reached in the air for a pair of chopsticks, which materialized in his hand. Delicately, he picked up a goose foot, thrust it into his mouth, and went through the entire chomping-machine-gunfire routine. "The tongue and the cheeks," he said, "have certain muscles which atrophy if you're not used to a diet of fowl feet."

Before I could stop Oren, he had already reached for another, and was trying it, unsuccessfully, into a napkin.

"Good," said Cornelius Huang, "there goes another lump. It's time for us to discuss your new job, Mr. President...."

"What happened to my old job?"

"Oh, I see, your old job." Mr. Huang suppressed a little chuckle; just your typical arch archvillain. "Unfortunately, your old job never really existed, you see. The life you have lived for the last, oh, seven years or so, has not been entirely real. Something terrible has happened. The fabric of the cosmos has shattered, you see. Think of each parallel universe as a jillion-piece jigsaw puzzle, each picture just a little bit different from the last. Well, what has happened is that someone has taken all the possible puzzles and mixed up all the pieces, so that when we travel from piece to piece in the great map of our existence, we are also leapfrogging from reality to reality; do you understand?"

"You mean," Oren said, "that little frisson I experience whenever I step into the en suite bathroom in the presidential bedchamber, and I suddenly get the feeling I'm a completely different person, that I'm not even supposed to be there at all —"

"Oh, you're so bright, Oren. May I call you Oren? Seeing you are not president after all."

"What about me?" I shouted. Was I being selfish? My lover's position in life, after all, affected the lives of millions of others; my own, perhaps, was less important in a way. But there was something I had to know. "The real me," I said. "I don't know why, but I suddenly just have to know. Am I fat or thin? In the real world, I mean."

"Profoundly banal," said Cornelius Huang, sighing.

But it was more important than you might think. You are what you eat, and I seemed to remember one life that was one long eating disorder. Hadn't I been fat once? Hadn't I catapulted from bulimia to anorexia and back again? Was that my real life, or some fantasy of self-loathing? And if I wasn't screwing the president of the United States, who was I screwing?

From somewhere in the distance, I could hear the rushing of a river. Perhaps I was wrong about the food. Perhaps it was only food. It did smell tempting. More tempting than food had a right to be. That was why I couldn't trust myself.

I closed my eyes and I saw someone else I knew I had once loved. He was flying high, riding the back of a dragon, careening over a flaming world. Who was he? Not the man I was sitting with now.

"But if I'm not president in the true world, who is?" Oren asked. "Don't tell me. Clinton won for a second term, and then ... no! Surely not Perot! Or was it Robertson? Or that other guy, the way-outa-left-field candidate ... Danzig I think his name was...."

"You don't want to know," said Cornelius Huang.

"And who am I?"

"You'd want to know even less." He peered into Oren's eyes, did the old hypnotist on a vaudeville stage stare, and I could tell that there were sort of images of some kind, projecting, laser-like, into Oren's mind. I didn't want to look, but I couldn't help myself ... especially since the landscape that roared past was all snow, all white, all featureless.

I saw Oren change — change so completely it was like when a werewolf is hit by a silver bullet and dying turns vulnerably human, you know what I mean — one minute so full of power and ferocity, the next so completely frail, as in those few moments when I truly loved him, which were not many — I put my hand out to touch his shoulder and amazingly he shied away from me, flinched, looked out of the window.

"I wish," he said, "I wish things were different."

"Yes, I know," said Cornelius Huang.

"I don't always like being who I really am."

"I know," said Cornelius Huang. The refrain was ominous. There was a plan afoot, and it had to do with Oren's hunger. Oh, yes, he was like me when it came to hunger, though it wasn't as simple as with me, I mean with me it was just food, stuff myself, starve myself. He had another kind of hunger and it was all to do with power.

Not that he wasn't a good man, you know. I mean, his politics were very correct. We'd saved a lot of whales, me and my Mr. President. Women's rights, gay rights, everyone had a lot of rights now, I mean we were about as liberal as a couple as our world permitted, but sometimes, when the TV cameras were turned off, I knew that Oren yearned to nuke someone's ass to kingdom come.

And so we drove on, you see. We reached a river's edge and the road went on, ploughed right through into the river, and the limousine sort of grew fins and plunged into the water, well, it was mostly ice, and it cracked and clattered against the car that was now some kind of boat and was still growing, growing, a mast thrusting up from where the lazy susan with the Chinese food had been, black sails sprouting up, a pirate flag flapping, crewmen with surly faces creeping past us, stopping to stare when they didn't think we were looking; only the leather upholstery we were sitting on remained the same, but now the seat had transmogrified into a bloated divan on a deck that overlooked a prow that was the face of a stern but compassionate goddess, to be exact the face of Mary Etchison if I looked a little more closely. Couldn't be a hundred percent certain of it.

"The prow of this ship," I said —

And Cornelius Huang, suddenly very tall, with robes that shimmered with coruscating shades of cerulean, viridian, vermilion, chrome, and a gilded trumpet in his hand like one of those monstrous Tibetan things, he glared at me for a moment, then blew three blasts (my eardrums could barely take it) and put the trumpet down and said, "Yes, we've kidnapped the goddess, of course; it's the one way we can be sure we know where we're going," and then, in a kind of delayed reaction to the trumpet blasts, the ice of the river, the air itself seemed to shatter, disintegrate, we sort of dissolved, the way you go in a movie from one scene to the next, and we weren't in the snow country at all, but in another place altogether. No snow here. The sky was gray, featureless, without a sun or moon.

Still a river, you understand. I remember. There's a great river that connects the millions of known worlds, and the river itself is both itself and a metaphor of itself. The trumpet blasts had unlocked some kind of cosmic gateway, and now we were far beyond where we'd been a moment before. Light-years away, maybe, or even universes away.

Oren got up. Walked over to the prow, placed his hand idly over the goddess's stony curls. Here and there, in the water, were weathered artifacts — great Easter Island heads, sphinxes, Buddhas, even an angular Jesus swinging from a marble tree — and in the middle distance a castle climbed up out of the waves, and it really did climb, clinging to the chalky cliff-face like a granite vine, a twisty mess of turrets and landings and parapets and minarets and great windows like the eyes of a thousand skeletons. Suddenly I knew the castle's name: Thornstone Slaught. I had definitely been here before. Déjà vu in spades.

"My master, the Lord Thorn," said Cornelius to my lover, "has been killed. There is a vacuum in the cosmos. In the vacuum there is a castle. To enter the vacuum is to gain power. You crave that power, and you're never going to have it if you allow the world to sink back to its entropic reality. Which it will, Mr. President, if you don't fight it with all your might."

And I knew then what Oren had seen. He had become the most powerful man in the world, knowing full well that the world he ruled was a dream world, only half real; he had seen what he was in the real world. I could only guess. It couldn't have been flattering. I'd never realized how much he hated himself. And you know, his self-hatred was the only thing about him that I loved. That was the strangest thing of all.

The lazy susan whirled around and around, so fast that you couldn't see the food anymore, like a roulette wheel.

"Will you bet everything on the red?" said Mr. Huang. You could hear the ball skittering. Then, as the wheel slowed, we were back to the table d'hôte. Two fortune cookies sat in a silver platter. "Surely, Serena, you'll have dessert."

"There's this game that —" I began. Who played the game? How did I know these things? "You take a cookie and ... the other person asks a question, any question, and you open it, and whatever it says is the answer to that question."

"An absurd sort of game," said Oren. "Will I lose you?"

I opened my cookie.

"Loss," said the fortune cookie, "is part and parcel of the karmic balance. Live with it."

"Seems pretty clear," said Oren. He seized the other cookie, gazed thoughtfully at it, and waited for me to ask my question.

"What kind of question is that," I said, "for a fortune cookie to answer, 'Will I lose you?'"

"That's two questions," said Oren, laughing. He opened his cookie, and read to me: "Life is a slow dance between death and desire."

"I don't get it," I said.

Oren tossed his cookie into the water. A dozen hands popped up to drag it under. Mermen, I supposed, or some other mythical creatures. "Better get rid of yours, too," he said. "You're the one who thought of the whole Queen of Hades linkage."

It was too late. I had bitten into the cookie.

"Not a moment too soon," said Cornelius Huang. He pointed at the castle, which had become suddenly much closer. There was some kind of commotion. A flock of birds — or were they dragons? — flinging themselves against the walls, bursting into flame. "Thornstone Slaught is under attack. Master, you simply must seize control. Or else there will be chaos. You see, there is an absolute need for you, here, now, even though the place and time is other than your own."

As the ship docked beside a wharf lined with human skulls, I could see that the castle was indeed under attack. But it didn't seem like a big deal. They were bats, or maybe baby dragons. The reason that I couldn't really think about Oren's plight was that something seemed to be happening to me, too. I was choking on the fortune cookie.

A steaming goblet appeared by magic in my hand — a bubbling, crimson fluid — and I started to drink without thinking, and the pieces of cookie started to slide down my throat — they were sharp-edged. I felt as if I was swallowing glass.

Drink the wine and chew the wafer —

Suddenly this whole scene popped into my mind, one big bleeding chunk of a scene, a fragment of lost memory. A hotel lobby in Mexico, just over the border, next to a Laetrile clinic. Oren's lobbying, too. He's only a congressman, though. He's about to use the clinic as a photo-op, something to do with alternative medicine, or some new health plan, maybe? And I'm a lot younger; this is a whole lot more than seven years ago, although it can't really be longer than that because it's the year 2000 now, isn't it? But well, there's Oren and he's pounding away on the lobby piano and singing The Vatican Rag, and it's one big politically incorrect singalong because everyone knows and loves that irreverent old Tom Lehrer song, and standing by the elevator, watching him, feeling a surge of love for him even though I know he's been sexually harassing me since I was a congressional page in my mid-teens....

I felt the fortune cookie settling in me like a lump of lead.

I looked up. A walkway now extended to the shore, and the crew of the ship was unloading, hastening down to the castle. They were about as gothic a crew as you could imagine, with bald heads and silver earrings and pierced tongues and lips and eyebrows and armed with scimitars and dressed in black, and some weren't even people but were sort of skeletons or something and a three-headed dog was yapping at my heels. Oren and Huang had already left the ship. The dragon-bats were swooping down from the turrets, and Huang was picking them off with a sort of laser-tipped staff. They sizzled and plopped into the sea, and each corpse was set on by a feeding frenzy of mer-creatures, their tails slapping up columns of black water.

Somehow I was unmoved by all this spectacle. It was like I'd lived through it all before. Somehow I was no longer feeling my age, either; years were peeling off me; I understood the truth of what Milt Stone had said earlier, that the last seven years had all been a dream.

The fortune cookie was a sort of lump inside me, and I could feel it sort of metastasizing within me. Something was invading me. Something wanted to control me.

Someone I knew well. Someone I'd once fought. To a draw, if not to victory, because you can't beat an archetype at her own game.

But she was dead, wasn't she? I had defeated her in proper mythic fashion by the good old power of love. Her name was Katastrofa.

How right you are, said a voice in my head. I cannot die so easily. I am immortal. You can kill the image of the dragon, but you can't kill the dragon within.

It was gnawing at my guts. It felt like, I don't know, the worst kind of constipation plus a choking feeling plus a vomiting feeling, all at the same time. Maybe I was about to give birth. Mrs. E. once told me it was like shitting a watermelon. Oh, God, I felt sick. Fire and ice in my belly. PMS and heartbreak all rolled into one. I started to scream. I caught up with Oren and Huang. They'd turned into some kind of dark dynamic duo, lashing at the creatures who were storming the walls. Oren had some kind of laser-beam ray-things shooting from his eyes. Cornelius was laughing and laughing and now and then blowing his trumpet which made dozens of the bat-things plummet onto the flagstones.

It occurred to me that someone was taking over Oren, too.

Still on the brink of heaving, I dragged myself over to the battle scene. They were dashing up the steps toward the first gray parapet. The stairs were littered with the corpses of the bat-things, but as we reached the parapet most were already turning away, heading skyward toward the lowering cloudscape. Still no sun, I thought. Although there was a dismal kind of light that suffused the battered bricks and weatherbeaten balustrades of Thornstone Slaught.

At the head of the steps, more ghoul-like beings stood, but these were clearly not attacking. They fell to their knees at the sight of Oren Karpovsky.

"Deliverance, deliverance," they murmured.

"No!" I screamed. "I'm not going to deliver anything!" But the dragon within me wanted to get out. She was willing to rip me apart. I just wanted to die, I really did. But I knew that if I did die, I wouldn't come back; I'd be inside the dragon, instead of the dragon being inside me. I had to fight it.

I grabbed onto the railing of the parapet. I shoved a loose brick off the edge. I belched fire. That was how powerful Katastrofa was.

And meanwhile, the citizens of Thornstone Slaught were raising up Oren on their shoulders, parading him about the parapet, cheering and gibbering. And all of them had dark and hollow eyes and you know, bad skin, the way you expect bad guys to look in books and movies. Their cheering was like the chattering of baboons or loons, really grating on the ears.

"Stay down there," I said to the dragon woman. My gorge rose again, but I forced it down by thinking of Josh.

Josh, who didn't exist anymore, who never existed, who somehow Chris Etchison reminded me of so strongly that I could feel a kind of sexual tractor beam shooting from his eyes and reeling me in....

"Come on up," Oren shouted.

He was a level higher, now, up another sweeping flight of steps, dark basalt, bloodstained; there was a kind of throne on this parapet, a throne of human skulls and bones, all black with ash and coagulated gore. At a mighty blast from Huang's trumpet, the assemblage of ghouls fell prostrate, repeating the words Oren, Oren, Oren, Rex, like a mantra. I threaded my way through the throng. As I got closer to Oren I realized that he too had been going through changes. Oh, I don't mean being able to kill with a death-beam from his eyes. I mean there was a different person in him.

"Hi, sis," he said to me, leering. "Ready for Ragnarok?"

That was how I was sure who that different person was. It had to be Thorn, the vampire; and that meant that the battle we had thought was almost over was about to enter its third and most devastating phase.

"You look a whole lot younger," he said to me. "Crossing the river's taken years off you."

"I know," I said.   "The last seven years was like, a dream, and now I'm almost as young as when you tried to rape me in your office on the hill."

"That's a fine way to talk to your one true love," he said.

"That's another that isn't true any more," I said. I was talking like a much younger woman too, someone barely out of her teens ... maybe even still in them. This was totally weird.

Cornelius Huang then said, in like this echoing, seplu-chral voice: "The Lord Thorn has defeated the creatures that have attempted to seize his castle during his period of, ah, involuntary indisposition."

"Listen to me, Oren!" I said.   "I know you're still in there somewhere. They're using us, Thorn and Katas-trofa I mean, trying to come back to finish off the war...."

"What the hell are you talking about?" Oren said. "I never had this much fun in the fucking White House. Diplomacy, diplomacy, diplomacy ... bullshit. I can do anything I want here. I have absolute power!"

"You're getting into the spirit of things," said Corne-lius Huang. "How about killing someone now?"

He beckoned with his little finger. One of the citizens crawled forward. She lifted up her eyes to my lover, and he decapitated her with a single glance. Huang plucked a golden goblet from the air and caught a brimful from the fountaining blood as she rolled down the steps.   He handed it to his new master, and Oren drank deep. His eyes reddened.

"Not bad, eh, sis?" he said to me.

"I'm not your sister," I said. "I'm still Serena Somers. I'm keeping the dragon caged up for now."

"Then I'll have to keep you caged up," said Oren. To no one in particular, he shouted: "Take her away!"

Burly arms pinned me. I shuddered. I taste the dragonbile in my throat, and then, suddenly, I sort of blinked out, and I found myself totally somewhere else....

Four
After We Stormed the Castle

Oren Karpovsky:

I am not a crook. (Try *that* one on for size!)

Don't blame me.

The buck never stops. It would have stopped here, but the idea of the buck stopping at all is just too, too *Euclidian* to pass muster in our multilateral, relativistic universe.

I had gazed into the emptiness that was my true self, and I knew that I had lost everything. You have to stop blaming me. Somebody was using me, and I was trapped inside myself, looking out at a harsh and savage world. I climbed up to the pinnacle of the castle, where there was a sort of war room, and I paced back and forth, planning out strategy with my new chief of staff, a cadaverous Chinaman who was a parody of the Yellow Peril, tall and beady-eyed and with one of those evil-looking goatees, constantly spouting words of ambiguous Confucian wisdom; and I'd locked up Serena and thrown away the key.

We were in a room. I was pacing. He was playing chess, actually. You know, the kind where the pieces actually fight each other to the death, on sixty-four squares of carpet in the middle of the room, and you can hear the clank of armor and the clash of swords and oh yes, the groans of the dying, and now and then even the rattle of an M-16 and yes, there's the odor of napalm in the air. He was sitting in a high chair and waving his arms, making the chess pieces move, playing, it seems, both sides, solitaire.

I said, "I would like to have Serena back."

"Why not?" he said, barely looking up. "You have absolute power, don't you? You stormed the castle and now you own all the territories of my former master. You have but to say the word and she will be returned to you."

"But I *am* saying the word, and I don't see her."

"Perhaps you don't really mean it," said Cornelius Huang, and then added a somehow condescending "O Master," as if to say, "Who the hell are you trying to kid?" and I thought, Perhaps I've only exchanged one hell for another.

"Perhaps," Cornelius said, "you'd care for another blood cocktail."

"I don't get it," I said. "I have nothing to do with any war that's going on here; you just picked me off the street to fill the shoes of some archetypal bad guy or something; you sit around calling me master, and an hour ago you made me drunk with power, but now you show me that there's really nothing for me to do here except drink blood and execute people I don't even know personally...."

"No, no, Mr. President. You have it all wrong. I didn't pick you to fill anyone's shoes. You were already trying to play that role before, in your stumbling way. We have simply upgraded you to the real thing."

"An impotent real thing."

"Not as such." Huang clapped his hands, and a beautiful woman materialized out of the air: the kind I used to lust after when I was running for office, and not just in my heart, either. Pouting, hair that wafted in slow motion like a hairspray commercial, and strange and unexpected curvatures, and dark and haunting eyes, you know the kind I mean, prom queen, gypsy, and slut all rolled into one, and she kneeled in front of me and clasped her arms around my buttocks and began to tug at the zipper. "And when you're through with her, you can drink her blood," said Cornelius Huang, "and you can toss her desiccated corpse out of the window, all the way down to the River. You've always wanted to try that, haven't you?"

"Of course not." But he had my number. I've always had fantasies. Bondage. Sadism. Blood. That's why I worked so hard to be a perfect liberal, the health plan, the safety net for the poor, helping the needy; oh, God, yes, I saw myself now in a different light; I saw the darkness that propelled every one of my oh-so-altruistic notions. I'm a hypocrite. I knew that now. Always had, I guess, but I'd managed to bury it under a megaton of health and welfare legislation.

I hated myself. That, in the end, was what it was all about. I hated myself so much that I didn't mind bringing down the whole goddamn universe, so long as I could get myself along with it.

Serena Somers:

I was in a dungeon, I guess, somewhere in the bowels of Thornstone Slaught. I wasn't chained up or anything, and the dungeon didn't see like a dungeon on first viewing. Because the walls were a sort of sensurround projection of an outside world, a world of ice and snow. Snow just streaming down, and the wind howling like a pack of madwomen.

But in the little bubble that was the prison, there was no cold and there was no wind. It was like, utterly still, and toasty-warm, and that made the images of the arctic world outside seem quite unreal.

I had one of those snow-bubble paperweight things once when I was a kid. It showed a castle almost as baroque as the one I was trapped in. You shook it and watched the flakes fly. It was weird to be on the inside of one of those things looking out. I stood with my nose to the wall, or the forcefield, or whatever it was, and listened to the wind.

In the blinding whiteness, I started to see things. You stare into emptiness long enough and you start to hallucinate I guess. You start to see, and soon you're smelling and hearing and even touching, too. I don't know how long it was before the snow started to resolve into those ghostly pictures, but I guess I had been there a long time, without food and water, my stomach still feeling all lumpy from that fortune cookie.

I started seeing Joshua through the window, if it was a window. How old was he when he stopped existing, maybe seventeen? I saw Josh riding the dragon with the sun on his back and I thought, I could be the dragon if I wanted, now. Josh was all beautiful, more like a *Tiger Beat* pinup than a real guy. Maybe my memories had been edited. For sure they had, but I wondered if I had done it myself or whether it was just a side effect of the universe slingshotting back and forth.

I started to cry, I guess. I don't know. I was so, whatever, cut off. Couldn't tell if even I was real. And there was this lump inside me, this Katastrofa-embryo, just itching to burst out of my stomach like in that scene in *Alien.* I lay back on the floor — there wasn't any furniture in the room, if it was a room, and the floor itself had the appearance and texture of the snow outside, but not the burning cold of it. I closed my eyes, but the whiteness of snow wouldn't go away, even when I cupped my hands over my eyelids. The snow here was more than mere snow, I guess. It was some kind of metaphor, which meant that it wasn't subject to the rules of reality; you couldn't make it disappear by shutting your eyes to it.

I lay there in the foetal position crying my eyes out. Gradually, it did get kind of dark; maybe it was night on this planet.

Joshua was standing on the other side of the force field. He seemed to be banging on the field, wordlessly begging, like a vampire, to be let in.

He was even more pale than when I'd least seen him in real life. He'd been a corpse last time. But now he moved, well, swayed back and forth, like a zombie; I couldn't tell if he was breathing or not.

"Josh," I whispered. Could he hear me? His lips started to part as though he was trying to remember how to speak. "Are you a zombie?" I asked him. I know, that was a pretty stupid thing to say, right up there with "Do you come here often?" but you could hardly blame me for being a little socially challenged.

Josh looked at me, then looked way past me at something else that was in the womb-room with me. Some*one* else, maybe. Katastrofa, I was sure. The dead, like animals, must have some kind of heightened sense about the presence of supernatural creatures. Josh *knew* that his nemesis was in here with me — was somehow *part* of me. She was standing behind me. She was my shadow, or maybe I was hers.

"Josh," I said again.

His lips moved again.

"Where are you?" I said. "*What* are you?"

This time his lips parted slowly and I thought I could hear like, this expulsion of breath, only maybe it was my own, because I knew I was gasping and my heart was beating fast.

Because I was remembering more and more including lying awake at night thinking of Josh and hiding my passion for him behind those great big eating binges. And I was remembering my imaginary friend I'd made up, not quite man and not quite woman, someone to talk to because I didn't dare talk to Joshua ... the imaginary friend who turned out to be real ... to be one of the sons of Strang, mad king of the cosmos.

"I —" said the pale Josh-zombie thing that stood in the snow, stretching his arms out toward me.

"You *can* talk!" I said softly.

He banged and banged against the solid nothingness. But he didn't say anything more, although I think he tried several times.

How could I let him in? How could I let myself out? I banged and banged, too, but to no avail, except that my fists became raw and I was crying so hard I could barely see.

At that moment, there came a tapping from somewhere. I whipped around to see a tray of food materializing and a gloved hand retreating into thin air, zipping up reality behind it as it disappeared.

It was a tray of fortune cookies. Better not eat them, I said to myself. Each bit of this neverland food's going to bring the dragon further up to the surface. I turned to look at Joshua again but discovered that he wasn't there anymore. Oh, he probably was, just playing some kind of now-you-see-it-now-you-don't.

I stared at the tray for the longest time. The cookies were stacked up to form a circle. There were chocolate fortune cookies and vanilla ones, and the way they were arranged was in the shape of a yin-yang symbol, a dozen cookies for the feminine, a dozen for the masculine.

The dragon growled inside me.

"Shut up," I said. "Didn't I defeat you once by sacrificing my virginity?"

So what are you going to do this time? Get a hymen implant?

I stared at the cookies hungrily.

Maybe if I didn't eat them ... maybe if I just opened them? The Etchisons had a game they would play ... oh, a hundred universes ago. If they ate Chinese, they wouldn't open the cookies just like that, at the end of the meal; they'd take turns asking one another questions.

The person questioned would respond by reading whatever was on his fortune cookie.   Mr. E. swore that any question whatsoever, no matter how recondite, personal, or ontological, could be answered by this method.   He said that in his freshman "how to read a poem" class, the one I audited, oh, a hundred universes ago, because Joshua wanted me to see that what his father did was a cool thing, after all, that being a poet wasn't the same as being just another stuffy old Dead White Male that you find on postage stamps.   He then doled out fortune cookies from a big old bag, and got the whole class of a hundred eighteen-year-olds playing the game.

Well, I thought it was totally brilliant, and then when I went back the next year just for kicks, some clown had substituted the porno fortune cookies from *Chest of Pleasures Bookstore* and you know what, Mr. E. even made all *those* answers work.

Maybe it was time to try.

I picked up one of the chocolate fortune cookies. Aloud, I asked it, "So, who am I?"

I cracked it open and read:

Serena Johanna Somers.

Underneath, it smaller print, was the legend: *Sometime babysitter to a family of Truthsayers on a world named earth; reluctant participant in the great war between the Darklings; in another universe, common-law-wife to the president of a non-existent country; in various other universes, the object of sexual harrassment from this same president, although he is only a congressman and never a serious candidate for the highest office in the land; fat pig.*

"That's ridiculous," I said. "I can't have been all those things; some of them actually preclude one another."

Even smaller print:

This isn't Schrödinger's cat; just because you've cracked open the cookie doesn't mean that all the answers but one are now untrue. Contrariwise, the act of the cracking the cookie does *determine whether the question gets answered at all.*

This was absurd. It occurred to me that it was one of those situations where the harder you look, the more obscure becomes the answer. I decided I was would just glance quickly at what was on the next cookie, then look away before my perceptions became dimmed with fine print.

I asked aloud: "Is Joshua still alive?"

IN YOUR HEART.

Did this mean he was actually dead? I *had* to read the small print after all. I peered at the slip of pink paper. The small print was beginning to swim into view now. It was sort of wavery, oscillating small print, small print that didn't want to keep saying the same thing.

— *if you build him, he will come* —

But Josh was not a baseball stadium ... was he?

— *hear the heartbeat of the universe* —

Some kind of New Age lesson to be learned here. If Josh was alive because he lived inside me somehow, was that the only reason Katastrofa was still alive — because we had fought, because we had wounded each other — because a piece of her was indelibly graved beneath my skin?

I had to ask another question.

"How," I said, "are we all going to get home?" knowing that *home* is a relative concept, because every place we had been to on our odyssey had been home to at least one Serena Somers, just not the Serena Somers I felt I really was.

The paper in the fortune cookie was empty.

"What was *that* all about?" I asked the next cookie.

— *you can write your own ticket* —

said the next cookie, before dissolving into a blur of gibberish.

I looked at the blank cookie slip from the cookie before. There was a pile of cracked cookies on the floor where I was kneeling, and the odor of chocolate was starting to get to me. They say chocolate contains an addictive chemical that makes you feel loved, and it sure was working on me. It was as seductive as the phantom lover of my teenage years. Well, I *was* a teenager again, I guess.

— *if you build him, he will come* —

Right. Build him out of what? When I looked down at the plate of fortune cookies, however, I suddenly saw that, in removing the cookies I had removed, I'd destroyed the yin-yang pattern; and what was left was the shape of a fierce, coiled dragon; and then I saw the crumbs all around me on the floor, and I wondered if they could be moulded, voodoo-style, into a little Joshua....

Book Two:

*Exposition: Second Subject
The Darklings*

"Her untitled mamafesta memorialising the Mosthighest
has gone by many names at disjointed times ... the pro-
teiform graph itself is a polyhedron of scripture."
—*Finnegans Wake*

from a Sotheby's Catalogue:

On Truth
by
Philip Etchison

My writing block, it seems, is permanent. As a result, I find my annual address from the poetry chair of this august institution to be more and more of a joke, year after year. What can one talk about, when one has been struck dumb? What eternal verities may I discourse on? Do I have a right to discourse at all?

I have decided to venture into the treacherous shoals of ontology....

What is truth?

Last night, I came very close to an answer. You see, I was dining with the president ... oh, I see you're laughing already. How could a third-rate holder of the poetry chair at a third-rate institution such as this even know the president? Well, what you've got to realize is that it was in an alternate reality. Well, what, you may ask, is an alternate reality? It's a place where truth is different. There are an infinite number of alternate realities. You remember Schrödinger's cat? But it's not just the cat, you see. Everything that is capable of being

in that box *is;* possibility, therefore, is
the unseen womb of truth.

The truth is in that wombbox. But
which truth? *All* of them. Think of the
truth as the slip of paper you find in a
fortune cookie; what it means hangs on
what you mean to ask.

*— coffee-stained ms. found stuck in a
shredder at Blair House, Washington, DC ,
along with a prescription for Prozac.
Believed to be in the handwriting of
Philip Etchison. (Analysis available for
viewing one week before the auction, 9
a.m. through 4:30 p.m.)*

— offered by an Anonymous Source.

— reserve $10

Five
A Bad Hair Day in Hell

Theo Etchison:

It was the 90s, the time before the mad millennium. But all the money in the world couldn't buy a Coke and a candy bar....

Today's a bad hair day for the mad king. He staggers up and down in the snow, that mane of his flying every which way. Okay, you see the sorcerer king dude in a movie, his hair's always all cool, with the wind whipping it and you flick your head one way and your hair all streams the other way, together as shit, and it should with all the fucking hairspray they use, but here in the hell world of ice and snow there's no hairspray.

King Strang shambles through the slush, Here and there his hair stands on end like he's been electrocute. Other places it's all flat, and then it's wavy, too, and bald in patches.

I stand and watch.

"Am I mad?" the mad king screams.

We're at the edge of the river, but the river's impassable. It's a river with icebergs and dead fish. We've been camped here for a while, I don't know how long, maybe a whole year. I don't really know because time seems to be standing still. I haven't aged. Every day's the same. I don't mean that we're repeating the same day over and over, but it does feel that way sometimes.

"Tell me, boy! Am I mad?" says the king again. The wounds on his forehead are festering. He waves the scepter at me.

"I'm your Truthsayer," I tell him. "You know you don't want to hear the answer to that question, because you know it'll be the truth, and truth could kill you."

"What are we doing here? Why are we still trying to get back on the river?"

"We're going to the source," I say.

"What for?"

"So you can start over," I say.

"Well, let's get on with it."

It's started to snow again. The sky is completely black. I don't think this world *has* sunlight; if it does, I've never seen it. I think of this as hell because it's a place that doesn't know the meaning of warmth, of love; because I feel so totally cut off that I want to just fucking die. But then again, I am dead, I remind myself. Dead to all the people who really matter to me. In fact, for them, I've never even really existed.

We have a little raft that's mostly made of ice and few planks here and there, and right now it sits jammed against the bank of the river, jutting into the snowbank. It's a pretty raft. It has a prow, of thoughts, that's sculpted into the image of a woman, a naked woman with arms outstretched and her lips slightly parted as though to say she loves me. I made that sculpture myself; in the weeks upon weeks that we've been here, unable to go anywhere, I've just been chiselling away at that chunk of ice with a little Swiss Army knife that I picked up in some other universe long ago and far away.

The mad king rants again, and I go back to work on the sculpture. I'm working on her eyes now. I carve and carve the cold ice and still her eyes are blind. Why can't I go back to her? I know the answer to that, of course. It's the original sin thing. It's a great mystery, what me and my mom did together; we danced the universe back from the brink of chaos; but the universe is still teetering. You know how it is. *The darkness comprehendeth it not.* I am a Truthsayer who is losing my power, and my mother is a goddess who has lost hers, and the king is mad.

"Still carving?" says the king. I turn to look at him. His eyes are wild. "I'll make breakfast," he says, and clambers over jagged ice to retrieve two frozen fish. Back on the river bank, he takes his scepter and bangs it on the snow a couple of times, and blue fire spurts up from the ground; he stabs the two fish with the butt end of the scepter and, grasping the great jewel in both hands, waves the whole shish kebab over the flames. This is how we eat here in hell. "Hungry?" he says.

"Yeah, dude," I say. I leave my carving for a while and chow down. The fish is bitter. I don't bother to skin it, I just sort of gnaw at it and pull out the bones.

"How much longer until you find the way?" says the king.

I pull the cosmos-marble out of the pocket of my jeans. Squint, hold it up to one eye. In the old days I could just reach inside it with my mind and I'd unravel all the strands of the river in my head, but now the crystal ball has become murky. I still don't see where we are exactly. I only know we have to struggle on, battle the current, track our destinies to their source, or else I'll never be able to go home. Jesus, home: what a concept. Just to be able to go to the mall. Just to be able to wolf down a Big Mac. I stare into the marble some more. There's a million strands down there, and they twist and wriggle and I can't seem to be able to grab one loose end so I can start the untangling.

"What kind of a Truthsayer are you?" says the mad king.

"I'm not that good anymore," I say. His hair really is exceptionally messy today. You could build a cuckoo's nest in it and you'd never notice. "But you know, there should be a new Truthsayer coming soon."

"How do you know?"

"I made him to take my place." I start to think about original sin again. It haunts me. I've had sex with mom. Oh, I know, we were gods at the time, all gods commit incest, I mean, when you're at the top of the food chain who else is there to fuck, right, but now it makes me feel like shit. Okay, so it had to happen. Joshua was dead, totally fucking dead. But I could bring him back if only I would give up the thing that made me the perfect Truth- sayer — my purity.

I can lie now. I've practiced on the mad king. Oh, little things like, "I feel fine," or "It's a nice day." Every- one says these things all the time. They're kind of these little pinprick untruths that shore up the house of cards that is all that humans have for security. I couldn't say those things before, but now I'm starting to.

"Who is he, this new Truthsayer? We'd better find him, or we'll never get anywhere."

I put the marble away. The only alternative is to sort of slog away at the ice itself, hack at it with icepicks until it gives and we can go on. What use is a map if you can't read it?

I don't want to tell him who the new Truthsayer is ... I guess I just don't want to admit the truth, that I've cre- ated someone better than myself, something that has to take my place ... who's going to be the one to stand at the edge of the precipice at the end of the story ... I don't want to admit that I can't see it all, can't see the clear white line all the way from the beginning of the world until its end ... not like before. So I don't tell Strang the truth. And even my not telling him, which isn't an out- right lie, only an evasion, chips away at who I was, and pushes me a little more towards who I will become ... draws me astray.

So here I am in front of the boat of ice with a fish head in my hand, staring at a blind statue of my mother,

the goddess of the cosmos; and the fish head's blind because it's dead, and I'm blind because I threw away my
sight to save the world, and I get to thinking, all three of
us don't have to be.

And this little scene springs to my mind from back
in the real world (which real world? I mean world one,
the world we started off in) and —

— we're in Virginia, see, and it's before Mom was
diagnosed with the cancer so I guess I'm just little, it's
even before the 90s, cause I'm eating out of my *Return of
the Jedi* plastic plate. And we're having fish, and I'm
playing with my food.

"Finish it up," Dad says, "because your mother has
made this cake, you see, and it's crammed with chocolate
and cherries and cream, and we're all salivating for dessert but we can't do anything because you're not finishing the entrée."

So I'm all, "Dad, I hate mackerel. I can't stand looking into its eyes."

So Dad says: "There's a lesson to be learned from
that, my son," and he goes into his PBS Joseph Campbell
lecturing mode, and he says (meanwhile, Joshua has
slipped away to call Serena, who secretly loves him but
he has no idea about that and only I do because it's a
time when I still see the truth) "a fish, you see, being the
ancient symbol of the Christian faith; but of course it
goes back much further than that. It's also the sacred
penis of Osiris. You may recall that, in Egyptian mythology, mean old Set cut the god Osiris into thirteen pieces
and threw him into the Nile; and Isis wept for, what was
it, three days and nights? or was it forty? are we confusing mythologies here? and she never found the last piece,
but she brought him back to life anyway, and that's why
people used to eat fish on Fridays: not just in memory of
Jesus' death, but also because the penis is the fish is the
male element of the yin-yang creative power that is the
river of life...."

"You're saying that I don't want to eat this fish because I have a subconscious fear of eating dick."

Dad smiles a little.

"Well, bullshit," I say. "I'm not afraid of anything." And I started devouring the animal with gusto. Except for the head. "Okay, I *am* afraid of the eyes. They're like, watching me."

"A very neolithic way to behave," Dad says. "Treating the dead as living, I mean. Everything having its own resident spirit. Animism. Very potent. Very profound."

"Oh, Phil," Mom says, "do you have to intellectualize quite that much? Maybe he just doesn't like to stare at fish eyes...."

"Windows of the soul, huh," I say.

"If thine eye offend thee, pluck it out," says Dad.

"The Bible?" Mom says.

"Actually no," he says, "it's from this great Roger Corman movie, *X — The Man with the X-Ray Eyes.* Saw it when I was young. It's a movie about someone who can see through *everything* ... he can see all the way into the mind of God ... and finally it drives him crazy and he ... rips out his own eyeballs." Odd movie for him to talk about in a way, I mean, we're a PBS *Janus Collection* family, we spend more time looking at *Alexander Nevsky* than at Freddie Krueger's latest exploits. It must be one of Dad's secret vices. I store away the info.

I stare into the eyes ... into the eyes ...

... and finally I do pluck them out, one by one, like in the Tom Lehrer song about Oedipus, using the left edge tine of the salad fork, and I keep staring at them all through the Black Forest cake, and you know, in time, they do seem to stare back after all, there does seem to be a flash of life in them....

While I'm remembering that little scene I'm still scraping away at the ice on the statue's face. On a whim, I pry out the fish eyes and pop them in those icy sockets.

Now she almost looks human.

I put my arms around her, woman of ice.

Wait. I think she's coming to life.

I think she's moving. Breathing. I think, I think … a veil of mist that's come between us that's maybe like her breath, all hanging in the air, mingling with my own. Fucking Jesus don't play tricks on me, I think.

At that moment I hear Strang yelling.

I turn around.

He's standing on like this big old white crag. He too is craggy, and his hair's all standing straight up like he's got his fist up a light socket. And he's screaming: "The music, the music, the music —!" at the top of his lungs and for a moment I hear another fragment of my sundered childhood —

— *turn off the fucking stereo I'm trying to write poetry* —

"Turn it off, turn it off," the king screams, with his hands over his ears. I listen. At first I don't hear anything at all. But then, there does come a sound, at last —

It's kind of a flute sound but really sweet, really high. The melody seems to be part of the whining of the wind until you really listen hard, and then you can make out a kind of melody. Not a simple tune, but one that undulates and twists in on itself, a tune like a tangle of knitting; it reminds me of the millions of lightstrands inside the little marble that's supposed to show me where I'm supposed to go.

As I listen I realize that there's an absolute truth in this music. Now there's a weird concept. But only someone who has Truthsaying in his genes can maybe feel it this way, in his bones. There's a chill that doesn't come from the snow, the knowledge that here's a truth truer than I ever saw. Why? Because no matter what I see, I still have to filter it through language, and language is distortion; it's a lens that changes reality.

This is a scary thing.

"The new Truthayer is coming," I say softly.

The king screams: "No, no, no, turn off the music!" and I see why: the music is showing him things about himself he never knew, never wanted to know; the music is pushing him closer to falling into the abyss.

I can't explain what's going through me. I mean, this is what I made, the savior of the world, the fruit of my sacrifice, and now he's coming down the pike to fulfil everything and set us all free, right? Then why does it piss me off so much? Is it because like, *I'm* not the fucking kwisatz haderach after all? Is it because I was better than everyone once, could see further, deeper, and now I've discovered I've only been a one-eyed man in the country of the blind, and here comes old two-eyes, my son, my Frankenstein's monster? The music is really getting to me, each shrill note jabbing into me like a lancet. Fucking Jesus. I'm scared. Really scared. "I think I want my mother," I say softly.

And that's when I feel the hand on my shoulder.

A soft hand, warm, womanly; the first warm thing I've ever encountered on this whole fucking planet. "Mom —" I start to say, and turn to see the ice-sculpture unhitching itself from the prow of our ice-raft, spreading out her arms, slowly, and begin to cry from those fish-eyes, and the tears are melting her cheeks, rilling down the crags of ice we've foundered against, and yeah, she's crying me a river, dissolving herself in the process of it —

"Don't leave me!" I cry out.

"I'm not leaving you," she whispers. "I'll see you at the end of your journey."

"Why can't you stay? You're still my mother, aren't you? Even though we —"

"But I'm also the fish-eyed goddess. The river needs the male as well as the female in order to flow. Salmon swim a thousand miles upstream to spawn. You did well, Theo."

"Then why am I so confused? Why can't I see the way ahead anymore?"

"Maybe the way to understand ordinary people is to become more like them," she says.

"Mom!"

But she's already dissipating into the mist, and then I hear her voice again: *Theo Theo Theo* in the wail of the distant flute, and I see her sort of wafting away from me, liquefying the ice as she flutters upriver. So I'm all, "Mom, mom, mom," but she doesn't turn back.

The river is melting like crazy now. Ice boulders are smashing into each other and grinding and squeaking against each other and disintegrating. I start to untie the raft but the raft too is melting, melting. King Strang still stands on the ledge of ice, railing at the empty sky. He howls, he shrieks. "Come on," I shout, and then I stride up the bank toward him and start to tug at his sleeve.

"Whither?" he cries out. "What am I? Where am I going?"

"The river is thawing out," I say, "and it's time to move on."

"Thawing? thawing? what river?"

Even the gods have Alzheimer's! "The source. The beginning. The end." The river is roaring now, and the sound of shattering icebergs is like a hundred-car pileup on the Beltway. And above it all comes the fluting. He's near, he really is. All that's left of the raft is a couple of pieces of driftwood; the rest was all ice. My mother, a translucent goddess, is all dancing on the water in the distance. Maybe there's even sunlight there, at the horizon where the river seems to lead.

"I don't know how to get there," I say, "but I am your Truthsayer, King Strang, and I have to lead you. Now move your ass or we'll drown." I pull the king off his slope (he's frail now, easy to pull) and then I sort of half carry, half drag him to the water's edge. I step into the water and so does the king, and the shards of the raft sort of drift our way and we are able to clamber on top. And look, there's more wood now, blackened planks that have been buried beneath the ice, and they're all bobbing up and down around us, there's even rope to last them together with ... "We're finally on our way," I say.

The king sits down, sort of squats, by the edge of the raft. "I think I remember now. I had three children once. I divided my kingdom up according to who loved me the most. The one who told the truth I exiled from my sight."

That's pretty much *King Lear*, but it's close enough to the truth. "Thorn and Katastrofa are dead," I say, "fighting over the pieces of your kingdom. The river flows through a million universes, but the gates are shutting off, one by one, because your kingdom's falling apart, because of your own foolishness."

"Foolishness! How dare you! Guards!" He reaches over to slap me.

"You have a third child," I say. "Where is Ash?"

"Don't speak to me of him. What I've spoken, I've spoken. I'm a king, and that's how a king should be."

I don't speak. It'll take a while to lead him to the truth, especially since I'm grasping it less and less myself these days. And now that we're moving again, I also have to paddle, which I do with a sort of oar that seems to have drifted alongside us; the king uses his his scepter, which gives off sparks whenever it touches the water; the scepter is death and the water is life, you see....

There's a bend in the river, and suddenly there's a whole new vista. That happens a lot when you travel along the river; you switch from world to world in a split second, and here's a world that I know too well. Shit it scares me.

See, the river broadens out, and the waters become a little less turbulent, and the snow thins out a little, and then there's like these old Easter Island heads looming out of the water, and sphinxes, and pyramids, and even the top of the Empire State Building. And in the distance, by the bank, there's a tall black cliff, and perched on the cliff like a tarantula is a castle I know well: Thornstone Slaught.

Nothing to fear, I tell myself. Thorn is dead, and the castle is probably abandoned. Or maybe it's full of squatters. Those miserable subjects of Thorn's, from whom he used to drink blood.

"You know this place?" I say to the king.

"No," he says. He looks shiftily from side to side.

I know that he does, though, somewhere inside that festering brain of his; I know there's something in the castle he's going to have to confront, which is why we have to go through it on our way to the source of the river; thing is, I'm no longer navigating.

The music of truth is in the air.

Someone else has taken over the job of guiding us all upriver. I have to trust him. I have to believe that he's going to lead us all through all the right tribulations and through to the healing of the world; if I didn't believe that, I might as well give the fuck up.

And yet I have to admit I'm angry about it.

Why isn't it me?

I never wanted to be the messiah before, but now that I'm not, why I am full of such rage and envy?

Can't think about it now. Mermaids are swimming up to us. They're stretching out their arms and throwing flower-wreaths at us. The flowers are long dead, rotting, but they are probably all they have. They are shouting at us: "Save us, save us, save us," and the king is staring at the castle, which we're approaching rapidly, his eyes filled with loathing and longing.

Six
Christmas in the White House

Phil Etchison:

We hadn't gone that far when it all changed. I should have known it would, but I didn't expect it quite so soon. All we did, it seemed, was to round a corner, trudge across a narrow ledge athwart a precarious precipice that felt like it was going to collapse at any moment; and then, by that familiar old Joycean "commodius vicus of recirculation" I suppose it was, we found ourselves face to face again with the icy statue that was my wife; only, while Chris twirled the magic flute and the notes flew twittering about our heads, so sharp and fluttery you could see their feathers before they soared, swooped, scattered into the flurrying snow, the statue wept, and I could not console my wife, because I was merely flesh and blood.

"Where are we?" I asked Corvus. I knew Chris wasn't going to tell me anything. "Did we just circle back to the crossroads one more time, and we've really gone nowhere?"

"Maybe," said Milt.

"Maybe? What kind of an answer is that?"

"Living in the white man's world," he said, "sometimes the forked tongue thing does come rather glibly to one's lips. Sorry. I'll think of a good answer in a moment."

As I waited for a good answer — and I knew that with Milt, a good answer could be a long time coming, because he'd have to consider and ponder the eternal verities for a while first — I saw that behind my wife there was a blizzard — well, just a sort of sheet of whiteness that hung oppressively like a Shakespearean arras — but I could make out dim shapes. Perhaps a castle. Yes, that was it. A gray, twisted silhouette, a sort of bulimic parody of Castle Dracula. Heard thunder too, though maybe it was just the percussive accompaniment to Chris's music.

"What I mean to say," said Milt, "is that you don't step in the same river twice."

"Is that all you can come up with?"

"Seriously, this may or may not be the same crossroads, Phil, but you are definitely not the same person. For one thing, you know who you are now."

"I do?"

I had to think about that for a long time. My name was Philip Etchison. I held the poetry chair at a modest university in Northern Virginia, and I was the author of a number of books poetry, undistinguished in sales figures, undistinguished, also, perhaps, in quality, though this was not something I much liked to reflect upon....

"How many children do you have, Phil? Quick now! Say the first thing that comes into your head."

"Two. No, what am I saying, one, one!"

"Right the first time. Names?"

"Josh and Theo."

"Why does your woman weep?"

"She is dying of cancer."

Was I making all this up? No. I knew these implausible nuggets to be the simple truth. How could that be?

"Do you know the name of that castle?" Milt said. His eyes glowed. Children of the Damned, I thought, suddenly remembering some old movie. What was a movie now? Never mind. It would come back to me.

"Thornstone Slaught," I said, mouthing the mouthful as though it were a household word. And suddenly, it was.

"Good," he said softly. "Let's go."

A limousine pulled up. All of a sudden, Milt Stone was the uniformed and white-gloved driver. We piled in — Chris, in his favorite blue silk tuxedo, the one he'd appeared on Oprah in — my wife still a creature of ice and marble, and I in the secondhand dinner jacket I had worn to give my half-assed speech about ontology to the college — and we sat down, and the invitation from President Karpovsky was suddenly in my hand, on the ivory linen stationery, in the Basildon Bond envelope.

"My name is Philip Etchison," I said softly. "I am a second-rate poet with powerful friends. I have two sons."

Chris turned to me. He put his flute back in his pocket. He put his arms around me. His cheek touched my cheek. Close-lipped, he hummed a single highpitched note, and all at once I felt coldness and loss. He can transmit emotions this way, just by the sheer vibrations. In a way it's so much more profound than speech, yet how can I respond, I whose whole life has been the manipulation of words, those airy packets of compacted meaning? I'm like a man blind from birth, trying to gaze up at the Sistine Chapel ceiling, intuiting awe from the reverberant hush of the sighted.

"Yes," he's telling me, I think, "you have two sons, and one of them isn't me, and it hurts me even more than it hurts you."

We drove on. The Potomac was unusually icy; Washington usually only has a few days of bitter snow; winter is ambiguous here. People were actually skating, but here and there strange shapes peered up from the ice floes: I thought I saw one of those Easter Island heads ... here a great stone Anubis, baying the invisible moon with a soundless howling ...

We crossed the Fourteenth Street Bridge, made a left and eased our way over to Sixteenth and Pennsylvania. The gates of Thornstone Slaught were also the gates of the White House. A marine saluted us and the iron portals swung open. Another marine ushered us into a foyer; another into a corridor; another into an elegant antechamber; everywhere we went, the walls were lined with living hands, clutching torches, buried wrist-deep in the concrete, swaying back and forth in time with a melody that seemed to issue from Chris's lips.

I said to Mary: "I feel a strange kind of déjà vu."

She didn't speak; she was still a statue, her arms outstretched, standing on a golden dolly wheeled along by oiled and kilted Nubian slaves, and fanned by a child of indeterminate gender, nude but for a peacock feather strapped over its genitalia.

Indeed, I had done all this before, but it was somehow not the same. The corridors had not seemed to lead ever downward before, and the walls were not quite so echoey ... or were they? Certainly the limestone facings, with their phosphorescent specks, seemed familiar ... the stalactites and stalagmites ... the ever-dripping sound of water ... drip, drip, drip, drip, drip. The little shrines set into the walls, the wailing women with joss-sticks clasped to their bosoms, the statuettes of gods with many heads and animal faces ... all these things seemed more and more familiar even though I knew I had never encountered them quite in this combination before.

Finally, we were in the dining room, and there was President Oren Karpovsky. "Ah," he said, "you're here. I did so want to listen to your son's celebrated music of madness. Is it true that you can experience more layers of truth by hearing his music even than by shrooming or peyote?"

"Just the sort of thing an ex-hippie president is expected to say," I said, "this close to the end of the mad millennium."

"Exactly." He smiled, and Milt Stone came into the room. He was a homeless Indian in shabby clothes, but I knew that underneath the filthy clothes and rancid body odor was a powerful shaman.

"Where's Serena?" I asked the president.

"Uh, I don't know. Changing, perhaps. Women. You know. Your wife, on the other hand —"

"She's already changed," I said, "beyond recognition, even."

What was happening between us, here in this room that was clearly not really this room at all, but a twisted simulacrum of another room in another universe? Sure, we were standing around making small talk, but the conversation wasn't quite connecting — it was a sort of a simulacrum of a conversation, if you know what I mean. Hot air, vowels, consonants, lexemes, phonemes, fragments of meaning being shuttlecocked back and forth, feeding the illusion of communication, but in reality....

We sat down at the dinner table.

"I'm afraid that this is going to be a rather frugal Christmas dinner after all," said Oren. "I couldn't bear to keep the staff away from their families this evening ... the marines are another matter, of course, being marines ... so I've sent out for Chinese."

Chinese!

We were, indeed, recycling crazily back to the beginning of our story. Because I knew more and more of what was going on. I knew that I had two sons. Chris, the apple of my eye, wasn't my real son at all.

"It's a strange kind of a Chinese restaurant," said the president. "It's called the Blue Moon, and usually, when you call, the line's busy. It's a *Brigadoon* kind of a restaurant if you know what I mean; it only pops into existence now and then; otherwise it floats inside its own sort of reality. But the food — it's beyond belief."

"I think I've eaten there," I said slowly. "But it was in Arizona."

"Yeah, that was its last documented appearance; read about it in the Enquirer," said president Karpovsky, and it was at that point that a cadaverous Chinese maître d' in Mandarin attire, followed by a bevy of pigtailed ladies in pink silk cheongsams, came gliding into the dining room carrying silver platters of wildly exotic foods.

"Mr. Huang, isn't it?" I said.

"We meet from time to time," said the Chinese gentleman, more an ethnic caricature than a real person. "Aren't you the Etchisons? What has happened to your good wife?"

"Apotheosis," I said.

"And your sons. Dead, are they not?"

"I —"

"Cornelius Huang, at your service," he said, bowing low. "We always seem to meet at times like this — at the beginnings of apocalyptic journeys."

"This isn't the beginning of a journey," I protested. "Actually I seem to have been traveling for far too long already ... I'm trying to yank the emergency cord, stop the train, damn the penalty for improper use, but I can't find it anywhere, and the scenery's starting to repeat itself —"

"We'd better start eating," said President Karpovsky, "or we'll never get to the fortune cookies."

Platter after platter, was being uncovered. "Here," said Cornelius Huang, "is a very fine sea-turtle soup. The turtle has been marinated in crocodile's tears for a hundred years, then braised in a bouillon-based herb medley for two hours before finally having its unfortunate throat slit."

"Great," I said listlessly. Chris was already attacking the soup. "Manners, Chris," I said, but he only looked at his statuesque mother with doleful, welling eyes.

"Here's a particularly fine dish," said Cornelius Huang, gesticulating with one arm (the other clenched an

impressive-looking horn tight between armpit and el-
bow) at a trolley that was being wheeled in by an entire
bevy of cheongsamed beauties. As they raised the cover,
he said, "It's the head of John the Baptist, basted in a lubricious Salome dressing."

The contents of the platter resembled the celebrated
painting by Caravaggio.

"Our lobster diablo," said Huang, and another dish
showed a giant crustacean — something out of Captain
Nemo, perhaps — writhing in agony as the flames of hell
seethed about him. The odor of brimstone filled the dining room. "Better shut that fast," Huang said, and, bowing, the oriental ladies slammed down the lid. This was
no ordinary takeout service, but a meal of allegorical pre-
tensions, a Dantean odyssey of a meal, and now I was
beginning to remember that other meal much more vividly, the meal in Arizona where all hell broke loose for
the first time.

I turned to Milt.

"Should I eat?" I said.

"Depends," he said.

Chris lifted up a shushing hand and sang one note.
Oren looked very uncomfortable. He started ladling food
onto my plate. Chris kept singing the note, over and over
in an ear-splitting ostinato, and that made the president
get ever more frantic and talk faster and faster.

"You'd better eat," said President Karpovsky. "You
don't know where your next meal is coming from. You
don't even know where you're coming from. In fact, you
don't even know —"

The president exploded.

Literally. I mean, it was the whole alien-pops-out-of-
stomach thing, only the alien was as big as he was, and it
sort of tipped him apart in a shower of blood and in-
nards. What suddenly stood in his place was someone
else altogether. Tall. Pale-skinned, and swathed in a
sweeping black cloak that sort of fluttered (there was no
wind) and gave off simmering, seething sounds; a crea-

ture with ruby-citrine eyes and thin, bloodless lips; a man with fangs, more handsome than Dracula, more frightening than Death.

"Master! You made it through!" said Cornelius, and prostrated himself.

"It was pretty simple," said Thorn — for that was who it was. I recognized him right away, and another piece of my jigsaw past settled into place. "Mr. Karpovsky was not exactly one of your more strong-willed psyches. After all, he got to be president by playing up the wishy-washy factor — no one really wanted to do anything on the eve of the Mad Millennium."

"How do you know so much about Washington politics? You're not even a human being," I said.

"True," Thorn said, "but I've been stuck inside one, trying to get out, for several days."

"What's more," I said, "you're dead, supposedly."

"Love never dies," said Thorn, "and the same might be said of hate, which, as you poets are always fond of saying, is but the reverse side of the coin."

It was hard for me to answer, soaked as I was with the president's blood, standing as I was in a room that was growing steadily gloomier and more musty. The wallpaper was peeling off the walls and behind it was the pitted stone of a mediaeval castle. The chandeliers had gone from crystal to smoky candlelight. Shadows danced, leaped, rippled. Thorn spread his cloak wide open.

"I've gotta have blood," he said.

The platters full of food were no longer even pretending to be Chinese. Each one held a young human being, folded, trussed up, arms and legs broken in order to be squashed into the space of a serving dish, and very much alive. Some moaned; most looked ahead with that lifeless, listless gaze that characterizes the irredeemably condemned; they had the Auschwitz stare. Thorn wandered among the platters — there were dozens more in the shadows, and the cheongsam-clad waitresses were now a ghoulish army of the grave, their flesh rotting from their bones — and now and then he stooped to sample a few drops of blood. "Gotta savor it," he said. "It's been too long."

Too long, too long.

When would I stand beside the river once again and greet my two sons, my two real sons, beneath the cottonwoods in the Virginia sunset?

I ached for a world that no longer was save in a few lines of poetry in my mind. How can you yearn for what doesn't exist, has never existed? This place was reality.

"I want —" I began. I felt Milt's hand on my shoulder.

"Patience," he said softly. "Before salvation comes the harrowing of hell."

Thorn laughed. "That's what you think," he said, "but the longer you harrow, the deeper you'll burrow; the more you sound, the less you'll breach; the spiral downward is a möbius strip; there is no surface; to paraphrase Monty Python, your very existence is a dead parrot."

At this point, Milt Stone cast off the End of the World placard from around his neck, leaped up onto the dining-room table, and began to dance up a storm.

Chris laughed: a silvery, bright laugh, the only thing of light in the whole benighted castle.

"Catch!" Milt shouted, and plucked a drum out of the air. Chris caught it one-handed, and began pounding away with the mouthpiece end of the magic flute. Each drumbeat sent a bolt of light across the chamber. There were ankle bells on Milt's naked feet, and each jingle was another puddle of light, and Chris kept laughing until his very laughter became a song.

"Dancing'll do you no good, chief," said Thorn. "You people always think that if only you get the right moves, the old palefaces will go back across the sea and leave you to your buffalo hunting. You were wrong then and you're wrong now."

But Milt didn't stop dancing. Once again I was on the sidelines while the forces of light and dark were locked in some cosmic battle. I looked at my wife. Perhaps she looked at me; I could not tell. I looked at Cornelius Huang, who attempted now and then to fend off the blasts of light with blasts of his trumpet. Occasionally, he would hit one, and the light-beam would shatter and scatter. From around us, out of the walls themselves, there issued another kind of music: clanking, industrial, electronic cacophonies that seemed to challenge the music of voice and drum. Duelling banjos of a sort — a David and Goliath sort, I thought in despair. "Mary, Mary, do something," I said, but I knew she could not intervene; the sickness in her soul was the sickness of the world; to cure one we would have to cure the other.

Milt danced. His body seemed to become more curvy, more ambiguous; sometimes he seemed to have a dozen arms and legs. Light darted from the drum, ran rings about his features. The vampire stood and waved his arms about and laughed, and Chris too laughed, the evil-villain laugh versus the pure-child laugh; and Huang trumpeted about while the silk-clad zombie Huangettes pom-pomed in the background.

And me? The spectacle was so confusing that I simply started to tune it out — like a hundred MTV videos crammed into one minute — image after image and nothing to cling to — and so I reached out for something else, something solid, something I could truly believe in —

And I saw Theo.

Running towards me across a plain of ice that stretched for all infinity ... a small boy in shorts and grunge teeshirt, hastening towards me, his father, his truth ... "Forgive me!" I cried out. "I didn't know what I was doing."

At this moment of supreme, grotesque despair, the walls in the dining room began to crack, and there was an intense, blue, blinding radiance pouring into the darkness. Someone was coming — crashing through the stone — a woman. Serena Somers. The warring music ceased abruptly.

"Sorry I'm late," she said.

Seven
Attack of the 50 Foot Woman

Serena Somers:

Well like, I wanted to wait to see if I could conjure up Joshua, but all of a sudden, I felt this irresistable force pulling me away, somehow, somewhere ... I was being summoned by some mighty power. I gathered up the cookie crumbs into a napkin, folded it up carefully, stuck it in a pocket, and then I allowed myself to be caught up in what seemed to be a giant tornado or whirlwind — thank you, Dorothy — that was sweeping me some- where, somehow. I was much bigger than myself, and I was smashing through the wall of my imprisonment, and it turned out I wasn't as far away from Oren and the oth- ers as I thought at all, because there I was, in the middle of the Christmas party that started this whole thing off, and my live-in-lover was exploding in a mass of gore and tissue ... sort of a Texas Chainsaw Massacre kind of thing, I mean, gross.

Mr. E. was there. Milton was there. Chris was there. The shaman and the truthsayer were cooking up a crazy kind of music, howling, jangling, banging, whistling. Everyone looked up at me. I guess I must have looked a little different than my usual self.

"Sorry I'm late," I said. At the sound of my voice, a chandelier cracked and smashed down on the roast turkey.

"Greetings, sis," said the vampire prince who seemed to have pieces of my live-in lover's skin hanging from his clothes. "Glad you could make the party."

"I'm not your sister," I said.

"Sure you are," he said. "You've come back to me. We won't fight one another any more — learned that lesson pretty damn thoroughly. We need to stick together, or we'll never be able to get our pieces of the pie."

"I haven't come back at all," I said, and then I felt the dragon stirring inside my stomach again.

Yes I have, said the voice of the other woman inside me.

"Oh, come on, sis," said Thorn. "Crack open the egg, break free of that confining human flesh. We've worlds to conquer and all that, and there's not much time, what with the structure of the universe collapsing all around us."

"True," I said.

The dragon woman was growing inside my belly. I knew that Oren had already gone through the alien-busting-out-of-the-stomach routine, and I wasn't anxious to be next. But Katastrofa was, I mean, seriously getting out of hand. She had gone from embryo to about ten months in the last five minutes, and my belly was swelling. Mary Etchison once told me about childbirth, gave me the whole shitting-a-watermelon metaphor, and it wasn't something I was anxious to try, especially if the baby was a baby dragon and perfectly happy to rip me apart to get out.

I looked around anxiously. Mr. E. was staring at me with his mouth wide open, and I guess I realized something was amiss when my head collided with ceiling, bricks began to dislodge themselves, and my head would stop pushing against the stone.

"I feel like Alice in Wonderland," I said.

Thorn raised his arms, and his cloak flapped like the leathern wings of a giant bat ... the wings of Satan himself. I could feel the dragon within me, and she was rumbling and shaking, and any minute now she was going to figure out how to breathe fire, and then where would I be? I couldn't allow myself to let her out.

"What's happening to you?" Mr. E. shouted, and his voice seemed curiously far away, but then of course he was way down there.

"I can't help myself," I shouted back. I didn't know my own decibel capacity, I guess, for another chandelier shattered and sprayed all the people down there with shards of glass. Mr. E. dodged, and Milt and Chris took shelter beneath a great big drum. Only Cornelius and Thorn were unfazed ... and Mrs. E., of course, who was a statue in this universe. "There's a dragon inside me trying to bust loose. I can stay rigid, and explode, or I can go with the flow, try to stretch myself to contain her...."

Suddenly I realized there was a rightness to what I was doing, just as Oren had done completely the wrong thing and had perished as a result, though of course perishing was not necessarily the final word around here. I had to make myself big enough to accommodate the dragon. There is a dragon inside every woman, and if she can't stretch her soul wide enough to contain it, it's going eat its way out and destroy her.

"I don't care how big Katastrofa gets," I screeched. "I'm just going to grow along with her. She's always going to be inside me, not me inside her."

But the voice inside me screamed, "Let me out, let me out, let me out," and then its rage seemed to subside and its whined, "Let me out, let me out," in the voice of a suffering, imprisoned child, and I was tempted.

Thorn flew at me. He darted at my stomach, fangs bared. I had long since outgrown my garments, so I guess I was pretty much naked at this point, except for a couple of denim patches over my pudenda ... how strangely prudish the new me was ... Thorn wrapped his arms around me was was trying to gnaw his way in.

I slapped him aside. Flung my arms about a couple more times, and sent more stones tumbling. A gargoyle plummeted from its perch. Tapestries ripped from the walls and caught fire on the candles.

Thorn rushed at me again. He careened through the air like an F-15. I dodged. He circled. I swatted him. I was getting bigger now, and the dragon inside me was calling to him. I had to grow some more. I broke through a few more floors. The castle was becoming an encumbrance. I started to kick and pound. It began to fall apart. House of cards, really; just needed the right kind of blows to like, self-destruct, virtually.

He charged again, this time swooping at me from a great height, funneling through the holes I had gouged out of the stone floors. I smashed more walls. Through the gaps in the ceilings, there was light now, lancet-like shafts of white light ... cobwebs were catching fire. Stone was turning to brimstone. Flames were running up and down the corridors, and still Thorn kept attacking me, and I was aware of his minions all about him, too, an army of bats and zombies and creatures of the night ... but they were no more threatening to me than a swarm of mosquitoes.

I tried a mighty kick. The foundations began to rumble. Well, actually, I think the whole mountain was shaking. I felt as powerful as a goddess. Shit, maybe I was a goddess in this world — if Mrs. E. was one, why not me? I started to really get into this.

Smash! A gargoyle-topped pillar snapped like a toothpick. Dust flying everywhere. More light now, riddling the smoky air, a forest of needles. I punched, I elbowed, I hula-hooped.

Thorn changed tactics. He and his minions started to grab at the Etchisons. I knew they weren't going to kill

them because they were still needed in the final spectacle. Mr. E was running around, trying to fend them off
with a soup ladle. The bigger I got, the more comical
these little humans seemed ... no wonder God sees the
world as a divine comedy ... the world is so minuscule to
him, I mean her, I mean, well, me, actually.

I decided to start doing a Godzilla kind of routine, so
I began stomping in their direction. Each dinosaurian
plod caused rock and tile to fly. I got down on my hands
and knees and scooped up the Etchison family in the
palm of my right hand, flicking off the bats and demons
with the fingers of my left. And meanwhile, Mrs. E sat at
the edge of the table, now and then anointing the whole
shebang with a tear or two, but otherwise quite, quite
still.

I was woman. It was time for them to hear me roar,
and I did so, a ten-ton torpedo of a bellow that got what
remained to the castle shaking like a humungous tuning
fork. Pretty damn awesome, I thought.

"It's okay, Mr. E.," I said. I held his hands over his
ears. "Whoops," I whispered, "I forgot how huge I've become."

"You used to gain weight and lose it like a yoyo," Mr.
E. shouted, "but this takes the cake!"

Thorn was buzzing around my eyeball. I couldn't
swat him that easily, so I tried to shake him by nodding
furiously.

"I know you want out," he screamed at the dragon
inside my belly.

I exhaled. A burst of blue flame exploded from my
nostrils. I could smell singed hair. I've hated that smell
ever since Lisa Peoples accidentally flicked her Bic beside my bangs in fourth grade. Thorn flew out of the
way.

"As long as I keep her inside me," I cried, "Your sis is
on my team now, not on yours."

"I'll be back," Thorn shouted. But you know, there's
nothing remotely Schwarzeneggeresque about a shout

like that when it comes from a creature the size of a fruit fly.

Thorn and his troops swarmed about my head. They darted, they hovered, they swooped. They tried to sting me, but I hardly felt anything. Only once or twice, when a pinprick drew blood, did I feel that an opening had been made into my soul, an opening that the dragon might escape through if I wasn't careful. It was time for another shout.

"Hold your ears, dudes," I said to the Etchisons (and Milt, who was still dancing up a tempest on a little mound of flesh between my index and my middle fingers.) "I'm gonna sing."

And this time I really did. I mean, I took in lungfuls of flame-tinged air and expelled them in an eerie song. I could feel my diaphragm working like a bellows, could feel the dragon churning inside me, could feel the smoke and fire stream from my lips with every ear-splitting note.

I've done all this before, I thought. The Christmas dinner at the White House, the mysterious bursting into song ... only the last time it happened it was only a foreshadowing of this ... it's the same event again, only deeper, richer, more resonant ... yeah, more resonant.

Then the awful thing happened. He and Cornelius Huang landed right on my hand, grabbed a hold of Chris, and started to yank him away. I couldn't shake them loose without dislodging Mr. and Mrs. E. as well. Thorn threw a dark cloak over Chris's head, and they took off. Dimly, I could hear Chris screaming.

The swarms of batlike creatures began to scatter. A mighty rumbling punctuated my valkyrie shrieks. Slabs of stone shattered to powder. Mr. E was running around in circles on my hand, skittish as a hamster on a treadmill. I roared several more times for good measure, until we were standing in a pile of rubble, and the light of a pale blue star was playing over piles of rock, which stood in circles around us on the barren ground. With a single song, I had rearranged the dark into a dozen concentric stone circles. Now that's magic, I thought. But I had to go after Chris. I could see him still, his head peering from the cloak of darkness Thorn had thrown over him. The vampire's minions flew hither and thither, and I could hear thin mocking laughter in the wind.

"Chris!" Mr. E shouted. I could see them in the distance. I started to stampede through the mounds of stone, but I couldn't get a good footing. The swarm was gone. I was a failure as a goddess after all.

Chris looked back for a moment, then looked away. What was he hiding? He could not hide if for long, surely. He was a truthsayer. There was some truth he did not want to utter. It must hurt more deeply than any other truth he knew.

"Shit," I said. The dragon inside me was laughing, I was sure of it; I could feel the rumbling in my belly, the squirting plumes of flame.

"Do you think you could start shrinking?" Mr. E shouted. "It's rather difficult to converse with you in your current, you know, state."

"I don't know how," I said.

"I've got just the thing," said Milt. He laid down his arm. "Can you hoist me up?" I did so, and he reached into a medicine pouch around his neck and pulled out a lump of something. I had to really peer to see it. It looked pretty grungy. Couldn't figure it out.

"What is it?" I almost forgot to whisper.

"Mushroom," said the nadlé. "It ought to work, if you know your Alice in Wonderland."

Mr. E. came to the rescue. "One side will make you taller ... the other will make you smaller. I think it was a caterpillar who said that, though he was somewhat opiumed out at the time." He was giggling uncontrollably.

"Is something wrong?" I said.

"Something wrong!" he said, flustered. "I'm stuck in someone else's dream, nothing is real, and a 50-foot woman is being hookah'ed up with shrooms by an apocalyptic Indian, and my son is not my son, and now he's been kidnapped by a damn vampire, and you want me to remain calm?"

I lifted my palm to my lips. I opened my mouth. I think my teeth must have unnerved Mr. E. — he was not the Fay Wray type — because he shrank back against the inside of my index finger.

"Pop it in," I said.

Milt Stone took a deep breath. There was no music in the air. Not even the sound of a breeze. It was the first still moment I had experienced since this adventure began. Milt concentrated hard, then — with fluidity and follow-through of a major league pitcher — he projected the mushroom into my mouth.

I started shrinking. It happened so fast that Mr. E. and the gang almost didn't have time to get out of my hand. In a second we were standing at the center of the great stones, which towered over us, and Mr. E. was towering over me, which made me feel much safer.

"You were great," he said. "Just like Allison Hayes in that old movie."

"No I wasn't," I said. "I lost Chris, for God's sake! How can you say I was great?"

Softly, Milt said, "Do not be sorrowful, Serena. He's a truthsayer. He goes the way that he must go. That is his nature. He will come back to us in the end. Thorn needs him to get to the source of the river. Whatever he does, he won't harm him, or he will have lost the war."

Phil Etchison:

The place was definitely akin to the blasted heath from Macbeth. Menhirs surrounded us, and here and there, strange, stunted trees pushed up out of the stony ground. The sun was not our sun, but a pallid blue.

My son was not my son, either. He was something quite other. Now that Chris had been spirited away on some ambiguous quest, I felt the way Joseph must have

felt when his wife gave birth in a stable and all those
kings and shepherds and angels showed up; I felt pretty
damn useless, pretty much a token human amid the gods
and goddesses and mythical beasts. They were all taking
it pretty damn calmly, these people — a man-woman-
shaman and a woman who was suddenly a teenage girl
who was suddenly a goddess ... not to mention my time-
frozen wife. What could one say? What could one do?

"Are we nearly there yet?" I said to Milt, realizing as I
spoke that I sounded just like a little kid on a long car
trip, across the Arizona desert maybe, watching the miles
of endless desert, losing all sense of time.

"Almost," he said, "almost."

"What has to happen," Serena said, "before we can all
just be ourselves again, before we can go home?"

I had long despaired of finding home at all. When
Serena said those words, I felt a surge of hope, but it was
only for a few seconds.

Milt said, "It's all pretty simple. We have to restore
the world to the way it was."

"How?" I said.

"We have to chase down and neutralize Thorn, or
this Thorn-simulacrum which is just the shadow of
Thorn already dead; for those who are really dead must
be made to return to death; those who should really be
alive must be brought back out of the land of shadow."

"And Theo," I said. "Theo ... aren't we supposed to be
looking for him? He's with this mad king, right? Going
toward the source of the great river."

"He is already running towards you, but time moves
at different paces in different parts of this continuum."

"And Josh?" said Serena. "Don't we have to bring
Josh back too?"

Serena said, "Look here," and took a folded-up napkin out of her pocket. "I think Josh is in these fortune
cookie crumbs. And I'm a goddess now, aren't I? Now
that I have the dragon within me. I can blow myself up to
the size of the Empire State Building, and shrink back to

normal by gulping down a mushroom. You think I could breathe life into these crumbs?"

"I don't know," Milt said. "You want to try?"

Then he started gathering firewood. He piled it up in front of my wife the marble statue, and presently started a bonfire by rubbing two sticks together. There was an altar-like ledge at the center of the circles of stones, large enough for all us to crowd on.

Meanwhile, Serena was spitting into her hand, shaping the crumbs into the crude likeness of a human being.

The sun was setting, and several moons were in the sky, crescents, half-moons, full moons; some were pockmarked, some striped, and others were bright and featureless.

Serena blew softly on her hand. Her breath was edged with dragonfire.

Nothing happened to the little cookie man, and after several more attempts she wrapped it up again and put it away.

"We're still missing something," she said sadly.

After a while, we all went to sleep in front of my wife, who watched over us with stony, moist eyes, her arms outstretched in benediction.

When we woke up, we were completely surrounded by water. Oh, the standing stones were still there, peering up from what seemed to be a crystal-clear lake; and we were still lying on the altar before the smouldering fire. In the distance, the Easter Island heads, pyramids, sphinxes, and other ancient artifacts still lay submerged, only more so. We had not moved, and yet, through the gateway of sleep, we had entered another world.

Things had been so much simpler when we were just one dysfunctional American family, driving through the Arizona desert toward a laetrile clinic in Mexico, fighting, trying to make sense of our little lives. I wanted it back, I wanted it all back ... even, God forbid, my wife's dying, that strange sick-sweet odor of the cancer that was eating her flesh....

Serena and Milt were roasting fish over the fire. In the distance, I thought I saw something familiar. A glint on top of one of the standing stones that was now an island in the crystal lake. "Milt," I said, pointing, "isn't that ... isn't it...."

It did indeed appear to be a battered station wagon, the very same vehicle in which our journey had begun.

Milt smiled. "You see," he said, "the world is knitting itself back into shape, and though this is a dark moment, and there are fearsome battles ahead of us, you can see that the past is coming back, a piece at a time. Soon it will start to flood back, and you'll be amazed you ever forgot any of it."

I didn't care. I was stripping off my shirt. I knew I could swim out to the car if I was picked the right stones to go island-hopping. Then, of course, there was the question of driving in the middle of the lake. I'd cross that bridge later. That car, I recalled, had a tendency to sprout a few more gears than your usual PRNDLL....

As long as there weren't any sharks....

Eight
The Truthsayer Speaks

Chris Etchison:

— and —
— father —
— and —
suddenly
suddenly I can speak
words come
the wind the words the darkness
rushing

"So!" The tall man, fire-eyes, coming to rest on the mountaintop, down looking, snow snow snow. "So, you can suddenly talk, Truthsayer."

— I —

— father —

Up looking: the sky, gray, many suns hidden. Around: the demon hordes. Bat wings, slitty eyes, eyes: citrine, coal, fire, smoke, hell. Wings flap, flap, flap, leather.

"And I know why you can talk. It's because I've set you free. Isn't that true, Cornelius?"

Across looking: the very tall mandarin, the golden trumpet: when he blasts the demon hordes fall on their

faces in humblest obeisance, black leather in the snow, a
sea of leather, clustering, eyes downcast. I have music
too. But music is inside, won't come out, silenced, sullen.

"Indeed, my master," says the tall man.

— my father —

"He's not your father," says Thorn, "as you well know,
Chris Etchison."

"You've caught the big one," says Cornelius Huang.
"The truthsayer of truthsayers, the shall we say kwisatz
haderach of our times; when comes such another?"

"Come, little one. You know I won't harm you."

Forward-moving: the rustle of prostrate leather.

"They think I'm dead," he says (and I gaze upward at
his eyes and I know, he is dead, what is there is only a
shadow's shadow) "but maybe I've only become
stronger."

— not true, you are dead —

"Silence!" Kicks me in the shin, but —

— you said you weren't gonna hurt me —

"Right." Frowning. "Sorry."

— I want to go back to —

"You can't say it. Because you're a truthsayer. You
can't say the word, because it isn't true."

— I already said it —

"But you weren't referring specifically to that one, the
one who reared you, the one who isn't your father."

And-again I fall silent.

Cornelius comes forward. Barefoot in the snow, his
anklets tinkling, silver silver on snow snow. Not used to
thinking in words, first come pictures, pictures, pictures,
faster than can put words to, want to turn them into music but the song will be too-much-weeping. And I still,
still, biting back the truth, though it's burning me up.

Cornelius says, "We can't all be truthsayers, young
man, but there is something we all know. The innermost
truth you're hiding is bitter for yourself, although it may
heal the world. But not every truth is the holy grail, and
we can take this cup from you; we can, we can."

— that's true —

"You see!" Thorn says excitedly. "I was right. I may only be zombie recreation of my former self, but I can still win the game."

"All you needed to come back to life," says Cornelius Huang, "was the sort of homeopathic tincture of a human soul."

"Would you like to see where Oren Karpovsky is now?" Thorn says. "Look into my eyes, boy, gaze deep into them...."

He bends down and I peer. First the churning flaming whirlpool-well down down down and then yes there, I see him, two of them, twins, one in each eye, little President Karpovsky, the size of a mosquito, running back and forth and back and forth battering his body against the sides of the well and screaming his pinprick little screams.

— you're big and he's little — but you're dead and he's not-dead —

"Silence!" Slaps me again, pain stinging, bringing salt tears, fuck you I won't cry out. "You will take me to the source of the river."

— fuck you —

"Foul-mouthed, aren't you, for such a sweet little boy." Pulls me up roughly. "Where did you learn language like that from? And don't say from your brothers. You have no brothers. They never existed. Not if you exist."

— they exist inside me, all of it exists inside me, all the pathways, all the little rivulets and tributaries and stop hitting me you motherfucker you need me more than I need you and —

Starting to get into this talking stuff a little. But talking I don't have a voice, I have a hundred voices, a thousand; I'm parroting back little fragments of other people's conversations. Words are not true enough. They only nibble at the edges of truth. They never show the heart of things.

"Listen, you snivelling little moppet. I want to offer you, for lack of a better word for it, an unholy alliance. Right now, we have a common goal. We both have to get to the source. Now, you're going to go there regardless, because it's your destiny; the fact that you let me capture you so easily proves that, or you'd have conjured up some kind of symphony of terror, put up a major struggle, something. I mean, Serena Somers, pregnant with a dragon yet, is no match for me. You have the truth, but I have the strength; you see, truth isn't the only card one can have up one's sleeve, is it, now? You will take me to the source of the river, and once we get there, I'll have a sporting chance with my agenda, just as good a chance as you have with yours. And I have another major advantage. I want to conquer the universe. You, on the other hand, my squeamish messiah, are reluctant to reach the end of your song, because to do so would mean — what? — that's where we come to your dark truth, which I, of course, am not privy to."

What can I do what can I say? He's right of course. I have to go where I have to go, and if he keeps be chained up by his side he'll end up going there too.

And I can't lie. I'm a truthsayer.

Can I make the journey longer, make time for the others to get there too? Can I misdirect maybe, or is that going to destroy the thing I am?

I don't want to get to the end of the journey. That's true, too, isn't it? I can't lie about that either. How can he be so right when he's one of the bad guys?

— all right —

"I knew you'd come around," said Thorn. "But you're a far better truthsayer than the last one I had. You probably don't need any marbles or visual aids at all, do you? You can just close your eyes and spirit us there, and we can take over the whole show."

— the way is murky — a lot of tributaries dammed up — some sections of the river have run dry —

"I know, I know. Now go."

Around-looking: far away, clouds, beyond clouds, the lake; my mom and dad and Serena and the shaman, cooking fish by the fire, and —

Around-looking: even farther, farther, farther, my brother has abandoned his fish and is running towards us, but his moment of running is an eternity, that's relativity you see, and I'm afraid that they're going to be long gone before we can —

"Go, I say!" says Thorn.

I close my eyes.

— you — follow — I — lead —

Listen. Listen. The real universe has an underlying heartbeat. You can call it Love. You can call it Om. You can call it God. It's so slow that worlds can evolve, devolve, and perish between two beats, yet you can hear it if you know how to listen. Listen. Listen. How can it be that the others can't hear it when it when to me it's the rhythm that drives all other rhythms, the ostinato that anchors the cosmos? Listen, listen, listen.

"What are you doing, child? Don't zone out, just take us where we need to go."

— be quiet! I'm concentrating —

"Oh." Thorn steps back. Suddenly I'm the boss and he's the anxious, waiting attendant. Role reversal. All right!

— how many are traveling with us? —

"I guess ought to take the whole army. I'll have to fight my father for possession of everything. And who knows, maybe my dragon sister's gotten loose by now, and she'll be setting out for the source of the river too. And then there's Ash. Whatever the hell happened to him? Okay, so he's the wimpy, rah-rah sibling, always telling the truth — half truthsayer himself in a way — but what if he gets it into his head to run for the source? A four-way battle is coming up and I want to make absolutely sure I win."

Eyes-closed looking around: chaos. Where's the river? Sending out feelers. Reaching out. Listen. That

universal heartbeat ... slow slow slow ... listen. Listen. I
think the heart is diseased. The echo of the heartbeat
comes across the continuum, and it's all skipping, skipping, like the pulse of a man with a heart condition ...
slow, slow, slow, slow, stop, slow, slow.

A flicker. The trickle of a mountain stream. The
river's broken up, a lot of places it doesn't even flow
anymore, but I hear something. Close by. Tap tap tap the
rush of an underground river, just gotta smash my way
through to it.

— okay. All of us. Everyone who's coming with me.
Hold hands. I'm going smash through, make a new gateway —

Taking Thorn's hand in mine. Clammy. Cold. A hand
that sucks all the warmth out of you. Just how a vampire's hand should be. Listen. That heartbeat is still
pulsing, weak, weak, weak, pulsing still pulsing pulsing.
Be still. I think about the source —

Crystal pure lightness pure crystal

— I'm going to think a big dreaming-thought now.
I'm going to bring us closer to the source by —

"I knew it!" Thorn says excitedly. "You can change the
fabric of reality just by your will."

— I am a truthsayer. If I say a thing, it is not only true
— it has always been true. That's the curse I carry inside
me —

"Yes, yes, let's go!" Impatiently he thrusts his left
hand behind him, and Cornelius Huang diffidently takes
it in his right. Then Huang stretches out his left hand,
and one of the demon things shimmies up ad seizes it in a
gnarled paw; and so it goes on, all the way down the
mountainside and down the hierarchy, all the way to the
valley, as far as I can see; and I'm going to think a big
dream-thought and I'm going to carry them all with me
through the sheer force of my truthsaying and —

Now! I synchronize myself with that great heartbeat.
Now! I open my lips, and I sing.

The sound that I sing partakes of the breath of creation. It's the new-world-joy that sings in the wind of a
world that's just sprung into being at the hand of a god.
Thorn frowns. He doesn't like the sound of joy; he tries
not to smile, but I feel the smiling stir inside him, and I
know he hates that, loves to be the villain, loves to be the
darkness, but he must know that he has allied himself
with me and must accept that my truthsaying comes
from the light, the first light of the cosmos, the light that
burst forth in that great Big Bang that set the particles to
dancing at the dawn of time.

Fireworks! The fabric of spacetime rips, and we step
through, and now:

Around-looking: the edge of a mighty canyon, the living rock carved with ancient petroglyphs in a long-dead
language, and in the sky above, a flock of pterodactyls
craning. Demons hang on the stone facings, some upside
down like bats; the canyon side thick with leather and
fanged faces.

Below-looking: the river. I've carved a new gateway.
The river roaring, foaming, exhilarated. The pulse of the
universe beneath it all, more steady now, more smooth,
like a man who's just had a coronary bypass; because
that's really what I just did, bypass the clogged arteries
of the river. I'm already beginning to heal the universe
and I know that's not in Thorn's agenda.

"This isn't the source," Thorn says.

— still a long way off —

"I'm hungry!" He lets go my hand. He paces. A thousand demons pace in the background, shadowing him.

Cornelius says, "Perhaps one of your own subjects?"

"Boring," he says. He gazes at me and what's in his
eyes is akin to lust, akin to hunger, yet also a kind of love.
"We'll need some kind of boat," he says.

— around the bend of the canyon —

He seizes my hand again. Throws his cloak about me.
Dark, all dark. He leaps. No wind rushing, no landscape
flashing by, because in the dark cloak is like in the thick

womb of sleep, and it's like a dream of forever falling ...
and when he whisks away the cloak we're standing on
the deck of a monster ship, all iron, all rusty and smelling
of death, and the demons are swarming all over it.

Thorn laughs, throws his head back and does the
whole evil villain guffaw thing. "The Titanic! How singularly appropriate!"

Then he crooks a finger at one of the demons, who
bends down so he can drink his blood. Other demons
toss him, drained, into the water, and so my pristine path
to the source has already been polluted.

"I suppose we can move on now," Thorn says, and
waves at me. What do I do now? I close my eyes. Listen
to the heartbeat of the universe. I center my truth-saying
sense on the source of the river. I know that if I start to
move toward the source, the energy of that movement
will carry all these creatures along with it, and the dino-
saur of a ship, too. I listen. Listen. Listen. And then I
pluck out of the air the notes that resonate with the
heartstrings of the cosmos, tentatively at first, and the
more confidently, filling the space around me with the
music of pure joy; I know how uncomfortable that makes
Thorn, and it makes me smile a little, for the first time
since my abduction....

The ship rumbles into action, and we start to roll upstream.

Nine
Ash

Theo Etchison:

So, we're on the water racing toward the castle, but then what happens? There's like this big old explosion. The castle starts to shake. Flames leap up. The king starts and stares, and now and then he murmurs, "the dragon, the dragon," softly to himself, and cradles his scepter in his arms. But then the urgency of it strikes him and he plunges the scepter into the water once more, churning it up and sending up sparks.

The mermaids shriek and dive back into the depths. I have to get to that place ... I know that my father's there ... I can feel him with what remains of my truthsaying, try to reach out to him, and for a moment I see what he sees —

— me running to him along the riverbank, back in Virginia I guess, among the cottonwoods, calling out "Daddy, Daddy" to him, a million worlds ago —

The castle is on fire and there's a giantess stomping about in the distance. It's like watching a monster movie in the distance, all totally unreal. "It's Serena Somers," I say, but King Strang doesn't know who that is. There's a music in the air, too, a drumming and a highpitched keening. It's the music of the other truthsayer. The one I brought into the world. The son I got on my own mother. Sounds sick, huh. We were gods at the time. You know how it is with the gods: incest, incest, incest. Sex with mom, sex with mom, okay, I admit it, I'm obsessed with it, it's like a black clot in my head and it clouds my thinking all the time. And then there's the kid. When I think of him, I feel all sick inside, sick because of how he came into the world, sick because he's so much better than me, because he has my gift, a thousand times my gift, and mine is getting fuzzier every day. But I have to play this thing out to its end.

The raft moves on. On toward the castle. But the landscape keeps morphing, distorting itself. Sphinxes rear up and pop like balloons. Aztec gods in gold and nephrite peer up over the frothing waters. We're about to reach the castle when like, this humungous flock of bat-creatures comes soaring out of the flames. The castle crumbles and our raft rams against the shore and Strang and I get out, him brandishing the scepter like it's a magic wand, trying to silence the divine and maddening music.

For a second I see them all: Dad and Mom and Serena, who's towering above the whole big burning mess, but everything's all blurry again, and I try to call out to Dad through the wall of fire but the fumes are burning my eyes and then the walls are shimmering and fading and —

Dad turns to me. Does he really see me? Or is there one of those yawning abysses between us, are we really standing in separate universes?

"Daddy!" I scream.

Dad cries out: "Forgive me! I didn't know what I was doing —"

And there's kind of a double vision about it because I know he doesn't see me, Theo Truthsayer, navigator to the mad king, but some little kid running towards him across a plain of ice....

"Dad!" I scream again, but —

There's a tremendous explosion.

It's all gone. All of it. And now, just as suddenly, we're floating on a lake, a crystal lake, and it's all intensely calm.

"What happened?" says Strang.

"There's been another glitch in reality," I say. "We haven't moved, but the sands of the cosmos have shifted under our feet."

He looks up. "Clear. The sky. Bright and clear. Hasn't been this way in a while. Must be testing me."

He smashes his scepter at an imaginary enemy: the air.

"You're acting paranoid, Strang," I say.

He swings the scepter at me, but I dodge; I'm good at that, I'm still agile, still got my junior high school Super-Nintendo reflexes. "Get thee behind me, varmint," he growls. But he's not even looking at me. He's haunted, of course, and doesn't know that it's himself who haunts him.

"Cool it, O King," I say. Sometimes I can lighten his mood by talking that way. But he begins to weep, though he doesn't know that I'm looking at him, doesn't quite know I'm there, really, so many other creatures in his world, all creatures of illusion.

The place we're floating in: rocky structures jut up from the lake like little islands arranged in concentric circles. I think my mom and dad are close, real close; I try to reach out with my mind, but when I try, a fog kind of seizes my brain.

"I was a child once, you know," says King Strang. "Didn't always have the scepter. Maybe I was better off without it."

"You could always throw it away," I say. But I know that won't solve anything; there'll only be another Strang, and even if he means well at first, the sickness that's in the scepter would eventually drive him mad too. "Tell me about being a child," I say.

"Not just me. The whole world. Morning of my life, morning of the world."

"Must have been exciting."

"It was lonely. I wanted to be loved, but since there was no one to live me, I had to settle for being worshipped."

Suddenly I think I see something on one of the islands, further in, toward the center of the circle. Something flashing, chrome and pale blue-green, a station wagon maybe. I think I know this car, which is just sitting there, parked on a basalt ledge poking up in the middle of this lake. The way it glints. The Arizona desert, the heat, the smell of my mother dying; it's all wrapped up in the image of that beat-up car. I know my parents have to be near.

"Look," I tell the king, pointing. "I think we're about to rendezvous with my family."

I start paddling the raft. Despondently, the king begins to strike the water with his scepter. We move. It's a zigzag drifting as we skirt the many jutting stones. Isn't that a tendril of smoke swirling skyward from the center? Could it be a campfire maybe? I wish I could see more clearly....

"What about my family?" says the king. "What about my children, spinning in the void? What about the dragon woman and the boy with the slate-colored eyes?"

"You have another child too."

"I don't!"

"You do. Think about him."

We have reached the first of the islands — no more than a mound of basalt. I tie the raft to a knob of smouldering stone. I have to think. Maybe I'm wrong to think we're closer to the source. King Strang sits by the edge, dangling his feet, not worrying about the water that soaks his fraying robes.

"This used to be Thorn's castle," I say. "There's been a struggle. That's all I can figure out." The surface of the basalt is covered with a fine ash, some of it still glowing. I kneel down, take a handful of it. Here and there are crystals, like unpolished diamonds, white and hard.

I blow the ash into the still thin air.

That's when the ash starts to form into the shadowy image of a man.

"Hey, take a look, King Strang! Someone's come to see us."

The king doesn't turn around.

It's a shimmering figure, a dance of light, a wavering in the air; I think I'm just imagining it at first, and then I can hear him speak to me; it's a weird voice, a not-quite-man, not-quite-woman voice. "Theo," he says. "Good to see you again."

"Ash?" I say.

King String winces, and still won't look.

"I've been wondering when you would turn up again."

"I've always been here," Ash says. "When my siblings consume each other in their rage, I'm what's left behind; I'm the broken pieces of their love for each other."

"I'm losing my gift," I say sadly.

"And I never had much of a gift," he says, "though I have been known to tell the truth once too often."

The king looks up for a moment. "Are you crazy, boy?" he shouts at me. "Speaking to the air like that."

"You're in denial," I tell the king. "You know very well who I'm talking to...."

Strang turns stubbornly away. What's he doing with his scepter? He's swishing it through the water. A dead fish comes floating to the top. He tears it apart with his bare hands, peers at it, sniffs at the guts.

"Help me," Ash says. "I can't go on like this. It's not natural for me to live as the quintessence of dust. But without reconciliation with my father."

"I don't know what I can do," I say. "You know I'm losing my powers."

"We can help each other. I've never been a truth-sayer, but I think I have a little bit of the gift; it's telling the truth that got me in this bind in the first place."

That's true. He's the Cordelia in this King Lear story, putting his foot in his mouth by refusing to embroider the truth with flattery.

"You mean," I say, "that between us, we could figure out how to get to the source?"

"Why not?" he says.

"The blind leading the blind?"

"Something like that. Whatever happened to your big blue marble?"

"I guess it got lost somewhere in the mélée." I had a map once. It had the whole river scrunched up inside what seemed to be a crystal, a marble. There was another map, too. It was in the palace of Caliosper. An arena, a kind of mega-Nintendo virtual map. "Whatever happened to your flying city?" I say.

"Lost it somewhere, too. But I get the feeling it's close by."

"Yes. Close by. That's the problem. So near and yet —"

"My father has some of the answers. You should listen to him more."

"But he's mad."

"Maybe there's method in it."

I go and sit down beside the king. Ash comes behind me, a swirl of dust that wheels around my shoulders and catches the blue sunlight; it's as though I was wearing a necklace of stars. The king doesn't look at me.

But he says, "Amuse me."

I say, "All right, but then you have to answer one question, no matter how hard it is, no matter what the pain. Truth or dare kind of thing."

"Tell me about your silly world, boy. It's always good for a laugh."

Okay so I tell him one of my stupid stories. It's the time the British exchange students decided to tell us all cricket. So they get out all these wickets and bats and other weird paraphernalia and start explaining it to me and the other kids in Mr. Norris's P.E. class, with curious words like googly and maiden over andhowzat, and it's what sounds like a really really slow version of baseball, you know, except that there's two people running back and forth instead of in a circle ... well then we decide to try it out for a lark, and no one picks me because I'm such a dweeb, so I end up in, I guess the outfield kind of posi-tion, and I'm all lying in the grass, knowing that the ball will never come my way, dozing; it's already summer, feels like it anyways, you know how muggy Virginia gets, and school's gonna be out soon and the fucking Brits will go home.

By the edge of the field, the grass is super-tall and there's a creek. There's hornets too; I think there's a nest close by. There's only three kids from England, but they're explaining up a storm over there in the distance, and I don't think they'll ever get started; so like, I stop paying attention; I've got a beanbag for a pillow and I lean over on my side and part the grass a little and look out over the creek, because I can hear someone sobbing, very softly, to herself.

It's Serena Somers. And the thing is, she's all naked, and blubbery, and standing in the stream, and she looks like one of those Stone Age Venus idols that we learned about in Mrs. Hulan's class; she's not ugly but kind of beautiful. But what's she doing in the middle of the school day, butt naked at the edge of campus? What the hell is she thinking to herself?

Thing is, it's the first naked woman I've ever seen. So I don't care that she's a slug, I'm just so amazed at how it's all put together. I'm so in awe that I don't even pop a woody. Okay so she's fat, but it's amazing how beautiful she is, with her Venus-on-the-half-shell hair plastered to her plump breasts, and her clear eyes, looking fucking Jesus knows at what; and there's a kind of rustling in the air, I think at first it's the hornets, but she looks, straight at me it seems, yet straight through me too, and I let out a little startled cry or grunt; and she says, "Ash, Ash, is it you, is it really you?"

And I don't answer, because if I speak I have to speak the truth.

And she says, "Ash, but you only come at night."

And I'm all, "I'm not Ash."

But she hears something else. She's in another world, parallel to the world I'm lying in, but not totally congruent.

"Of course you are," she says. "But you only come, you know, when I'm about to go to sleep ... you're the whisperer before the dream."

She laughs. She splashes me with water. Her clothes are hanging on a nearby bush and suddenly I catch a whiff of, I don't know, underwear, and suddenly there comes the long-awaited stiffy after all.

So this is Serena's big secret; she ditches fourth period and skinny-dips within a stone's throw of the school ... I wonder if Joshua knows.

In the far distance, there's that hooting-cum-steam-whistle sound that passes for the bell in our school, an electronic racket cooked up by a computer class last year. Startled, she jumps out of the stream, grabs her clothes, starts to dash away, but not before she turns and looks me right in the eye, and smiles, and says, "Oh, it's only you." And thunders off through the bushes.

Only me? Only Ash, the imaginary friend, or only Theo, the pesky little bro of the boyfriend?

As I tell King Strang this story he continues to fish, and Ash himself continues to waft around my shoulders as a flurry of silvery dust. The king's not pleased that I've worked Ash into the conversation. He's silent for a long time.

"You're forcing me," he says.

"What?" I say.

"Forcing me to relive things. I don't like that. I'm old, boy, old, and those things were a long time ago."

"It'll be over soon," I say, "I promise. Because we're at the dawn of the mad millennium, and we're all almost at the end of our journey...."

"I know something you don't know."

"That's probably true," I say. "I know less and less these days. My truthsaying totally bites."

"I know you've been speaking to a certain someone who shall remain nameless." He shakes his head. His mane is soggy, and he asperges me with lake water, cold and smelling of fish. "I also know you're thinking of others, people close to you, and you think that all we have to do is swim out a little further, and meet up with them, and all convoy together to the source of the river where there'll be some big apocalyptic event and the world will be reborn. Isn't that right?"

"Something like that."

"How far is it to the next island?"

I look across the water. It seems a lot closer than it did before. I can see the stationwagon clearly now, I can even make out what seems to be my father, a thin balding man in a crumpled suit, banging at the car door; I guess he doesn't have the key. "I could swim it easy," I say. "But I wish I could give Dad the key."

"Sometimes you have to go the opposite direction," says the king, "to get where you want to go." He gets up suddenly. Grabs me by the shoulders. He may be stooped and emaciated but when he wants to grip you he can dig right into your flesh. "Let's go another way," he says. He lets go of my shoulders, grabs onto my hand, brandishes his scepter with his free hand.

"Go where? You're crazy ..."

"I certainly am! Stark staring bonkers, mad as a hatter, ho ho ho!" And he's all waving the scepter and pulling me in circles, staggering around the perimeter of the island which is after all less than fifty yards maybe, with the Ash-dust streaming behind me. "You want to get to the end," he says, "you have to come to the beginning! Now run, run, run!"

And we're all running hard, running in a spiral toward the center of the rock. The king's robes, stained with blood and bile, are flapping in the breeze he's made by his running. And suddenly it seems that the world is spinning around us and we've like become still. The still point of the turning world as Dad would have put it. Still, still, still, and the universe rushing like mad, circling us, pushing us squarely toward the center, and —

"Ash," the king says.

"Ash is with us," I say, astounded that he has finally brought himself to say his child's name.

"No, no, no, you idiot, you be Ash, you stand in for him; see with his eyes, know what he knows; because Ash was with me, you know, when the world was young; he was there at the moment of original sin."

Now I understand the spinning. It's like in those Superman comics when Superman flies so fast he overtakes the speed of light and catapults himself back in time so he can explain some paradox.

The king's opening up to me now. He's carrying me with him down the river of remembrance. "Are you listening to this, Ash?" I whisper, as the world whirls so fast it's no more than a blur of rainbow streaks. Then I see like this desk calendar whizzing around, with the pages tearing off one by one ... yeah, just another of those visual metaphors that comes to me when there's no rational way to analyze what you see around you. "Ash, Ash," I say.

Ash doesn't answer. I guess it's true. He's inside me now. Or I'm inside him. The world begins to settle down. King Strang is still holding onto my hand. But when I look at him I can't believe the transformation. He's all, you know, tall and goldenhaired and his complexion is all golden; and his robes are white and shiny.

"Come, Ash," he says to me.

We step out into the morning of the world.

Book Three:

Development
The Mad King

"In my end is my beginning."
—*T.S. Eliot*

from a Sotheby's Catalogue:

On Truth
by
Philip Etchison

My writing block, it seems, is permanent. As a result, I find my annual address from the poetry chair of this
august institution to be more and more
of a joke, year after year. What can one
talk about, when one has been struck
dumb?

I have decided to venture into the
treacherous shoals of ontology....

What is truth?

We all long to believe in the existence of
an Ultimate Truth. A truth that is the
touchstone by which we can measure all
our private little falsehoods, beside
which even the whitest lie is black as
night and death. This Ultimate Truth,
we believe, is the thing that will "sets us
free", as it says, not only in the Bible, but
in that old protest song — but of course,
you're all too young to remember that.

What would happen to us, if it were
suddenly revealed that this Ultimate

Truth does not exist? If this Ultimate Truth is the rock on which our faith in our perceptions is founded, does it not follow that to negate its existence — to say that it has no clothes — would automatically plunge humanity into a dark, suicidal despair?

History shows that this has already happened on a number of occasions. And, in a smaller way, we all experience that moment of gravest doubt. I know I have. I think it is that moment of doubt that propels us, causes us to yearn for, to strive for, to demand artistic perma-nence.

— coffee-stained ms. found stuck in a shredder at the Kremlin, along with a prescription for Prozac. Believed to be in the handwriting of Philip Etchison.

— reserve $10,000

Ten
At the Morning of the World

Theo Etchison:

I'm still Theo Etchison, but I'm inside someone else, watching through his eyes. I'm a kid I guess, and the place we're in is a rambling palace that goes on and on. Ivory pilasters and tile floors, and murals with scenes from unfamiliar mythologies; but the place we're in now is like, some kind of playroom. And I've got two older siblings, a boy and a girl. I'm sitting in the corner. Maybe I shouldn't be playing with dolls, but I kind of am; it's like an alien Barbie Doll kind of thing, all heads and tentacles and slimy skin yet giving off a strange seductiveness.

"Ash, Ash," says a strange voice from above.

I look up at the ceiling and there like, this Michelangelo Sistine Chapel God-thing floating among the holographic clouds, only it's animated. I call it the Godfather. "Stop playing with dolls," says the voice from above. "You want to grow up like your sister?"

My sister Katastrofa is breathing fire over a city made of chalcedony building blocks, and my slate-eyed brother Thorn is torturing one of the servant children with a little needlegun. No fear that I'm going to be like either of them.

My father's not really in the ceiling. The ceiling has only been imbued with his personality, the better to control us. After all, it's hard to be ruler of a planetary fiefdom; one doesn't necessarily have time to spend with one's kids. And certainly no quality time.

There are no people at all in this wing of the palace. Occasionally servants, but even those are mostly spirits. I'm looking through Ash's eyes but because I'm me, Theo, from the 90s, the time before the mad millennium, I see and taste and smell things differently; the scent in the air, decaying flowers maybe, a hint of a chemical smell, it all evokes a sadness for me, a feeling of loneliness; maybe it's because I've smelled this smell before and it's the smell of visiting my mother in the hospital, the smell that says goodbye, I'm dying.

And because I know Ash, Thorn, Katastrofa from a much later time, I can see the future in their childish games.

Thorn says, "Let's get Ash."

Katastrofa does a flip through the air, wraps her scaly arms around my neck, throws back her head and sends out a fountain of flame; Thorn laughs; I'm on the verge of crying; abruptly, she lets go of me and I go sprawling onto the stone floor, and Thorn says, "He'll only go crying to you-know-who."

I look up at the Godfather, who wags a finger. "Stop picking on your little brother," comes the booming admonition, like the voice of God in The Ten Commandments.

"Sissy," hisses Thorn.

Katastrofa flies up to the ceiling; I think she's going to lob a fireball at the Godfather, but she doesn't dare. It may be a computer simulacrum, but it slings real lightning bolts. So she only swoops back down to glare at me. It's a typical morning in the nursery.

I don't hate my siblings, but they certainly hate me.

Suddenly, to everyone's surprise, there's a break in the routine. Softly at first. The tramp of lizard feet. Tramp-tramp, tramp-tramp, in a corridor far away, yet coming closer.

"Military exercise?" Thorn says.

Katastrofa listens. "Only a few of them. They're coming to the nursery."

Now they're in the doorway, my father's saurian henchmen, they of the hivemind and scaly complexion. They don't even glance at Thorn, the firstborn, or Katastrofa, who practices her gliding among the crowned pilasters of the nursery. They come straight up to me. They speak in tandem.

"His Imperial Majesty, your Father," says one —

"Commands you to see him in the throneroom —"

"Right away!"

"Five minutes to make yourself presentable!" Their voices grate like actors in a Japanese monster movie.

"We will wait."

Katastrofa and Thorn scowl at me with the kind of singleminded hatred that only ten-year-olds can feel. I look at the floor. "Could be anything," I say. "Could be a death sentence. You know how Father is. He could be disowning me."

"Fat chance," says Thorn. He sounds hard and bitter.

"He never summons us to the throneroom," says Katastrofa. She tries to sound hard but there's a hint of heartbreak in her voice.

The imperial lizards wait. Their scales glisten like anodized titanium. I clap my hands for a body-slave, who crawls into the room and changes my clothes for me before slinking away.

The palace is a labyrinth, but prince of the House of Strang must not walk far. The two lizards lift me onto a litter that rests on a cushion of air; they levitate it; one on either side, they guide it out into a milelong cloister whose walls are empanelled with gold and malachite. We move swiftly; the lizards can run like machines, and the palanquin is one; the walls are a blur; we race dow more cloisters, more corridors, more passageways; and now we are levitating up along a flight of steps, and on either side are painted scenes from our family's history: the first Strang, forest-born, emerging from the wilderness with an army of jungle animals at his back; the second, floating down a river in a chest of gold, wrapped in the skins of marmosets; the third, a holy king, squatting in lotus position on the summit of a mountain, preaching to the monkeys; these are all scenes the three children have been required to commit to memory, along with the inscriptions, in archaic poetry, that run along the walls and are etched into the glazed-tiled steps; the palanquin glides up, smooth as a gilded hawk.

My father's throneroom: viziers and ministers are prostrate on the floor from which rises a rose-tinged mist. Cherums with censers flit above our heads, and the air is filled with the sweet fragrance of frankincense, myrrh, and copal. A major domo with a golden, Anubis-tipped staff stands sentinel. I tweak his wig as the litter sails past him, over the sea of suppliants, all the way to the foot of my father's throne; and there he sits, the Seventh Strang, the father of Ash, and also my father, because I'm still inside of Ash, seeing with the eyes of a young Virginia boy. This isn't a Strang I've ever seen before. This Strang is bright-eyed, vigorous, decisive; his hair is a mane of reddish-brown. A torc of gold and amber hugs his neck, and within each nugget of amber is the remains of an ancient creature.

"Father, father," I say. In a piping little voice. How old am I really, seven or eight? I can't tell because Ash isn't thinking about that, but I know that his kind don't age at the same speed as humans.

He doesn't look at me at first. One of the many viziers is at his side, and they are poring through documents. It's Cornelius Huang, who doesn't like any younger than when I first saw him at the Chinese restaurant in the wilderness.

"Yes," Strang says, "yes, yes," and with each yes
there's like a sigh of pleasure from the suppliants, and
then, one time, he says "No," and there's like this hush
that falls over the crowd, and Corny frowns a little, and
turns to one of the lizard guards that flank the throne
and raises just one eyebrow; and a detachment of guards
runs off to execute the king's command; and Strang looks
at me at last, and I'm all, to myself, He's tired sometimes,
he doesn't like his job sometimes, and I'm the only one
he lets see this; and it moves me.

"Son," he says. Really softly. But suddenly, as though
he has spoken with the voice of thunder, the suppliants
begin backing away, the lizards turn their backs on us,
the advisors and viziers look at the floor and shuffle their
feet so as not to intrude on this totally private moment in
this totally public place; and I think, Shit, that's power.

"You wanted to see me, father?" I can't help trem-
bling.

He smiles. The viziers, of course, have turned their
backs to us, and yet they too are smiling; they've picked
up on his mood, understand that he's not displeased with
me, and this makes their jobs all easier too.

"I haven't seen you for days," says Strang. "Come on
up."

I climb out of the palanquin and hop down onto the
lowest step of the throne where there's a velvet foot-
stool, and I sit down, but he crooks his finger and makes
me crawl up onto his lap, and he gazes into my eyes and
I'm thinking, Yes, it's true, how tired he is, all those
yesses followed by that single no, it must really have hurt
him to say it; and I know how much it pleases him to
have me there, bright-eyed, adoring him.

"If only you knew," he says. "There's got to be another way of doing this."

Abruptly, he rises.

"Come, child," he says. "We're going fishing."

Eleven
Dreams Within Dreams

Phil Etchison:

I swam toward the island of the station wagon. It was easy; the water was warm, and heavier, too, than regular sea water; I didn't have to struggle to stay afloat. I heard that swimming in the Dead Sea's like that, because the high salt content; you jump in and you just float, and float, and float. But this was no Dead Sea. I don't know what was in the water; maybe some of the peyote tea that Milt was so fond of serving us. I felt wonderfully alive here. I felt nourished. The water of the lake had an amniotic quality. I swam ... no, I drifted. Slowly but surely, toward where my car was miraculously parked. But all of a sudden, night fell, just like that: like switching off a light and going to bed. I tingled. I felt secure. I knew I would arrive at my destination even if I fell asleep in the arms of mother darkness....

Night fell and I dreamt, dreams within dreams, and with each dream I came closer to awakening from the grand dream that had been my whole existence.

I'm a king on a throne, dispensing justice, picking life or death for my erring subjects. I have three children; one is the apple of my eye. In this dream there are corridors lined with scenes of my many pasts. In this dream, the child I love most is flying to see me on mechanical wings. All morning, I order executions. My child drifts toward me over a field of prostrate suppliants; I am both god and king.

I see my child, goldenhaired and swathed in light, and I think to myself, but of the other children, lost in the darknesses of alien worlds, what of them? And I'm torn, because this is my son, yet but for him the others would be here, imperfect though they are, the sullen brooding one and the bright-eyed truthsayer.

I say to Chris, "Son, let's go fishing."

And he says, "You see yourself as the Fisher King now, Dad?"

And I say, "You can talk!"

He says, "This is a dream, Dad; truths are spoken in dreams that dare not be spoken in life."

"True," I say. The strange thing is, I know the place I'm in is real, though I've never been here; I know that the body I inhabit is a real person, even though I'm interpreting the world around me through the lens of what I've seen and known; I know that what's in this dream has really happened, but to me and not to my son.

"What do you want to fish for, Dad?" Chris says. "Are you sick of the old 'fishers of men' thing? You want something bigger and better than a few miserable souls?"

"Maybe."

"Okay then. I'll take you. Come."

He pulls me up from the throne and the next thing I know I'm —

Theo Etchison:

— floating —

Through Ash's eyes, I see Strang, rowing with a fe-vered energy I've never seen in him before. This is some boat; first we were carried to the edge of a crystal lake, then we rode like this hovercraft thing, its prow a mass of writhing serpents, across the lake to this stream, and the stream fed into a river that was descended lower and lower into a canyon where the guards finally left us; this boat, a battered old dinghy, was moored to a post, and there were cataracts beyond, thunderous and foamy; and I got into the boat with king, and he straps me down with chains of silver, and I'm all, "Where's the bait? We're not really going fishing at all, are we?" And a wild thought races through my mind, that he's brought me to this wild place to dispose of me, to fake some kind of accident. King Strang doesn't answer me, but just rows; he closes his eyes, and we plunge down the first cataract, and I think, Fucking Jesus this water is bitter, it's like carbon-ated Robitussin or something, and it's cold and it's pour-ing down my nose and throat and like I'll drown or some-thing if it doesn't stop and I think oh shit I'm maybe drowning or something, I'm going to die —

And then — my eyes are closed — we're all flying through the air and then, bam, we hit something hard and I'm all, This has got to be the end. Water just slams into me, winds me, I'm puking it up and coughing, and then, suddenly, there's calm.

"Open your eyes, boy," says Strang.

I do. This is what I see: we're drifting smoothly down a river of blood and mud, and where we are is the bottom of a chasm whose walls are etched with petro-glyphs and images of hell, souls being tortured, brim-stone, demons; the river banks are carved out of the rock, they're totally straight, artificial-looking.

"What do you see?" says Strang.

"I don't know ... ancient artifacts maybe, the work of some lost civilization, something like that?"

"I think so," says my father. "I stumbled on it quite by accident. An old truthsayer told me there's a fork in the river and one channel leads straight to the darkest of all places."

"But why are you taking me? It scares me."

The walls are so high that there seems to be no sky; the walls simply meet up there somewhere, and I feel caged in, trapped in an endless tunnel, and there's a whooshing, wuthering wind that sears my eardrums.

"I'm taking you," my father says, "because this is a big thing, and I must share it with someone, and because of all my children you are the only one who tells me the truth."

"I can't help it," I hear myself say out of Ash's lips, "there's a little voice inside me, someone else, not me, and he whispers to me, and what he whispers is always true."

"What's he like, this other voice?"

"I think it's a boy. But it's someone on another world, a world where reality doesn't shift around as much."

Strang laughs. "Are you possessed," he says, "by the ghost of some Truthsayer yet unborn? Or do you maybe think you could have the gift?"

Holy shit, I think to myself, how many times have I haunted Ash's dreams, slunk into his thoughts before? When I thought I was dreaming, was I really living this totally other life? Are we like mystic twins or something? I answer him (Ash answers him) "It's not my gift, father, but I sometimes feel it, some big alien thing, tickling the back of my mind."

"Then let's test your skill. Come on. We're coming to a fork in the river. Pick the right path."

That's when Ash realizes there's an ulterior motive, perhaps, why his father has brought him on this journey. He needs a guide, and he has no truthsayer. There was one in the palace, but no one has seen him for years; perhaps the old man crawled away to die somewhere. I remember him vaguely; they used to trot him out on holidays to give a few pointers at banquets, the future of the nation, the direction of the king's policies; I never saw him myself, only on the palace's closed-circuit babysitting television. Ash really loves his father, though there's as much fear as there is love there; he's happy his father wants to do something with him, doesn't much care what it is as long as they're together.

The stream narrows. The walls darken. Somehow we've gone from canyon to cavern. The paintings on the walls become more realistic. I think they're moving, some of them; there are demons with pitchforks, lost souls lashed to fiery wheels, tongues of fire, glowing eyes that seem to follow us as we drift. Strang rows and I sit back, watching him, worshipping him, in a way; and pretty soon the stream does seem to divide; one fork is well lit, and in the other the light grows dim, and the cavern walls press in harder, and stalactites hang down like rows of sharks' teeth.

"Which way, son?" says my father. "Listen to your inner voice."

Ash does listen. He makes his mind very empty, and what fills the void is me, smartass little kid from some future millenium. "I think we should go —"

Phil Etchison:

"— into the dark side," my son tells me in this increasingly baroque dream that has me playing the role of a bearded, ancient god-king, an Osiris.

"Are you sure, Chris?" I say. "Doesn't it scare you?"

He says, "Sure, Dad. But we have to face it sooner or later."

The walls of the subterranean stream are painted with murals, and there are scenes that I know all too well: Mary, standing in the rain; Joshua and Theo playing by the river bank back in Spotsylvania County, a dog barking, the cottonwoods with their deep russet sunset shadows; so why I do I feel that behind the lurid hues of this sunset are the flames of hell? I reach into the water and let the minnows nibble at my fingers.

"This isn't where we usually go fishing," I say to my son.

He says, "That's true."

Then I say, "Son, I get the feeling that this journey we're taking is —

Theo Etchison:

— a timeless journey," Strang says, "a journey that a billion fathers and sons have taken together, down into the darkest depths of their own souls, and yet —

Phil Etchison:

— this is different," I tell my son, "because I'm not really a king, or a high-priest, or some mythic hero, I'm not the arch-guru of reality, I'm not Prince Siddhartha seeking enlightenment; I'm just an ordinary guy trapped in these cosmic events —

Theo Etchison:

— because we are kings and princes, you and I," says Strang, "not ordinary people; because the petty do-mestic tragicomedies of our lives are writ large, because whole worlds and civilizations can fall to dust if we utter a wrong word, a mistaken command."

"Yes, father," says Ash (and me too, listening intently) "Yes, I know."

The tunnel narrows. It's like we're little micronauts sailing through the bloodstream of a giant creature. "Do you know why I was so upset this morning?" Strang says.

"You had to have someone killed, didn't you?"

"You have to understand, boy. I need a better way. I need to know things. I'm a good king, mostly, I think, but it never seems to be enough. If only I could change the way men feel ... if only I could make them see how great they can become when they join their dreams with mine...."

"You think the better way is to have more power?"

Strang looks away. Into the distance, where the tunnel has narrowed to virtually nothing. Ash understands him, knows that each time he exercises his kingly authority, it eats away a little piece of his soul; I too understand a little more, although I'm seeing him from a whole 'nother vantage point, although I know how corrupted he's become, how much of his soul has been eaten away by the time I'm journeying with him, a thousand years later, in the wilderness of ice.

"Now which way?" Strang says.

"Left."

More and more. Twisting and turning. Bends in the river. Down, down, down. No silken thread to guide us back out of this labyrinth. Ash tells his father the way; I tell him the way because here in the past I still have all my powers, I haven't yet gone blind.

Now there are three pathways; darker, darker, and most dark. Ash knows the answer; so, I think, does Strang; he doesn't need truthsaying to figure that out. I point; Strang steers the boat; we go on. It's tough steering now, but Strang doesn't ask me to help him row; we both know why; it's a journey he has to undertake entirely with his own muscle; this is a game that you just can't cheat at. The waters are brackish. A corpse floats by, stinking, draped over driftwood. I think, it can't be this easy. There's got to be obstacles. You can't just sail right up the river into the mouth of hell without battling a few monsters.

That's when the boat thuds against rock.

The river can't be blocked. It's still flowing. But there's an island in our path, and the water's rushing through the living rock like it's not even there ... and there's the obstacle! The guardian of the abyss! A humungous three-headed dog —

Phil Etchison:

A sphinx, standing before a wall of impenetrable flame! Not the serene, pharaoh-headed sphinx of the desert, but the sphinx of the Oedipus legend, a winged yenta with the body of a lioness. Her shrieks make me shiver, and from her withered dugs runs blood, and her eyes are like ice.

"What'll we do?" I ask my son. The boat is about to be sucked into the flames.

"You know what to do," Chris says.

"Answer a riddle?" I said.

"I guess," Chris says. "Meanwhile, I'll try to keep you cool."

Chris spreads his wings, sheltering me from the heat of the flames; I can see that it pains him. But he smiles bravely and says, "Just call me Mr. Asbestos."

The sphinx has a curiously plaintive voice, like a cat, like a woman dying of cancer, my wife; she has my wife's eyes, too, those wild, wide, dark post-chemo eyes. "Phil Etchison," she calls, her soft voice echoing above the roaring flames, "why do you want to pass through the impenetrable fire?"

In the background, you hear a sort of Wagnerian mêlée of themes from The Ring, as in the scene where the god Wotan declares that only the hero who knows no fear shall pass through the flames to the sleeping goddess. Where is the orchestra, I wonder, just sawing away behind the curtain of fire, is it only a scrim, a projection, an illusion? I think, I can handle the sphinx, for god's sake! I'm an English major. I know my Greek mythology.

"Answer her, Dad," Chris says.

"Is it one of the riddles?" I say.

"Maybe," he says.

I call out to the sphinx, "I'm here because I'm dreaming. I think I'm living through someone else's experiences, but somehow making them my own —"

"Good answer," says the sphinx. "But now it's time for the riddle."

"Oh," I say, "I know the answer to your riddle. It's man. Four legs in the morning — as a baby — two in the daytime, three, with a cane, in the twilight of his life."

She laughs.

At this point, the sphinx is supposed to leap off a cliff to her doom, and then I enter the city in triumph and have sex with my own mother, and I end up having to pluck out my eyes. I know the score. But she only laughs and laughs and laughs, till the whole cavern echoes with the sound of witchery.

"I have a much question to answer than that," she says at last. "Come on, little man who would be a poet. You think I'd let you get away with Mythology 101?"

"I guess you're right." Standing in the pool of coolness, fanned by my son's bright wings, I still can't quite feel it's all real. "Fire away."

"The riddle of the sphinx is this: If God commanded you to do it, would you sacrifice your own son?"

"That's easy," I say. "I don't believe in God."

But my words ring false. There've been gods in my very own home, after all. But there's a difference between gods and God, I tell myself. The flames leap up higher, and there is definitely a stench of brimstone in my nostrils.

"Since you don't believe, you say — and I am not here to argue theology with you — I'll rephrase the question. To save the universe, would you sacrifice your own son?" —

I stare at her. I stare at Chris. This is more than a riddle. The question is actually the answer. "Is this why you don't speak to me?" I cry out to my son.

"But I am speaking, Dad," he says, so softly his voice is almost one with the hiss of the spurting flames.

"But I'm dreaming," I tell him, and I look at the sphinx in consternation as she shrugs, awaiting my answer, and —

Theo Etchison:

— Cerberus, guardian of the underworld — I know all about him because he was on the boat when Thorn first abducted me from the Chinese Restaurant, way back in, as it were, the first volume of the trilogy, because when you're in an adventure like this you always think of it as a trilogy — okay so there he is, guarding the gateway to the underworld, barking up a storm from his three slavering mouths — he was a fuck of a lot tamer when I saw him way back then, but I've got to realize that though this is later in my stream of consciousness, it's earlier in the stream of time —

"Watch out for him, Father," I say. "He's probably rabid."

"No dog is going to stop me from pursuing this river to its beginning." His ice-blue eyes are already beginning to acquire that deadness that I first saw in him, when I first looked on him and wrote about him in my dream book; the obsession's there. But Ash can't know what I know. Unless I slip the images into his mind....

The three-headed dog is charging us now. His three mouths are flecked with foam. Water churns around us. There's no way past him. "I can't very well throw him a piece of steak," says Strang. "I'm not prepared for this."

The dog growls, gnaws at the boat, chomps off a big chunk of the prow. We spring a leak. Strang leaps down and I follow. The dog rips off a piece of his robe. Ash cries out, "Throw me to him, Daddy —" and I think, you fool, it's not worth it, not for this, but I feel the force of his love for his father, I know there's no way I can break it.

Strang says, "I can't —"

I huddle in his arms. He throws his robe around me. The cloth, infused with spells of protection, feels cold, smells faintly of frankincense. The dog throws himself at us. Ash thrusts his hand into one of his mouths.

"He'll bite you!" Strang screams. "You'll lose your hand!"

But Cerberus seems to quiet down a little. He backs away to slab of rock that blocks our access to the next leg of the stream. But I know he won't let us go on. He snarls. He froths.

"What do I have to do?" Strang grips me/Ash by the shoulders. His big hands clamp down and I feel the lust that drives him, the terrible need to control men's destinies. "This is important, Ash. Call the truthsayer inside you. Make him tell you what I must do."

And that's when I speak, through Ash's lips: "If thine eye offend thee, pluck it out."

Yeah. The Bible and The Man with the X-Ray Eyes. Suddenly I picture Dad in the living room expounding about how the same myths blow through both bible and B movie. And Odin exchanging his eye as the price of knowledge. And Oedipus, too, losing both eyes because he can't face his new knowledge about himself. Yeah, all the stories, from Sophocles to Roger Corman, all jangling inside my head, all told in my father's deep, patient voice, each one a shiny jewel for the magpie's nest of my imagination. How true it is. King Strang looks at his son, sees me, standing there in the back of Ash's consciousness, knows me, though he will not meet me until much later in time; knows that what I'm saying is true, because a truthsayer's truthsaying always rings true.

And he howls. It's the first time I've heard this howl, though I've heard its future echo many times before. Howl, howl, howl. Oh, I'm afraid. This howl comes from the despair of knowing for the first time that the first step in any journey is the first step to that journey's end; that after Oz, the next exit off the yellow brick road is Death. Oh, God, he howls, and Ash, not understanding, howls with him; and then, indeed, he covers his face in his hands, and reaches in with his thumbs, and wrenches out his right eye, and thrusts it at the dog, howling, howling, howling; and then the dog trots forward, gulps it down, lies down at our feet, whimpering, our slave now; and I look at Strang, I look at the bleeding socket and the gore that spurts down his face and spatters his beard and his robe, and I see that the wall of rock is starting to crumble, and —

Phil Etchison:

— and looking at my son I learn an awful new truth, the reason he hides behind silence, the reason he won't run into my arms and cry out Dad Dad Dad, the reason he will never say how much he loves me —

And I scream at the sphinx, at the top of my lungs, "No, no, I won't answer, you can't make me answer that question," and furiously I rush at the sphinx and I start pummeling her with my fists while my son wheels overhead, his wings burnished by the flames' reflection —

Theo Etchison:

We step through the wall of rock. Ash (and I with him) holding his father's hand, guiding him gently. The dog follows us. He's meek now, sniffing our heels, whimpering.

And there it is.

The still point of the turning world.

The whirlpool, and, in the whirlpool's center, an eye of calm; and in that eye, floating to the surface, glittering, thousand-faceted like the compound eyes of an insect, is a crystal.

"Son," says Strang, "reach out there and grab it for me."

And I say, "No, father. It's for you to take."

Strang steps into the water. The water sears him. He howls again and again as he thrusts through the whirlpool to reach the quiet center.

"What is it?" he cries out to me.

And I say, through Ash's lips: "It's what you gave up your eye for.   It's knowledge.   It's the power to steal men's souls."

The king's fist closes around the jewel. We gaze at each other over the turbulent waters. I see that the light has fled from his good eye; that this moment contains a future moment, a moment we're all inexorably rushing to; and Jesus it scares me because I can see what that moment contains, because in this moment, I am a truth-sayer, and I have not lost my vision —

Phil Etchison:

— the sphinx shatters and spills into my arms and it's my wife and we're making love in the fireworks in a small Mexican town near a laetrile clinic and —

Theo Etchison:

— and I call out to my real father, my other father, lost in another labyrinth, and I —

Phil Etchison:

— laughing, she says to me, "Aren't you lucky this is only a dream? Aren't you lucky you don't really have to answer the question?" and —

Theo Etchison:

— the king, closing his eyes, cries out, "I dream, I dream, I dream" —

Phil Etchison:

— and sobbing I wake up, on the shore of the island where stands the chariot of the sun, Odysseus' ship, the Titanic, the rusted station wagon of my life —

Theo Etchison:

— and now more images, floods of memories —

The King implanting the jewel in the scepter. Fashioning a new eye from an iolite crystal, emerging triumphant on the balcony of the palace. Stealing his first soul. Feeling that first pang of guilt and terror.

And withdrawing further into himself.

And one by one, the lights darkening in the palace over the years, the turrents falling into disrepair, the minarets shrouding themselves with rust and dust and birdshit. And the kingdom growing. Growing. But not like a tree. No vegetable love here, as Dad would say. The kingdom grew like a cancer. The kingdom was its own sickness, its own corruption —

Phil Etchison:

— and the dream was etched in my mind, every byway and fork and crossing, so that at last, I, Philip Etchison, the plainest Everyman who ever lived, possessed a piece of my sons' magic: I too had a map, I too knew the way to the source of the river that runs between worlds.

But I wasn't sure I could read the map....

Theo Etchison:

— and there, on the island, sitting beside the mad king, I know that the jewel in the scepter is the same jewel as the eye of knowledge. Ash has gone to ashes, but I can bring them back, I can bring them all back. Death is pregnant with renewal.

King Strang says to me, "I've seen things I shouldn't have seen. If I had my real eye back, I would be blind again. I wish I were."

"What would you say to Ash," I ask him, "if he were sitting with us now?"

The King says: "I don't know. We'd have to try it. A little at a time."

I say, "You wanted me to lead the way to the source even though I've lost my gift."

"You people never lose it all the way."

"Well yeah, I wanted to tell you, I didn't know the way before. But now I do. Because, in a way, I've been there."

The ashes swirl in the bright air, sparkling, star dust. The ashes settle a little. They fleck his beard. They clog the creases in his brow. I wonder if he knows how close Ash is, how little time he still has.

Twelve
The Battle over the Amethyst City

Chris Etchison:

— navigating —

I raise up my arms. I split the iceberg. The ship busts through. Cold. Cold. Funnels belch dark smoke. Satanic mills. Demons blacken the sky.

Thorn paces up and down on the ship's uppermost deck. Cerberus is running amok, worrying at three old bones. Cornelius Huang paces too, a few paces behind his lord and master so he won't intrude on him. All I'm thinking about is —

— navigating —

— navigating —

The ship shatters more ice. Ice scatters. Million itty-bitty rainbow prism fractures hailing down, the whole sky shivery and shimmery.

Thorn says: "How soon, how soon? I'm hungry."

— carving great channels in the ice floes —

Cornelius Huang: "Your hunger is a great consuming flame, my lord; soon it will swallow up the world."

"Bullshit!" says Thorn. "I'm just hungry."

The slate-colored eyes are the color of the gray gray sky.

— listen listen listen —

Thorn and Cornelius buzz around my thoughts. Like horseflies, worrying at me. Shutting out the heartbeat I need to hear.

— we'll never get there if you don't —

"Stop for a moment! Look, isn't that a city?" says Thorn.

Across-looking, beyond the ice: a patch of lavender light. A city all in amethyst.

Huang says: "My lord, we have to hurry if we're going to reach the source before anyone else."

"I don't care. I'm hungry."

Not a physical need, this hunger. Thorn feeds on power, on subjugation, on submission. He needs to oppress someone. An itch that has to be scratched.

"Truthsayer," he says, "lead us to that city. We'll lay it waste, eat up a few souls, then go on to the source when we're all full."

I won't need to delay the journey. Thorn's own greed will do it for me.

Serena Somers:

Mr. E. came cruising toward us in this kind of speedboat thing that also looked like an old station wagon. "Pile in," he said. I got in on the passenger side.

"What about you?" Mr. E. said to Milt, who was still putting away his fishing pole.

"First things first," Milt said. "We have to make sure the mother-goddess is comfortable." He and I carried the Mary statue, placed her reverently in the back seat, made sure she was adequately belted in.

"Think I'll just ride on the hood," Milt said. He swirled around and at first I thought he was going into one of his man-woman transformation things, but no, with every twist he seemed more and more feathery, and more and more black. He spread his arms and did like, this flapping, springing sort of dance, eerily graceful.

He flapped and flapped and flapped himself into a great black raven and perched himself where the hood ornament should have been if Joshua hadn't stolen it years ago to use as part of a collage in Mrs. Shigenaka's art class. He wasn't all raven, either; sometimes he looked completely human. Guess it shouldn't have surprised me.

Mr. E. said, "Serena, Serena, I've had the strangest dream. I think I know where we're going now."

I said, "Cool, Mr. E. Where's that?"

"It's a place I visited in the dream. I can't really explain. I've got a kind of map of it in my head. But I don't know how to read it."

"Joshua could read it if he were here."

"I know," he said. "And Chris wouldn't need a map at all. And Theo...."

"Can we find them?"

"I think I already have. At least, inside the dream I did. I just have to get back."

The raven screeched, a word that sounded something like "Shebabalah."

He put the car into drive. There were a lot more gears on the gearshift than I thought cars were supposed to have.

"Mr. E., we're on an island. How far are you going to drive, maybe a hundred feet?"

"I got the car here, didn't I?   Let's take it as it comes."

The engine purred.

"The gas gauge is on E," I pointed out.

"This car apparently doesn't run on gas at all," he said, "but on the stuff of dreams. Close your eyes and make a wish."

Joshua, I thought, hard, with all my might.

Joshua at the edge of the bed, Joshua smiling, Joshua picking at a zit, Joshua in an oversize sweater, reaching out to me, Joshua in my arms, dead —

The car began to move.

I opened my eyes.

"Good," Mr. E. said. "Your dreams are very lucid. Look in the side mirror. Your side, not mine."

I did. And there he was, standing by the car door, in the oversize sweater, picking a zit, smiling, laughing even, but he vanished into thin air as soon as I tried to concentrate.

The car pushed off into the water. Zoomed, in fact, churning up a wall of water on either side. We zigzagged around the standing stones, rounded the tip of a sphinx, vaulted all the way the side of a pyramid, hung in mid-air for the splittest of seconds, crashed hard into the crystal foam. The raven turned to us. His eyes were shining. In a moment we were just skimming along.

Reached the bank. A road ran alongside the river. A autobahn with signs in hieroglyphics. We were speeding now, and the woods and hills were a blur of green-gold-icy-blue. The sky flashed with purple lightning — the lights of a city just over the horizon.

The raven shrieked: Shebabalah! Shebabalah!

"What the hell does that mean?" said I said.

"My wife would probably know."

I turned to look at Mrs. E., but she was, of course, a statue. When she is in this state, it takes her a thousand years to take a single breath. She can't exactly answer questions, but she does the enigma of godhood thing really well. Mr. E. drove on. The landscape was alien and rural: checkerboard fields in garish hues of neon pink and lime, mountains shaped like fists, shaking at the setting sun.

"Are you hungry?" Mr. E. said.

"Hungry? I guess so. We could fish, I maybe. I think it's unlikely that we'll find a McDonald's around here." You know, when there's a furious dragon, gnawing away at the pit of your stomach, the thought of food seems totally distasteful.

"You never know. There is a city up ahead. We should stop. Maybe get a decent night's sleep in a hotel. Take a shower. Watch cable. You know, all the things one does on the road."

"You're daydreaming, Mr. E.!"

"Maybe not."

We're swiftly passing by signs that say GAS FOOD LODGING. Say other things too: CHEAP SEX. FACTORY OUTLET MALLS. PUBLIC EXECUTIONS. This is quite a town we're racing to.

"Stop for a moment," I said. Mr. E. pulled over. We got out and stood by a clump of saguaro under a purple-brown sky. "I've got an idea."

The raven, who had detached himself from the hood, and was circling overhead, came down and perched by the side mirror, tapping at the window as if he needed to talk.

"I see you agree with me," I said. "The goddess goes on the hood, not the shaman."

I remembered that Mary Etchison was much worshipped in the many worlds we'd passed through. We'd get a much better reception in a strange city if we were preceded by divinity.

"So we'll tie her to the bumper, like a — like a dead deer?" said Mr. E., appalled.

"No," I said. "I think she'll find her own way of adapting. She usually does."

The raven cawed out that weird-sounded word, over and over. "What's he talking about?" I asked Mr. E., because he always seemed to know such things.

"It sounds to me like Xibalba," he said, "which is to say, the labyrinth of nightmares. It's some ancient Maya thing," he added with a glance at the raven; he probably felt a twinge of political incorrectness, lecturing about Native Americans in the presence of a real-live one.

Milt Stone morphed back to humanoid for a moment. "You're right," he said. "For a paleface, you're pretty perceptive."

"Good," I said, "you're human enough to help us with Mrs. E."

We sort of hefted her onto the hood, and you know, the very first thing that statue did was to like, shrink into about the size of a hood ornament, and to stand, her robes fluttering, with open wings, the way they do on Rolls Royces — or is it Bentleys? — or on the prow of an ancient ship. It was totally cool. But why not?

"Fascinating," Mr. E. said. "She's very adaptable, isn't she? She's had many shapes and sizes. She's been in a lot of places at the same time. One of the rules seems to be that, if two of her are in roughly the same location, one of them gets subsumed into the other. Two of her can't occupy the same perceptual cosmos as each other. ..."

"That's pretty intellectual-sounding, Mr. E.," I said. One of Mr. E.'s problems is that he's always trying to figure out the underlying rules of whatever cosmos he finds himself in. This is okay, to some extent, but the rules always end up breaking down, don't they? Better to take it as it comes....

"Okay," he said.

So now we're in a battered old station wagon with a wheezing airconditioner with a goddess as a hood ornament, and a raven wheeling overhead. And we're closing in on the Amethyst City, kilometer by kilometer. That's how I thought of it in my mind. It makes sense, once you're in Oz, that there should be a city for every precious stone.

Chris Etchison:

— swooping —

Demons are spreading their wings. Diving off the
upper deck of the ship and flinging themselves against
the purple minarets. Screeching, howling, shrilling.
Thorn watches with me.

"Come on, boy," he says.

— what about the pursuit of the source? —

"First, dinner." He claps his hands and they roll out
a blood-red carpet woven with designs of skulls and
crossbones. "You like Arabian food?" he says.

— not if it's sucked from the living —

Thorn laughs.

He spreads out his cloak on it. Motions me to sit
down beside him; then, knocking on the cloak three
times, causes the carpet to levitate. I hold on tight. The
carpet ripples, threatens to throw me off. I cling to the
frayed fringe. We're in the midst of the squadron of demons. Their gargoyle faces spit fire. They black out the
bloody sun.

Down-looking now: streets full of panicking citizens.
Men in bejewelled turbans fending off the diving demons. Naked children dashing through the alleys, veiled
women running in circles.

We flit over an avenue, careen down a twisty muddy
lane; a woman being raped against the side of a great
stone statue of the goddess, a bewildered zebra running
wild with his gold chain clanking against the gutter, a
man trying to ward off the demons by flinging stones ...
Thorn's very smug, very satisfied; he feeds as much off
the commotion and the confusion as off blood; as we
speed over gardens of rose and lilac, we watch one of his
minions twist the head off a child and toss it in the air so
that it lands in Thorn's lap, and he bends over and slurps
up the hot carotid blood but I look away; but I can still
see it of course, I can feel it, a sharp dissonance in the

music of my mind; I can't help seeing it because I'm a Truthsayer.

The flying carpet comes to rest at last. A purple parapet overlooking the city's central square. Thorn tosses the head into the street. On the terrace, priestesses in sweeping lilac robes are propitiating a huge statue of a weeping woman. My mother. Clouds of lavender-tinged incense. The women beat their breasts, tear at their hair, wail, moan, make a ferocious noise. The high priestess wears silver horns, and one breast has been replaced by a breast-shaped crystal of deepest amethyst; and when she sees Thorn she holds up her hand. At once, the cries of lamentation cease. The priestesses regroup. They stand in a semi-circle, protecting the statue of the mother goddess. We are in a little pocket of silence, but from beyond the parapet the dying can be heard screaming.

Thorn says, "You've turned your back on me."

The priestess says, "We heard you were dead."

"Never dead," says Thorn, "not so long as my name lives on. Now let's get rid of your goddess and put up the proper statues; it's fine to worship her in secret, in the catacombs, in the gutter, but this city's my turf." The priestess throws herself at Thorn, tries to scratch out those slate-colored eyes. But Thorn merely laughs, slaps her around a little — casually — stoops to kiss her fingertips and draw a drop or two of hieratic blood — then cries out: "Time to topple the bitch!"

A passel of demons hovering around Thorn's head like a black halo; at his command, they switch direction, swirl, reconstitute, gather into an arrow of dark flesh and smashes into the statue. The statue totters, tumbles. The priestesses scream. Thorn laughs like an evil scientist. He guffaws, he yawps, and the wind picks up his laughter and sends it echoing back and forth and back and forth.

The statue: suddenly: just before it hits the ground: a burst of purple radiance from the sky ... lightning ...

thunder, like the crack of a great stone heart ... then, all at once, the statue disappearing in a flash of white light.

Thorn stops laughing.

"The goddess has disappeared," says one of the priestesses. "That means —"

Another says, "— that another incarnation of the goddess has entered the city — that means —"

"That the battle isn't over yet —"

Thorn turns to me. "Quick! Where is the goddess? Who's brought that bitch into the city?"

I close my eyes and:

Listen, listen:

First the heartbeat of the world. Then, above it, the pounding surf that is life, human and alien, angel and demon; high above, the pinprick birth and death pangs of the stars.

Mother, I cry out in my mind.

And this is what I see:

The hood of a beat-up stationwagon, wheezing up a freeway somewhere ... Arizona? Perhaps it was Arizona once, before the river changed its course.

Behind the wheel are Philip and Serena. Wheeling in the sky is a black raven; and the hood ornament is the triple goddess. Somewhere in that car there is also a dragon, but she is invisible.

— the goddess is at the gates —

Thorn stands tall but in his eyes there is consternation.

Phil Etchison:

— and so I drove up to the gates of amethyst — I was in about seventeenth gear by this time — and the gates shattered and I drove on past them. Fire was racing up and down the streets. Demons were swooping down from the sky. The cobblestones, the walls, the storefronts, even the fast-food places were a million shades of crystal purple, but the liquid fire that spewed over them all was neon green. Purple and green ... comic-book villain colors ... the colors of the Joker, who is also the Antichrist....

"Duck!" Serena screamed. I steered hard left to avoid a Temple-of-Doom-sized ball of flame, crashed through a lavender store window, could stop the car in time to hit a blank wall, but —

The wall just pulverized itself at the last minute and I sped through, did a sort of bounce down into an alley, zoomed on.

"How did that happen?" I said.

"Look," said Serena. "It's the goddess."

Sure enough, the hood ornament that had been my wife had changed position; she was standing up straight now, one arm held out in a warding-off-evil gesture, the other over her heart.

"Mary!" I cried.

The hood ornament turned and winked at me.

"Way to go, Mrs. E.!" cried Serena. Then, suddenly, she clutched her stomach as we swerved past a soda fountain that featured a ten-foot-high purple sundae in the window and a flock of festive demons inside.

"What's wrong?" I said, slowing down a little.

"My stomach," she said. "It's all ... churning...."

"Butterflies in your stomach?"

I heard a whirring from beneath her dress, like the sound of locusts hitting a wheatfield. "More than butterflies," she said.

"A dragon?"

Smoke belched up through cracks in the crystal pavement.

"Yes," she said.

Chris Etchison:

At that moment, I clutch a pure white tone that squeezes itself out of the heat-haze of the burning city and —

I weave that tone around me until it becomes a circle that is both light and music all at once, and —

Spin and spin and —

White-hot! Blue-hot! the music of the spheres and —

Mom, I cry out once more, and —

— Mom —

— Mom —

I hear her coming. She's raising up her right arm and with her right arm she's crossing her heart.

Thorn is glowering.

"Where's the fucking goddess?" he screams, and grabs me through the cocoon of light and tries to shake me by the shoulders but the power of the music is too strong for him, it burns him and he backs away and —

Serena Somers:

This time the dragon really wanted out, and I knew that if I grew into the fifty-foot woman again I'd bust through the roof of the station wagon and then I suppose we'd get rained on or something once we started back up the road. Wasn't thinking too straight, but I had the presence of mind to hop out of the passenger seat in a hurry. Not a second too late because as soon as my feet hit the sidewalk they started to grow. Meanwhile, my stomach was really churning and I was sure there was going to be a remake of the gut-popping scene from Alien right here in the middle of the street.

I reached out, grasped the cherry from the ten-foot sundae and it skittered down the burning pavement like a big purple marble.

I need something to settle my stomach! I thought to myself. The dragon was rearing this way and that inside me. I couldn't tell if Katastrofa wanted to get out to help her brother or to battle him, or whether she was just going to come bursting forth in a tumult of raw, ungovernable energy.

I looked up at the sky —

Chris Etchison:

— Mom —

Serena Somers:

I gazed at the hood ornament, which was spinning, its arms whizzing back and forth, palms held out, deflecting laser shafts as the demons in the sky blasted us with their burning eyes.

Milt Stone, too, wheeled overhead, dashing his beak against one demon after another, making them sizzle and plummet, but there was always a fresh gargoyle figure to attack; the sky was black with them.

I sure needed something to settle my stomach —

Thirteen
The Return of the Triple Goddess

Chris Etchison:

— Mom —

Serena Somers:

Well like, then I suddenly knew what I had to do. Oren always used to lecture me about checks and balances and branches of government when I was working for his campaign, oh, I don't know, fifty million universes ago. I was shooting up like, well, like Alice in Wonderland, and there was a dragon flailing around inside my belly, and now and then a tendril of smoke was totally pouring out of my nostrils, and I felt a hell of a tickle at the back of my throat, but I thought, oh, God, if I cough, the whole street will explode in a ball of flame. There was only one way to balance the dragon.

I knelt down beside the stationwagon. I cupped my hands around the hood ornament. Milt, approvingly, circled my head, and I could once more hear that other-worldly screech: Xibalba, Xibalba. Mr. E. looked pretty panicky, though.

"That's my wife," he cried out.

I said, trying hard not to boom, "It's okay, Mr. E. I'm only borrowing her for a few hours. The transformation wasn't complete before, but now it will be."

Mr. E. puzzled over this — the motor was still running — and then he suddenly cried out, "Why, of course! The triple goddess ... virgin, mother, crone ... or should I say, young woman, dragon, hood ornament? Without the third piece of the puzzle, you were almost the real thing, but now you can be it all ... and you can really fight the forces of darkness."

"It's not really a light versus dark thing, Mr. E.," I said. "It's more yin and yang ... it's more the feminine principle counteracting the masculine ... you know the kind of thing I mean."

I stood up ... I hadn't yet reached the full fifty feet, but I was about a couple of stories high now ... and I lifted the hood ornament to my lips. I looked around for a fire hydrant, kicked it open so that it spouted up laven-der water, took a swig, then swallowed the goddess as if it was the toughest pill in the universe.

Caught in my throat for a moment, and then, as though my saliva were an acid bath, it smoothed itself out and slid down to meet the dragon. I felt like a glass of water that you pop an alka-seltzer into ... when it hit my stomach, I started to hear the rumbling. Then I kind of stretched ... like a really big yawning kind of stretch ... and all of a sudden there were these lines of fire gridding up and down me. I was powerful. Not just tall and strong, but full of the pull of the earth itself; where my feet touched the ground they linked with the nervous system of a whole planet. My hair was a mess of fiery serpents.

"Here I come, Thorn," I shouted.

I was naked, too, and my hips and breasts were full, robust, like those obese prehistoric Venuses, bursting with fertility. I covered my vulva with my left hand because the dragon inside it might spew fire and devastate the alleyway.

Where was Thorn?

Chris Etchison:

— Mom —

— and then I see her. Rearing up above the parapets of amethyst and sugilite. A woman in flames, her eyes white-hot, her breasts brimming and fecund, yeah, I see her. She is beautiful. And then —

The priestesses are all falling to their knees and crying out, "The Goddess, the Goddess." Thorn stares about, Cornelius holds up the trumpet, the three-headed dog yaps.

"Muster the demons," Thorn cries. He pauses to suck the juices from a dead woman, then tosses her over the stone tiles down to the street beneath. The triple goddess towers over us. Her hair is a mass of fiery snakes.

Cornelius blows his horn: three sharp blasts that shatter the heartbeat of the cosmos into arhythmic cacophony.

Up-looking: the black sky splits into three stripes, three ranks of dark angels: mandibled, drooling, fanged. Each file is arrowed at the triple goddess.

Three more blasts —

Then Serena-Katastrofa-Mary flings her arms wide and her breasts heave like volcanoes, and I can hear the warm milk churning, the milk that is the manna that is the nectar of the gods.

"Get out of my city," she whispers: her whisper makes the pillars rattle.

"No, you slug," says Thorn, but he sounds listless, not at all defiant.   Turning to Cornelius, he orders him to sound the trumpet once more.

"Nobody calls me slug now!" screams Serena.

One at a time, the lines of demons hurl themselves at the goddess. The goddess spins; she twists; she dances. The demons shatter like glass. They snap in her hands. They dash themselves into pieces. Dead demon shards pelt down, obsidian rain.

The goddess shrieks, and from her lips stream moons and stars that flock up heavenward, each planetary body thrumming with the crystal harmony that makes up the music of the spheres.

And I say:

— Mom —

but suddenly I realize for a fact that the man I call my father has entered the city, is nearby, and I know too that I soon will lose the power of speech, because I can't say what I have to say and still remain his son, can't break his heart, can't stop the spinning cycle of our fate (and I hear my father's voice now in my memories, making some curious dry pun about spin cycles and washing machines), can't say what I have to say because the moment isn't right yet, feel all wrung out inside and out because what I have to say is so, you know, so, so, so fucking crucial to the world.

The priestesses are still prostrate — those that survived the attack of Thorn. The goddess slams her fist on the parapet and a crystal causeway arches up and over and down to the lowest story of the palace.

Thorn says, "Come on, boy. We've been here too long anyway."

Cornelius says, "My lord, we seem to have lost the advantage."

Thorn says, "Fuck the advantage. I came here to eat, and I'm full now."

"But I thought you wanted to recapture the Amethyst City from the Triple Goddess," Cornelius Huang says.

"Don't give a flying fuck about that bitch," says Thorn. "Grab the kid and let's get out."

And I can't speak, because, inching up the causeway at a gravity-defying angle, a battered station wagon is creeping, led by a raven with bright eyes and open wings; and because he's so close, I'm frozen, I'm back to the state of dumbness.

"What are you staring at, kid?" Thorn screams.

— * —

— * and * —

— * father * —

— * and * —

I can't even get out one syllable. But I feel a great music welling up inside me, a music of desire and loss and the impermanence of the world; and that is weird because I'm a truthsayer and I see the things that are real, firm, permanent, the bedrock beneath the shifting sands of illusion, and here I am hearing the counterpoint pound louder than the theme. I open my lips and a few notes come tearing out and the notes sunder the sky, and then Thorn and Cornelius grab hold of me and drag me, carry me, across the parapet, away from the triple goddess and the car, and the car has screeched to a halt and Phil is standing there and he's calling to me, "Chris, Chris," but I wonder if what he sees is really me because for those few seconds I can't hear the real music. And in that split second of doubt Cornelius Huang kind of wraps me in a bubble of his trumpet's blasting. The blast is piercing, crimson-sounding; it coils around me, renders me helpless long enough for Thorn to cast his cloak of darkness over me, and then we're flying again, flying and fleeing, to where the ship of lost souls is docked beside the sundered city —

"Quick, boy!" Thorn cries out. "Make us a new gateway! Get us to the source, the fastest way you can!"

— and I —

— fly —

Phil Etchison:

I saw him. I really saw him. Chris just the way I saw him last. Looking back at us, being flown up into the sky, staring fixedly at me with an expression I couldn't fathom: oh, I know he is brighter than me, and sees more, hears more, understands more, but still he's a child, and it breaks my heart, that's what it does to me.

We pulled up to about the middle of the parapet and parked. There was a broken altar. The priestesses were getting up, helping each other up, adjusting their head-dresses, re-coiling the silver snakes they wore around their bare breasts.

Serena still loomed above us; there was a hint of sunlight behind her hair; we watched at the edge of the terrace; Thorn's ship, which might or might not have been the Titanic, lumbered off upstream, past floes and icebergs, toward a shimmering circle of light that I knew was Chris's gateway to the next portion of the journey toward the source.

The priestesses all turned and fell prostrate once more, this time in front of the congressional page turned live-in president's lover turned giantess. Serena blinked, and a beam of laser light ignited the altar, and it soon glowed, deep, rich purple. Violet smoke curled skyward.

"I guess I should come back to earth now," she said.

She put her hands together in a Buddha-like gesture. And started to shrink, but not before coughing out the hood ornament, which landed with perfect precision on a plinth, where once my wife's statue had doubtless stood. I wondered whether she would disgorge the dragon as well — there was a lot of fire still whirling about her body — but I guess she managed to hold it down. She was no longer naked, by the way, but dressed in an unassuming pair of jeans and a shapeless, oversized Beavis and Butthead sweater.

"You seem younger, somehow," I said.

Serena said, "I am, Phil. I've shed about seven years since we all got back into this adventure; what I thought were seven years, Oren winning the presidency, my moving into the White House, all those years of banquets, speeches, and congress-wrangling, they all turned out to have been a dream, didn't they? And like, now I'm barely out of high school again."

"Where's the dragon?" I said.

"Around my neck," she said, and pointed to a shiny amulet. I came closer, and I saw now that she wore the dragon; that the coin-sized creature was alive, spluttering up tiny tendrils of smoke, squirming against the space between Serena's breasts, clawing at her skin. "And she'll stay there until I need her again."

Serena, for once, seemed to live up to her name. There was a kind of tranquility in her features that, once or twice, I'd seen in my wife's face; sometimes it would be when she and I stood in the doorway and watched our babies sleeping; sometimes it was after she and I made love.

Milt Stone, all raven now, perched on my shoulder and stared out at the world with icy eyes.

One of the priestesses — a head priestess of some kind, I guess, because she wore a plumed crown and a silver torc above her bare breasts, came up to me — stretched out her palm reverentially toward me as in an Egyptian mural — touched her lips, bowed deeply.

"I am," she said, "the priestess Polydora. Thank you for bringing our goddess back to life. I take it you're the Mortal Consort, the hero who keeps the flame."

"I didn't realize I was anything at all in this drama. I mean, my sons have become seers, my wife is a goddess, even my former babysitter has turned into a sacred cow and then — I thought I was the one guy left out of everything — you know, like Joseph, shut out of the whole Madonna and Child situation, always suffering from a complex at having been cuckolded by the Holy Ghost."

I said, "The way this goddess keeps coming and going, vanishing and reappearing — it's very confusing."

"I know," the priestess said. "The goddess is real,
and the goddess is alive, and the goddess is omnipresent,
but her physical manifestation can't occupy the same
general area in more than one form; that would violate
the paradox of allness-in-oneness."

"So if two statues of my wife are near one another,
one of them disintegrates?"

"That's how we knew that the goddess was on her
way to rescue us. Well, perhaps you'd like to attend a
celebratory banquet, since the City of Amethyst has been
rescued from the forces of darkness one more time."

This was all wonderful and good, you know, but I had
to confess that there was a certain remoteness about all
this frantic, mythic warfare. I really could have cared
less that there were goddess-cities and Strang-cities and
there was a perpetual state of Manichaean tension between them. I just wanted to get on with the journey.
"Can't we forge ahead?" I said. "They'll get to the source
before us if we don't hurry."

Serena said, "They may, Phil, but the final conflict
can't be fought without all the protagonists present; the
sensible thing would be to get a little food into your
stomach."

"And then?" I said.

"And then resume our quest," said Milt, or rather
croaked, since he was still a raven; then he craned back
his neck and shrieked, "Xibalba."

Fourteen
The Leap

Theo Etchison:

So here I am, the blind leading the one-eyed king. I look through the eyes of Ash, who knows the way because he once looked through my eyes. As Dad would say, paradoxes within paradoxes. Cool. He loves paradoxes. Thinks they have a sparkle to them, like brilliant-cut diamonds.

"So you do know the way," says King Strang.

"I guess so, dude," I say.

Around us, the water ripples. The blue sun dances on the lake. The concentric stones are all shiny and metallic, like they've just been minted, glittering against the deep.

"I bet," says Strang, "that it's down."

"Yeah," I say. The journey to the heart of things is always down. That's a new truth that I see clearly now, even without my gift. The path to the summit of the world is through the center of hell. Fucking Jesus I see it all so clearly now, that shiny paradox, I can just imagine Dad holding it out to me in the palm of his hand and grinning, probably muttering something about the human condition.

"You've been a good fool," says Strang, "you've never lied to me."

"I know the way now, nuncle.   It's like, totally through the darkness and out the other side. Like a black hole."

The water swirls around our little island. We are the eye of the whirlpool. We climb a little higher up on the standing stone, using the basalt ledges that are barely wide enough to hold our feet. Strang goes ahead of me, his scepter under one arm, now and then reaching for me so I can steady him. He seems frail, but there are sinews beneath the soft skin; he has one last great act of power left inside him; but since I am no longer a truthsayer, I can't know what it is exactly; I can only feel the surge of energy. Clutching the rock as he does, he draws strength. Perhaps it is because he's a child of earth, and the earth still suckles him.

"Do you know where we're going?" he says again. It's one of those magic questions, the ones that you have to ask three times before the answer actually comes true.

"Yeah," I say. "Into the arms of darkness."

We have reached the topmost ledge.   The king squats, stares out at the churning lake; his face is as furrowed and pitted as the moon. I can't tell his good eye from his bad; they're both like ice. "So you're saying," the king says, "that I just have to stand up, open my arms, and leap."

"I think so," I say.   "We've reached a place where thousands of pieces of the river intermingle ... maybe every molecule that jostles every other molecule is a molecule from a different universe ... you see what I mean? We're going to have to rely on instinct ... well, faith, maybe."

"You still are a truthsayer, boy."

"I can't see the truth anymore, but maybe the memory is in the cells of my body ... you know, the way Dad gets in a car sometimes, and he's all talking about Keats and Shelley, and he never once looks at the road, but the

way home is imprinted deep inside him so that he always
makes the right turns, doesn't exit the Beltway at the
wrong place; so what I'm saying is, that you and I were
there once ... well, you were physically there, and I was
there inside of someone else who is now inside of me ..."
I know that Ash is around because, now and then, I
sneeze.

I scramble up onto the topmost ledge beside him.

"Hair-raising, isn't it, boy?"

"I guess."

The wind rises a little. I shiver. "And we just jump?"

"Yeah."

"What? So momentous an event, one small step, one
giant leap and all that, and there's not even a modicum of
thunder and lightning to portend the drama of the moment?"

Far, far away, a lone fork of lightning tickles the horizon.

Far, far away, a burp of thunder; or maybe it's just
the splash of a pebble, or a blind bird braining itself
against the standing stones ... not with a bang but with a
whimper, that's what Dad would've said, declaiming his
T.S. Eliot over a massive pot roast. To travel to other
worlds, you first have to die a little. Dying can be a
metaphor or dying can be real. I wonder which it's going
to be this time.

"C'mon, King Strang," I say. "Time for the chicken to
cross the road."

"Are you saying I'm a coward?"

I laugh. "Let's go, already."

King Strang stretches up to his full, majestic height;
yes, there is still one great spell inside him, one final
making or unmaking. He scares me. The sky darkens
and yes, there's another thunderbolt, a little closer; and
when he lifts up his arms, the wind begins to whistle, to
encircle him, and his hair starts flying, and yeah, he is
like King Lear after all, old, mad, possessive; his robes
begin to flap and they are more thunderous than the

thunder; his eyes flash and they are brighter than the lightning.

"Do you know me?" he screams. "Do you know who I am?"

I try to answer until I realize he's not shouting at me. He's shouting at the elements, the storm, the lake.

"I'm the king of the whole damn universe," he cries, and he twirls his scepter above his head like a demented cheerleader. "I'm the head honcho, the judge, the reckoner, the destroyer of worlds!" He doesn't say it like he means it though. There's a lot of despair here. I feel it. The storm around us has been wrought by the turbulence within him. "You know how many souls have been sucked into the jewel in my scepter? Do you know how many deaths have fed my power? Millions, billions, trillions."

"But you need one more death," I scream back at him.

"My own?"

Thunder and lightning. His eyes darken, redden. There is a hint of the dragon about him. I sneeze again. Ash is filling my lungs.

"Hold on to me," I say, and grasp his gnarled hand, and then, together, we both jump —

Phil Etchison:

— and ride in triumph through Persepolis? —

I thought to myself, Is it not passing brave to be a king? There were too many great poets jangling in my head. Maybe that's why I could never quite become one myself. The women of the Amethyst City were crowning me, robing me in ermine and purple, while Serena looked on and Milt wheeled above my head. Below, the gutted streets were full of people, and they were cheering, and there were fireworks.

"Why are you crowning me?" I asked the high priestess.

"Because you saved our city."

"But I'm leaving. Got a train to catch, as they say."

"It's all right," she said. "It's just a formality; this city is really a matriarchy anyway. But we do need a quick dose of spectacle to make up for the carnage we've been through."

That night, there came to me another woman, in a palace apartment overlooking the river. I was alone this time; Serena and Milt had found other things to do; I think they were a lot more in tune with the goddess-ruled religiosity of the place than I.

The woman's name was Porphyria, and, true to her name, was pale and purple-haired, and her hair was her only clothing. She seemed very young — well, maybe not her eyes — but she carried herself like a queen.

"Your Majesty," she said to me (a weird thing to say to a man in a teeshirt and faded boxer shorts) "is there anything I can do for you?" I took it that she meant in a sexual sense, because why else would a naked woman show up in a man's bedroom and smile brazenly at him with her hair fluttering just a little in the breeze from the river, and a tallow candle in her hand, set in a heart-shaped candleholder?

I said, "But I'm married." Not that I had a wedding band or anything bourgeois like that.

She said, "I know."

"I can't go through with —"

"It is traditional for the conquering hero to take the goddess herself to bride."

And still she came toward me. She smelled of rain. Like the first time I saw Mary. "Is it raining?" I asked Rapunzel of the purple tresses.

She laughed, shook her hair, sprayed me a little. "Only in your memories," she said.

And then I understood what she meant. My wife is a statue in this world, a mysteriously self-replicating statue that obeys a whole different set of laws of physics. I can't make love to a statue, but....

She shakes her hair again. Between the curve of her breasts, I see an amulet that bears a remarkable resemblance to a certain hood ornament....

"Mary?" I said softly.

Porphyria smiled.

I thought: What is it about this woman that reminds me of my wife? Is it only the smell of rain, that lashing, scalding Virginia rain that reeks of fertility? Because that was the first time we met, that wetness clinging to her. She smiled. My wife had a crooked way of smiling sometimes; I wonder if she always knew she was sick, that every breath she took was pregnant with impending death. Porphyria smiled and moved a little closer, and when she touched my cheek I could feel Mary's soul.

"How do you do that?" I asked her.

"Prayer," Porphyria said, "and meditation. We breathe in the goddess's essence with a special kind of incense."

"Mary," I said, "Oh, Mary, Mary," because we rarely made love anymore, not since Chris was born, and it was taking a moment for my body to remember how it was supposed to react; but she touched my lips with a pungent finger, and said only, "Not Mary, not Mary; I am only her shadow's shadow."

Then she enveloped me in herself, and I too breathed in the essence of the great mother, my wife. Porphyria seemed to grow and grow; I don't mean she became bloated and hideous, like those two-thousand-pound women on Donahue, but that her womanliness seemed to spread out from her so that she was in the bedsheets, in the air, in the dust, in the walls, in the carpeting, in the feathers in the pillows. If I had not loved her I might have found the experience disquietingly arachnoid.

We made love, and the next morning Porphyria baked me a loaf of bread, wrapped two baked fishes in a banana leaf, and put them in a basket for me; and she said to me, kissing me awake, "These are for your journey." She also made a fresh pot of coffee, and we drank it from amethyst coffee mugs, and I could hear the whisper of the river from the open window, and I could see the gauze curtains shifting in the breeze.

I left the apartment and walked over to the parapet of the goddess. The stationwagon had been buffed, and it shone as though it were the chariot of the sun. Milt was back in human form now, robed in black feathers from head to toe, and looking as sexually ambiguous as ever, with his eyes heavily mascara'd and his lips painted goth-black..

Serena Somers:

That night, they put me up in the goddess suite — that's how it seemed — a penthouse overlooking the river. It was even better than the White House. For one thing, you didn't have to call down to the kitchen for room service; you could just clap your hands, and whatever came to mind would appear, probably on a silver platter, trumpets blaring. To think we decided to stop here for a burger and fries on our way to the great rendezvous....

In the middle of the night, in the moonlight, after I had hung the dragon pendant over the mirror, a man came to me. He wore nothing but his own purple hair, twined and twisted around his body so that it was like a silky tunic. His eyes had a silvery tinge to them, like the moon; his fingernails, too, were painted silver.

"Goddess," said the man — more boy than man, perhaps — "is there anything I can do?"

I realized that I hadn't had sex in a very, very long time. Moreover, I had never had sex since becoming a goddess. It certainly put a different spin on things. It wasn't that I felt the way I think men feel, when they see women as a garden, and they go through plucking a violet here, a tulip there; but there was a certain, like, appraising quality to the way I was able to look at this of-

fering. I looked, and I liked, and, after a moment's con-
sideration, I fucked.

I don't know what kind of training these priests of
the goddess have, but I do know that I didn't get any
sleep at all that night.

Phil Etchison:

And then we got into the car ... we started to move
up the yellow brick causeway that had sprung up over-
night by a miracle of the goddess ... the causeway
climbed and climbed, arrowing skyward at a dizzying
sixty degrees ... the sun was out and I could barely see to
drive. And no goddess hood ornament to protect us, because we were still within range of the goddess of the
city ... the law of conservation of goddesses still held
firm. Higher and higher we climbed. I sweated. I shifted
all the different gears, even the ones I'd never heard of,
trying to reduce the strain on the stationwagon. But you
know, the gearshift itself kept shifting; one minute it
would be the usual PRNDLL, the next a mind-boggling
PRNDZSDFGEWLZ, and one time it even read PRINCE.
Unless the bright sun was driving me mad.

Sitting next to me, Serena watched me, strangely
calm. Radiant, even. I wondered what kind of interest-
ing sexual experience she had had the previous night. I
wondered whether Milt, the raven, had been vouchsafed
an experience himself, or whether, as a sacred hermaph-
rodite, he was allowed only to conjugate with himself.
Milt was occupying the back seat, tapping slowly and
methodically on a drum, and muttering to himself in Navajo.

I floored the gas.

Higher! Higher! Higher! Around us, the crystal sky-
scrapers dazzled! Ahead, below, the river sparkled!

"Do you know where we're going?" said Serena.

"No, I don't!" I said. "But my body knows." Because
the dream that I'd had while floating in the waters of the

lake had etched that memory in every cell of me; it was as though I had a special piece of DNA now that knew where the source of the river lay.

"Xibalba," said Milt Stone. "Nifty-sounding word, isn't it? Native American words always roll around the tongue that way. Mythic resonance, you know."

The car was morphing every few seconds now. Sometimes it was a golden swan whose wings flapped mightily against the gusting wind. Sometimes it was a spaceship, sometimes a galleon, sometimes a pink Cadillac, and always accelerating. And then ... just as the causeway was starting to become more and more and more perpendicular, just as we reached the crest of it, just as we reached that moment, you know, on the first hill of a roller coaster when you are magically suspended, defying gravity, and we hung there, waiting for the great fall —

That's when I noticed the gap in the causeway —

That's when I noticed the sheer drop into the churning river.

"Shit," I said, "I didn't put on my seat belt." I fumbled for it, but there wasn't one.

Serena screamed. We plummeted.

"You said you knew the way!" Serena shouted.

"This is better than peyote," Milt said. "No external chemicals; all the synthesizing's done right inside your brain."

We plummeted faster.

"We should hit terminal velocity soon," said Milt.

"We're gonna crash!" Serena shrieked. I, on the other hand, was too terrified to say anything at all.

The station wagon hurtled toward ground zero. My face smacked into the windshield. The wipers went on, the air conditioning went berserk, and the car radio burst into Strauss's Also sprach Zarathustra.

The goddess materialized on the hood —

Then impact.

Fifteen
20,000 Leagues Under the Sea

Theo Etchison:

— and hit the water hard.   Bubbles flying, liquid flooding our nostrils. Fucking Jesus I think, I've made the wrong choice, this death is the one true death after all and not another metamorphosis —

Chris Etchison:

— the iceberg —
— smash and —
Concentrate! Hard! The whistling wind, you blink and your iced-up tears break off your lashes and glide down your cheeks and —
— the ship! capsizing! —
— no wonder it was the Titanic —
Demons are dashing around me. Their webbed feet slide on the steep, slippery decks. They scream, they belch fumes of brimstone.

Phil Etchison:

— striking the water, the car morphed rapidly into a kind of subaquatic vessel, sprouting dials, levers, periscopes, computer screens, and —

Theo Etchison:

— Confusion!   Slowly we turn, while around us churn —
— the moon the stars the cavernous earth —
Strang clutches my hand hard.   He's almost like a child, and I'm almost a grownup, teetering on the brink of it at least; I get a glimpse of how things may be one day, when I'm a lot older, and when the power of truthsaying has left me forever —
— bubbles —
I close my eyes. I can't breathe. I'm drowning. Got to find a straw to grasp and it has to be the right straw. Over there, what's that, a hint of yellow, a half-brick bobbing up and down? How can I even see it when my eyes are closed?   Or it is the memory of the journey burned into my brain?

Phil Etchison:

Then came a miracle.   The water smoothed out somehow.   The station wagon was a surrounded by a bubble of still, sweet air. My wife had reconstituted herself on the hood of the car. We were still descending. The depth gauge read 100, 1000, 7000, 9000 feet ... way beyond the car's physical tolerance. We went down gently.   Serena began to hum, and Milt began tapping out a slow, syncopated rhythm on his drum.
The view as we sank was a bit like the Captain Nemo ride in Disneyland; the lake we swam in was all the lakes and oceans of our dreams. You could see the things you dream about, but only a glimpse at a time — here a flash of the Loch Ness Monster, there a glint of pirate treasure;

here a barnacled turret of lost Atlantis, there a mermaid, shimmying past, only to turn and whisk herself away in shock at seeing a carload of human beings....

A glimpse of yellow. A piece of golden brick drifted by.

More bricks. A rain of gold, ping-ping-pinging against the side of the car, tinkling against the windows. I could feel it in my bones ... the road was close by.

"I hope you know where we're going," Serena said.

"I've been there," I said.

"Tripping," said Milt Stone.

Suddenly something went by ... sinking a lot faster than us ... the hull of a gigantic ship ... I thought I could see the word Titanic. The metal sheets had gaping, woundlike gashes, and through those gashes we could see Thorn's demons, spinning, twisting, grimacing. How could Thorn have so many creatures at his beck and call, when he wasn't even the real Thorn? Were they self-replicating, regenerating, so that there was always an infinite supply of gargoyle-like spear-carriers to enhance Thorn's powers?

I didn't really have time to think about it because the whole ship when barreling down into the depths. And at the topmost corner I could see Thorn himself, his trumpet-blowing sidekick, and my son-that-was-not-my-son, each of them encased in a bubble of air.

"After them!" said Milt.

"Yeah, right," said Serena, "one sinking stone chasing after another."

"We can't catch up," I said.

"Stop dodging the bricks," said Milt.

One brick after another pelted us. I said, "But they'll smash the windshield ... we'll drown!"

"They're not those kind of bricks," Milt said. He rolled down his window.

"We'll drown!" I screamed.

"Have a little faith," he said, "we're inside an air pocket of some kind." He reached out and grabbed a brick on the fly, then rolled the window back up again. He held it up; I watched in the rear view mirror, fascinated, as he squeezed it — it made little whiffling noises — and I realized that this was like one of the bricks they sell in Universal Studios — a fantasy brick, a latex brick, a movie special-effects brick — though it was just as glinting-yellow as a block of gold. "Fool's gold," said Milt.

"So we're all fools?"

Milt said, "Yes, sure we are, in a way. Only a fool would set out on a quest. And only a pure fool can see the holy grail...."

"Oh, Milt, you're always mixing mythologies," Serena said, giggling a little.

"You can talk," said Milt. "You're about the most mixed-up triple goddess I can imagine."

"Wait a minute," I said. I wasn't avoiding the bricks anymore, and in fact they were sort of coalescing into the faint outline of a road. "Why did the Titanic sink faster than us?" I saw the Leaning Tower of Pisa poking up from a bank of ruddy coral. "I thought everything fell at the same speed. Laws of physics."

We spun around and were suddenly face to face once more with that hull.

"One of the rules of this place," Milt said, "seems to be that nothing is true until the moment that you know it's true. Everything is in flux, waiting for the pronouncement of a truthsayer."

We and the hull were falling at the same speed now. From the gaps in the metal, the creatures stared at us, hollow-eyed, hollow-cheeked. I stared back, since there didn't seem to be much steering to be done. The yellow brick road formed and unformed itself beneath us, and we sort of hovered above it, now and then passing through a school of manta rays or coming eye to eye with a humpback whale or a sea-monster, though none seemed quite as malevolent as the packs of Thorn's creatures.

Slowly we kept sinking....

Theo Etchison:

Slowly we find ourselves inside a pocket of air; slowly the water seems to drain from our lungs. The air pocket grows; soon it's almost the size of a toilet, and we can see out clearly and it's the old underwater wonderland that we see, all garish colors and singing clams and dancing mermaids.

It's raining yellow bricks.

The bricks are drifting, dancing, spiralling, spawning....

Making a road beneath our feet....

But here's the weird part. We don't seem to be following that yellow brick road. The road seems to be following us. See like, I'm leading the way (walking in the middle of the water, still falling, the ocean floor nowhere in sight)and I just seem to tread wherever instinct leads me, and the minute my foot lands somewhere there's a yellow brick to receive it, materializing out of nowhere or just floating up from the depths.

"You do know the way," King Strang says.

I'm relieved that now we can talk, we don't have to just say glub glub glub to each other. I keep walking ... walking ...

Chris Etchison:

— falling —
— and I hear —
— the heartbeat of the cosmos —

Serena Somers:

That's just it: we were descending, the Titanic was descending, somewhere out there the mad king and Theo were probably descending too, dropping faster and faster into the abyss. Mr. E. was attempting to drive, in a way, mostly just steering a little to avoid the odd whale or coral reef. The yellow bricks were forming and unforming beneath us. They made pretty patterns ... little Figaro chains ... little herringbones necklaces ... when would we hit bottom?

Glimmering in the depths were hints of moments long forgotten. The shaft of moonlight in my Virginia bedroom, where I first saw Ash and thought he was just like, my imaginary companion even though I was too old for imaginary companions ... I saw that moonlight once again, heard the drapes rustle, held up my dappled hand to the soft radiance....

But I was still in a stationwagon, sinking to the bottom of the ocean....

Or were we sinking backwards in time? Were we heading back toward some intersection in our lives, when we could have made other choices, become different people?

I saw another glimmer: me naked in the creek by the school, ditching; that was wild! I smiled at my own audacity. I fingered the dragon around my neck and stared at the Mary-shaped hood ornament, and I knew that I was going to have to be the goddess again soon.

Then I thought about Joshua....

Phil Etchison:

If existence was like a symphony, were we now heading into the recapitulation, when the themes articulated at the beginning are replayed straight through, only now they carry the weight of all the passions that we've lived through?

Because I was starting to see things in the deep ocean. Little flashes. Mary suckling Theo in front of the fireplace. Theo bigger now, me declaiming Whitman at him while he jabbed at his cereal, the chocolate milk mottling his cheeks; Joshua running through the cottonwoods. The real world. So long ago, so far, it had become like a fairy tale; it was as though myth had become reality, and reality myth.

Swimming in and out of those images: fantastical deep sea fish, with flashlight eyes and spiny fins and outlandish neon colors....

We were going back. Not just in memory, but in time itself.

We were returning to the big bang, the place where all worlds began.

Book Four:

Recapitulation
Howl, Howl, Howl

"Hirou mono
Mina ugoku nari
Shiohi-gata"

"Everything I pick up
Is moving, awash
On the beach at low tide."

—*Chiyojo*

from a Christie's Catalogue:

On Truth
by
Philip Etchison

My writing block, it seems, is may not be
permanent after all. Still, I find my annual address from the poetry chair of
this august institution to be more and
more of a joke, year after year. I have
managed to shit out one half-baked lyric
this year (pardon my French, Mr.
Chairman). The poem appeared in Poetry magazine, unnoticed except by an
advertising firm who paid me $25,000
to adapt it slightly for the tagline of a
deodorant soap commercial.

Having thus sunk to the very depths of
poetic despond, I have decided to venture into the treacherous shoals of ontology....

What is Truth? Is Beauty Truth, or is
that just Keats's wishful thinking?

My son, who in some ways does not ex-
ist, has an instinctive grasp of Truth.
But he cannot express it in words at all.
So how can I presume to do so?

I had another son once, who has since
ceased to exist; he knew truth well, and
could articulate it. But it wasn't enough
to keep him in this world. He vanished
without a trace, and thus became an
Untruth.

I had a wife once, but she became a
goddess and deserted me.

Have I gone crazy?

*— coffee-stained ms. found stuck in a
shredder at the University of Northern
Virginia, along with a prescription for
Prozac. Not believed to be in the handwriting of Philip Etchison by most handwriting experts; one, Mr. Pinkham, dis-
agrees, and attributes its variation to an
excessive conception of hallucinogens.*

— reserve £500

Sixteen
Disjunctive Fugue

Theo Etchison:

The time before the mad millennium....

The shimmering sand. My father's cold cold eyes. The smell of my mother dying, hanging in the wheeze of the dying air conditioner ... somewhere in Arizona ... so fucking long ago I don't even know that it was ever real ... so vivid that it's now.

Flash. Flash.

Fighting Joshua in the men's room of a phantasmagorical Chinese Restaurant in the middle of nowhere.

Flash. Flash.

Now it's the present, and we're running in place somewhere at the bottom of an ocean of chaos, the truthsayer who's lost his truth and the king who's lost his kingdom. I used to be so young and a dollar could still buy a Coke and a candy bar, and every new truth was fresh and shiny and spanky-bright, and now, running in place, with the weight of the universe pressing down on me, I feel so old, so blind, so tired, so decayed, so fucking senseless, I don't know why I don't just die.

And the yellow bricks are streaming down, and the road is forming and unforming beneath our feet, and I know that we are getting closer to a place where the universe is young and still coming into being. And the king, striding beside me, he seems younger too; or maybe it's just that I'm taking on part of his age, his blindness, his tiredness, his decay. His white robes billow around us. We are trapped in a bubble of air and time. The ocean we're in is a place where quadrillions of little pieces of the river have come together in a rich confluence of pathways. We could go anywhere that the river goes, if only we knew the sequence.

A turn in the road. So familiar. Are we in a battered station wagon once again, are we turned south toward Tucson, are there billboards advertising weird Chinese delicacies, is the desert air stifling? No. I'm journeying toward the source of the river with the mad king, but I seem to be experiencing the many pasts all at the same time, too. That's how I know we're heading in the right direction.

Another turn, and then the brick road leads steeply down into a pitch-black chasm. King Strang turns to me questioningly. I nod, I guess. We descend. I have no maps, no knowledge of what we're doing; I'm hoping that the universe itself is snapping back on track, thrusting me down the right road, the path of least resistance.

And after the longest time — I would say that it seems forever but that's such a stupid cliché, but you know what I mean — we seem to bottom out, and there's a faint light ... a bluish light ... I can't see where it's coming from, but the bubble of air seems to have grown bigger, too.

I guess we're in some kind of caves. It always turns out to be caves somehow, caves, caverns, underground tunnels. Don't know what it is about caves. I never liked Dungeons and Dragons that much even when I was like eleven or twelve; never liked being trapped in level after level, getting killed, coming back to life, it's all totally claustrophobic. I know the universe is a metaphor, but why this metaphor? It sucks. Deeper and deeper into the labyrinth that's really inside our collective heads.

"Quiet," the king says.

"I didn't say anything," I say.

"But your thoughts are thundering in my ears."

Okay, so we both laugh, a little, at least, I laugh and the king smiles. "Come on," I say. I recognize something — a little grotto with a statue of my mother, candlelight, Mexicans in skeleton costumes. The Day of the Dead in that little town next to the laetrile clinic. We turn down another musty corridor. The tunnel swerves. It pulsates; it's almost organic; no, it is, we're in the guts of some cosmic creature.

Then, abruptly, we're somewhere else completely....

I'm a little kid and Daddy is writing next to the basement fireplace in the dead of winter. No one else is in the house. Mom went to pick up Joshua from somewhere. I'm watching him. He has a little notebook. He scribbles, he rips up, he trashes, the fire leaps up and I see little pieces of words before they shrivel and burn up:

love
darkness
energy
ensorcellment

I don't know all the words. But I think of how they must sound and their music jangles in my ears along with the hiss of the fire ... it's a fake fireplace ... fake logs ... but the pictures that dance in the flames are all too real ... yeah. I'm a little kid, maybe six or seven, but I can read pretty good. Around here, they make you read all the time: store signs, book covers, food labels, and of course those poems that I can't understand even, but the way the words tumble and crash make me feel mighty and powerful.

Daddy's scrunched over in a big old leather armchair by the fire. Too close to the fire really cause when you sit on it it makes you jump, the leather's so hot; I don't know how he can stand it and he's all sweating. And the words keep flying into the fireplace:

darkness

silence

gold-winged

sentinel

I creep up closer to him. He's scribbling like a maniac but only one or two words at a time, and the pieces of paper keep flurrying around him like snow. I want to say something but I'm scared of breaking his mood.

He cries out. He's in some kind of creative agony I guess, and he's all, "Oh shit, I'm nobody, I'm nothing."

Then suddenly I have to say something, and this is what it is: "Daddy," I say, "you're not nothing, you're a king."

Daddy stands up suddenly and he's a hundred feet tall and his hair is a white mane that billows in the wind, and he's wearing these big old Moses-type robes that billow right along with his hair. I step back. I'm scared. "I'm a king, huh," he says softly.

Then he picks me up and holds me in his arms (I smell him: Old Spice, sweat, a hint of liquor maybe, and something a little bit like dry leaves) and tosses me up in the air and I fall along with a thousand itty-bitty paper shreds all of them inscribed with letters and half-words all in a great big jumble and my Dad seems as tall as the sky.

"I'm a king, huh," he says. A laughs. "I wish."

"You are, Daddy, you are. You're a hundred feet tall and when you write a thing it becomes real."

"So it is written — so it is done," he says, I think that's a quote from some ancient Egyptian movie thing, we watch them late at night when I fall asleep in my mother's arms even though my brother keeps prodding me. And I reach up and touch my Daddy's face and I run my fingers along the deep, dry furrows ... and I know I've touched another person, a person Dad carries inside him.

"Why are you staring at me like that?" says Dad. "You act like I'm a strang —"

"Your eyes, Daddy," I say.

Because I've seen another's eyes: the cabochon iolite eyes that years later I'll know to be the eyes of the mad king; and he senses I'm having this strange disjunctive double vision thing and he says to me, "Kid, you've got too much imagination, too much, too much...."

And laughs, and throws me up, catches me, smothers me with security; I glare with pretend-angry eyes at the icicles in the two high windowpanes, the only way to see outside from our basement.

Then Daddy lets me go. I scrunch down on the floor and pick up the scraps of paper and I start putting them together and this is what comes out:

time river back

My Dad looks down at the words in amazement. I put together another pieces of the jigsaw:

two truths can both be true

My Dad slumps down on the armchair. He's not a king anymore. He's a tired man, and I think he's maybe feeling kind of old. "You're better than me," he whispers, "and you can barely read...."

I look into his eyes. One of his eyes is like a big blue marble filled with crisscrossing paths of light....

Strang's eyes....

Deeper in the caverns now, and the roar of water rushing, just behind some limestone wall; Strang and I are walking, walking ...

And then, somehow, we're driving I guess, we're back in the wheezing wagon with the stale smell of dying, and I'm slumped in the back with my dream book, watching the desert unreel behind me, sand upon sand upon sand; and I kind of creep forward, gaze up above the seat, look into the rear view mirror and I see my father's eyes,

Strang's eyes; the one eye false, the other true; and in the eye that is the marble that is the map of the cosmos I can suddenly see the way, clear and bright and terrible; I know we're going to have to die again before we can be born, and I'm so scared I could fucking shit myself right now, but I have to hold myself together, have to hold true to the path; I stare into the eye, into the map, and know that we're headed straight to —

Hiding in the bushes by the river by the school, I see the river-goddess rising naked out of the waves; don't know if she sees me, but there she is, wet and smiling in the muggy Virginia summer, and her name is Serena Somers....

Two truths can both be true....

... all comes to me in fragments, pieces of a great dream, someone else's dream maybe....

... Mom....

A halo of ash surrounds me....

"Trapped," the king cries out, "trapped inside my own madness!"

Then: suddenly: the wind takes us both —

What wind? There's a whirlwind in the tunnels, a wind that shrieks and wuthers, and it carries us up and twirls us and spins us and wrenches me around, a wind like the wind of a rollercoaster, endlessly plummeting. I'm holding onto King Strang's robes. He's holding out the scepter and the scepter's light darts back and forth, back and forth, in and out and across, and the dank walls glisten with phosphorescent stars, galaxies within galaxies. The river has a mind of its own now. There's no navigating to be done at all because the paths that we must go have been predestined since time began.

Ash dances in the black walls of the caverns.

Ash dances in the eaves, in the stalagmites, in the thick air.

Ash dances.

We're whisked further down the tunnel of stars. Round the seven-bended snake, up the down chute, down the upslope of the cavern. Every place we pass I know, I've been here before, but I don't know when. Maybe it's my birth canal. Maybe I'm inside myself. We whip around corners and spiral down stairwells.

The sphinx is there now, between the king and me and the great chasm that yawns between us and the holy of holies. She is a beautiful woman with fiery hair and coal-bright eyes. Her wings are black and leathery, and she prowls back and forth and she claws the sulphurous air. She looks like a scream queen from a B horror movie. She has vampire teeth, and when she roars you can tell she is part lioness.

"I'm not just any sphinx," she says. "My conundrums go far deeper than you can delve; even you, King Strang, who are finally but mortal."

"King, you can do it," I say, "you can answer her riddle and go on through." But I remember that last time there was no sphinx, no riddle, only the rabid Cerberus and the sacrifice of an eye, so this is a second test, a more difficult test.

"I can't give up my other eye," says King Strang.

The sphinx cries out, "Answer the question! Answer the question!" and she darts back and forth, her bat wings dripping slime.

"But you haven't even asked the fucking question," I scream. What is this, Jeopardy or something, are we supposed to guess the questions too?

"You're right," says the sphinx.

"Four legs in the morning, two in the daytime, three at night, is that it?" I ask her.

The sphinx laughs. Really laughs; and each time she laughs, lava erupts, pieces of the ceiling come pelting down, and the smell of brimstone becomes more and more choking. "The clichés never seem to change, do they?" she says at last.

She settles down, just a few feet from us. She's a real harpy despite her beautiful face, and her breath is totally kicking. She looks at us, waves and shakes at us like some Las Vegas showgirl.

"Maybe you don't think I'm that frightening," she says, and bares her teeth. Behind her, fire leaps up out of the chasm. "But I am." I know she is. "Here's the question: To save the universe, would you sacrifice your own child?"

"What kind of a riddle is that?" says King Strang. "I have no children."

I say to him, "O King, have you forgotten?"

"Did I once have children?" he murmurs. "Didn't they die? Didn't I myself kill them, not with my own hands, but with a few misspoken words?"

Ash dances in the sulphur fumes; Ash dances in the haze; Ash is a halo bright about my head, sparked by the brimstone's burning.

"No," says Strang, "no sons. No daughters. No one."

Ash swirls. Ash begins to form into a semblance of human shape; Ash glows, Ash dances.

I remember the first of my many dreams. A King is dividing his kingdom between three children. He holds his scepter in his palsied hand and the three children, vampire, dragon, and something unknown, they kneel to him, one by one, speaking in honeyed tones of the love they have for him ... all except the last one, the one who dares speak the truth.

"What about the one who was neither son nor daughter?" I ask him. "What about —"

"Don't speak to me of that one!" cries the king. "Ashes to ashes, dust to dust."

The sphinx waits, tapping her feet; she purrs and the floor of the cavern rumbles with her; her purring is the stirring of magma deep beneath our feet. "What's your answer?" she growls.

"Ash," says the king.

And when he says the name, the name he has refused to utter in all the time I've been with him, that's when Ash starts to become Ash. Ash of the still small voice; Ash, luminous, androgynous, kind of beautiful in a waif-like way; that's who Ash is, and he begins to form out of the cloud of Ash that's followed us all the way from the island in the crystal lake.

"Father," Ash says softly.

No longer speaking through my lips, no longer seeing through my eyes, Ash steps out of the spinning dust-cloud. He looks at his father and his father looks at him, while behind us the sphinx springs from crag to crag and roars and belches hellish fumes and waits for the answer to her riddle.

Strang says, "You told me the truth, child, didn't you?"

"Yes," says Ash.

And in my mind's eye I see Dad swinging me up in the air and I see the words that are pieces of unborn poems scattering, swirling, dancing like dead leaves in the autumn wind, and I see the fireplace in the basement in winter and I think, this place is not different from that place; they're the same somehow; because we're close to the source, the place that's the anchor for all places and times, and we see how the whole universe is intercon-nected. I see how I'm like Ash and Dad's like Strang; I always used to know the truth that Dad strove so hard to find, him the great poet and all and engaged in the great quest for the meaning of our existence, and me just some clear-eyed kid who had no right to know because I hadn't struggled to know, hadn't sacrificed one eye as the price of knowledge, was born with the right eyes, the right map, burned into the ROM of my brain ... fucking Jesus it must have pissed him off, I think to myself, I don't know why he even talked to me ... and now I remember the

poem that he wrote, the poem that was grown from the
seed of my putting together the scraps of paper:

... for in the momentary closure,
The blink's breadth between two truths, two truths
can both be true.

How would you answer the riddle? How could I answer it for him, when I could see that both answers to
the riddle were true and false?

I watch them embrace, father and son. I feel kind of
bitter because who am I in this? I've brought the king to
the edge of the abyss, to the last gateway, but all I am is
this blind navigator; the king's finding love again at the
eleventh hour, and I'm here on the outside, not even family, not even knowing when my own father's going to get
here, not even knowing if he'll know I still exist, because
in the universe he's in now, I never existed, there was
only Chris, the one true truthsayer.

Ash says, "I'm sorry I told the truth, father."

And Strang says, "Never be sorry, child." And kisses
Ash, solemnly, on the cheek, not like a father and son, but
like two world leaders on television, like President Karpovsky and President Yeltsin; and they stand, a little bit
apart; the moment is so big, it's too big even for tears, but
I cry, I cry for the two of them, feeling the truth of their
grief and their joy.

Finally, King Strang turns to me. "Which is it to be,
truthsayer?" he asks me. "What is the answer?"

I say to him, "It depends on whether you're a man or a
god."

The king sits down on a rock. He is more weary than
I've ever seen him. The journey is almost over. The
jewel in the scepter glows. All the light here is hell-hot;
only the scepter's radiance is cold. Ash sits at his feet.
How could the king have been so blind before, not to see
the difference between real and imagined love?

"I see what you mean," says Strang. "A god would sacrifice his son, wouldn't he?"

"Many have," I say.

"To heal the world, it's the natural thing to do. But what would a man do? Wouldn't a man put his child first, and let the world plunge to perdition?"

"Two truths," I say, "can both be true."

This is the final great piece of truth that I know; the last piece of truth I am able to divulge, before the big darkness of normality swallows me up and I become just Theo Etchison, just about to go into the tenth grade, dreamer, good-for-nothing, kid with too much imagination, kid who plays by himself in the forest in Spotsylvania County, loner who thinks too much.

"So what's it to be?" Strang says. "Man or god?"

"Well," I say, "you've been pretty godlike for the last couple of thousand years...."

"To be man," says Strang, "doesn't that mean I would have to —"

"Die?" I say. When I think of death, I think of my mom, I think of the close, dank air in the station wagon, I think of that awful smell.

"Die," says Strang, and the sphinx waits; she holds her breath; the whole chasm seems to have fallen silent; you can't hear the hissing flames, the screaming of lost souls, nothing like that. You can hear death itself in that big old silence. "Maybe there's another answer," Strang says. "You mythical creatures are always trying to force humans to choose, always putting us into an either-or situation. Heaven or Hell, black or white, truth or falsehood ... isn't there another path, one that lies in the cracks, a third, hidden answer to every question? For example —"

I know now what he's going to say. So does Ash. Ash steps back. He hasn't expected this, but now he realizes that Strang has chosen the right answer to the riddle; right, at least, for him. "Godlike," he says, "I will my own son's destruction. But like a man, I hold him to myself, I let the world go to keep his love for myself. What if I want both to be true? I have to give a death for a death. I give my own death for my son's death. I am old and foolish. I have lived too long. I shall go now."

Holding the scepter aloft, King Strang totters over to the edge of the precipice. The flames leap up. The sphinx appears panicky for the first time. "Don't jump," she shrieks. "It's hell down there. You'll choke on brimstone before you even land, and then you'll be consumed."

Strang turns to her. His face is wedged between the shadow and the fiery light. The ridges, the furrows, are deep as the mountains on the moon. His eyes are filled with terrible anguish; but there's like, a resurgence of power inside him. Like when my Dad gets the words right in his poems, and his whole body seems to zing and his eyes are full of fire.

"My scepter," he says, "has one last great magic in it."

He leaps off the edge of the world.

I see him fall, the scepter's jewel flashing like the head of a comet.

Ash grabs my shoulders. "Come on, Theo."

"Come on?"

"What are we waiting for?"

"Waiting for?"

"Yeah," says the sphinx, who now seems considerably drained of her fierceness; she's gone back to squatting on a rock and purring softly; she's more like a kitten than a lioness now.

"Let's follow him," Ash says.

"Follow?"

"Yeah," says the sphinx. "Stay, follow, whatever. Two truths can both be true. Makes me kind of useless, doesn't it? I mean, if people start answering the riddles any way they choose...."

"Follow?" I say. Gazing down at the comet that's blazing in the pitch blackness below. Teetering on the edge of ultimate darkness.

"Are you scared?" says Ash.

"Shitless."

"All right then."

The comet darted, did a three-sixty, zigzagged, spun round and round. We jumped.

Into the embrace of nothingness.

Seventeen
Doors and Tapestries

Serena Somers:

— a ship was wedged at the bottom of the sea. We parked the car beside the hull, which angled upward into the dimness. I could hear a high solitary voice, singing: it must have been Chris, though maybe he was singing in the language of the whales or something; it was a weird, keening, wailing kind of a song, and it echoed and echoed against fluid and metal, clanking, murmuring, burbling. God it was spooky.

We stepped out. It was all right because the air pocket grew to about the size of a football field. We were walled in by water, and above us was a great big dome of dark, cold, wet, opressive ocean.

"The Titanic," said Mr. E., "seems to have landed." He emerged from the car.

"Thorn and Chris must be inside," I said. But I couldn't see anyone at all. You know, before, we'd seen demons and gargoyles lurking in the rips in the ship's hull, but now it seemed totally abandoned. In fact, it was hard to believe that it had been seaworthy only hours ago, because now it was all rusted and twisted and looked as though it had been underwater for centuries ... then again, maybe we had been sinking for centuries. There was no way of telling. They call it time dilation, or something. It's in science fiction books. Speed of light. I don't get it, and I don't think anyone else does either.

Milt Stone stepped out of the back seat. He was still carrying his drum. We could still hear Chris's eerie singing, or whatever it was, reverberating around us. The air was sweating a cold salt moisture onto our hands and faces.

"I guess I should go look for Chris," said Mr. E., and he started to stride toward the ship. I watched him for a moment. He started to kind of waver, like a mirage. I started to follow him, but he got harder and harder to see. I mean, his outline was shimmering, and he was getting all distorted, like a special effect, folding in on himself.

"Mr. E!" I shouted. "Are you okay?" A stupid question to ask at the bottom of the ocean without an oxygen tank, but no question seemed to stupid for this mad universe. "Wait for me," I said. I hurried, trying to catch up. I could sense my own self wavering and contorting too, and when I looked down at my own arm, I noticed that it was twisting like a corkscrew, though I didn't feel any different. "Wait up!" I shouted again. He couldn't hear me I guess.

"Don't go," said Milt.

"Why not?"

"This is the classic moment in the drama," Milt said, "when the characters say to each other, 'Let's split up.'"

"What do you mean?" I asked him, as Mr. E. kind of twirled himself into a vortex and popped out of existence, a few yards in front of the wreck of the Titanic.

"We are all here for a purpose," he said. "We all have unfinished business. What's yours?"

I had to think awhile. I mean, I had been the triple goddess. I'd trampled down cities. I'd spewed out dragons from my maw. What was there left to me? But then I remembered: there'd been men in my life. "Oren Karpovsky," I said ... "and Joshua Etchison."

"See what I mean?"

"What am I supposed to do?"

Milt Stone began to beat on his drum. He did a kind of dance around me; feet together, feet apart, slowly, slowly making a complete circle with me at its center. "This is the round dance," he said. "Women do it, because they are the encirclers, because they are the earth." With every step he became more and more feminine. I don't know how he did it. It was as if he had always been a woman. "Strictly speaking, this is not a Navajo dance," he said, "but a Plains Indian one; but you know how it is; cross-fertilization some call it, others cultural pollution. But it doesn't matter; I'm a a nadlé, a holy man-woman, and I can ransack the mythologies of the world if I want, so you'll see the truth. Look at me," he said, "look at me, love me."

He went on dancing, and the drumbeats made a weird counterpoint with the wailing that was Chris's whale music. After a while it seemed like Milt was moving faster and faster and faster and was maybe turning into more people ... or were they all the same person? ... there was Milt the tribal policeman in his uniform ... there was Milt the end-of-the-world homeless madman with the placard around his neck ... there was Milt in, oh my, a bridal gown, smiling on his way to the altar ... Milt in wild, made-in-Hong Kong-style Indian regalia, grimacing as he leaped up and down to the strains of a Hollywood movie score ... a hundred Milts were writhing and wriggling around me ... a kaleidoscope of blurring Milts. The music was confusing too: there was the whalesong and the drum, but also bits and pieces of reggae, hip-hop, and house leaking in — music from when I was fifteen or sixteen, music I used to turn my nose up at. It was like listening to the radio when you're driving through nowhere, just bits and pieces of weird stations.

Then, suddenly, I was inside the —

Phil Etchison:

— ship. But it was not what I expected to see. Yes, it was dank, and clammy, and musty, and there were barnacles and twists of seaweed coiled around broken shafts of metal, and there was a cold, blue light — that Spielbergian, sci-fi movie light that you always imagine as an accompaniment to a close encounter of any kind — lines, whorls and pools of this light fantastic. I stepped in a little farther. You could hear chimes, bells, and whistles in the distance ... or was it the tinkling of anvils?

I got a little more brave. Somewhere in this labyrinth was Chris, and a piece of unfinished business I dreaded more than anything in the world. I had spend a trilogy's worth of adventuring caught between Scylla of heroism and the Charybdis of mediocrity, and the way ahead wasn't really getting any more clear. Was I now expected to charge in, despatch the vampire (who was only the outer shell of a vampire, since within him lurked the soul of the President of the United States, my friend) and rescue the child who would soon prove not to be my child? In that dream I had had, submerged in the amniotic waters of the lake of the human unconscious, I'd faced the sphinx, and I'd failed to answer her question. This time, I supposed, it would be no dream — except insofar as our entire existence is a dream.

Perhaps it was time to try the direct approach.

"Come and get me, Thorn!" I screamed into the cavernous emptiness.

I didn't really expect a reply, but I went on in that vein for a while: the jig is up, come and face your doom, a swift and terrible justice is sweeping down the freeway towards you ... I shouted myself hoarse, and exhausted the clichés of poesy, and still there came no answer save my own voice, echoing, echoing in a metallic roundelay about my ears.

Presently my eyes became more used to the dimness. As I wandered, I became more aware of sounds, too: clickings, tickings, ratchet-like scrapings. There were cogs, wheels, fanbelts, all turning, whirring, painfully snapping into place. I was inside a monstrous machine. It was pretty damn Kafkaesque. All the way up one wall, as far as the eye could see, were anvils, and robot elf-arms swung hammers in complex, mechanistic patterns of pinging. The floor of the cavern was stone, and it was littered with broken cogs, loose spokes, tortured fragments of steel. There was a certain gigantism about some of the pieces: I mean, if I was meant to believe that I had been caught inside the workings of an immense, infernal machine, it would not have been difficult to convince me.

From far away ... somewhere in the high invisible vault of this clockwork cathedral ... I could hear Chris's voice ... part human, part whale, part angel ... a high pure sound that lanced through the dust and must like steel, like lightning.

The floor was rising ... that figured, I supposed, since the ship itself had struck bottom at a 45° angle ... but presently the slope softened into steps. I kept moving up them. Wheels spun. Gears shifted. Somewhere, a cuckoo announced the time. I went on climbing. I was vaguely aware of light, somewhere in the heights. I kept moving. The odd thing was, even though I was moving upward, against the pull of gravity, there was also an energy propelling me so strongly that I almost felt I was descending. Did this mean I had reached "the still point of the turning world"? There came the sound of another cuckoo, then another. Time did not precisely stand still here. Perhaps it ran around and around in circles. Or spirals. Or corkscrews. It moved and did not move. And the ticking and the tocking made a joyful, jangling noise in the back of my mind. This, I thought, is how the echo of the Big Bang sounds on radio telescope, to a being vast enough to be able to hear radio waves as a comprehensive music.

This, perhaps, is what Chris hears, the bedrock of ultimate truth that underlies all our disparate realities, the
ocean floor above which swirl the waters of consciousness. Tick, tick, cuckoo. The clockwork theory of creation. Newtonian physics in action.

I went on climbing. Not, you understand, thinking all
this through — I was not expostulating some mechanistic theory of the universe to myself as I ascended — just
keeping my mind open, letting random thoughts flit
through, flirting with cosmic concepts yet never quite
grappling with them — the Phil Etchison patented
method of dealing with things too big to understand, too
deep to find meaning in.

Perhaps, I told myself, you too are clockwork.

Perhaps you too are a machine.

At the top of the steps was a great iron door. It was
Brobdignagian in its proportions; I could see the door
handle about thirty feet above my head. The door was
one of those things you find in Italian cathedrals,
crowded with scenes moulded in high relief. Beyond the
door, doubtless, was the thing I most desired and feared
— the final locked room of Duke Bluebeard's castle —
the infamous Orwellian Room 101. There was nothing
for it but to try to reach the doorhandle, and the way to
get there was by climbing up the relief itself. It looked
like there were plenty of protruding footholds for me.

I too can be a hero, I told myself. I too can stop being
this nonentity, this brain-blocked poet who at best can
shit out only a line or two of advertising copy; I too can
brave the final door; I too can summon up the courage to
answer that fucking sphinx and send her spinning into
the void. Yeah, right. No bright sword, no .38 special;
just me and the blunted saber of my poesy.

So you know what?

I grabbed onto the first protuberance on that iron
door, which appeared to be the fangs of a great, coiled
dragon; I wedged my knee firmly into the crook of its

belly and planted one foot on one of the dragon's claws, and then —

— a great dimensional shift and —

Iron, iron, the whole world was iron —

The door was the gateway was the world. I too was sculpted in relief. Looked down. My hands, my arms glistened, polished, silvery. And there was no time to lose. The dragon threw me to the ground. The ground, boulders, grass, all metal — the blades were literally blades, needle-sharp, but I too was metal, and the grass scraped and whined against my robot skin. We were on the edge of a cliff, and the edge was the edge of the door.

The dragon clanked and whirred as it approached me. Reaching behind me, I found my sword, the traditional hero's sword, all chrome, its hilt studded with emeralds, but it wasn't much good; I could barely heft it. Meanwhile, the dragon snorted, and I smelled its sulphurous, fetid breath and felt like barfing. Behind the dragon was a cave. Treasure inside, no doubt. I could hear the whimpering of a woman; somewhere behind those rusted rocks was a the virginal princess I needs must rescue. I was doomed to reenact scenes from mythology — and bad fantasy novels — before I could find redemption. Since my adolescent son was the ultimate demiurge whose dreaming made the world the way it is, I guess I shouldn't have been surprised to find myself trapped in Tolkienland, wrapping my brass knuckles around some mediaeval weapon.

The dragon charged, and so did I. We missed each other. He ran into an iron wall that replicated the texture of limestone. Clanged against metallic rock. I landed on my butt but felt no pain — how could I? Iron can't feel. Iron never hurts.

The dragon, turned, sniffed the air, clawed at the ground. The wind was foul; it reeked of a carnivore's breath. It occurred to me that the dragon could not see me. It was blind. It was senile. It had lost its sense of focus. It rolled its empty eyes. A cloud of gas escaped its nostrils with a strained, mechanical wheeze. I wondered how longer the dragon had been there, and whether it longed for death after so much time guarding some treasure whose meaning, no doubt, had long been lost.

"Perhaps," I said aloud, "you want me to run up, deliver that killing thrust, return you to the earth."

The dragon stirred, cocked its ear in my general direction. "Oh, good," it said, "you can talk. So few of them ever talk. All they want to do is joust, joust, and be consumed."

"We all talk," I said softly, and I ventured a little closer. He was about as big as a two-bedroom apartment, and his tail stretched beyond the edge of the door. "It's just that most of us don't talk to dragons, because we don't know that dragons can talk back."

"A communication gap," the dragon sighed.

"Yes," I said.

"What kind of a creature are you?" said the dragon. Its voice, hollow, raspy, reverberated through the metal mountain, in a hundred virtual passageways. "I've fought so many, and I've lost my sense of smell and taste."

"Actually," I said, "I'm a human being."

"No shit," said the dragon. "Don't get many of those anymore."

"What do you mean, you don't get many of those anymore?" I said. "What about all those knights in shining armor that rush in to save the virginal princess? That is a princess you've got back there, isn't it?"

"Of sorts," said the dragon.

I heard a scream coming from behind an outcropping. The voice of the woman was oddly familiar, but I couldn't yet place it.

"I suppose," the dragon said, "that we should get on with it. I can barely smell you, or hear you, and of course, I can't see you, since I'm blind as a bat; perhaps you'd care to point me in the right direction?"

A kind of wind was gusting over us. I creaked, I squeaked; I wished I had been better oiled. Carefully I shifted my position to the upwind, and projected my voice against the side of the mountain so that it would bounce away. Nothing like a bit of trickery.

"I'm over here," I shouted.

The blind dragon charged — too fast, too far — and soon it was hanging over the cliff, clinging to the edge of the great iron door by a single frayed claw. I tried to lift that sword again, thinking I could perhaps chop it off at its most vulnerable link. Couldn't heft it. So I just walked over to that claw and I looked down, and I saw the dragon, dangling in a bizarre forced perspective, over a chasm of cogs, spokes, wheels, chains, gears, and intermittent cuckoos.

"Despatch me quickly," the dragon gasped. "One way or another, it always comes to this; there's always one hero too many; one can never retire in peace."

"Isn't there something you're supposed to do?" I said softly, leaning over the precipice. "Grant me a few wishes, answer my burning questions about the secret of the universe?"

"Not any more," the dragon gasped. "I've exhausted my supply of answers to burning questions. The questions, you see, got harder and harder; the heroes got dumber and dumber. As for granting wishes — you can see that I hardly have any power. I can barely even cling to a cliff."

"There's got to be something you know that you can teach me," I said. "For example — what is this place, what am I doing here, that sort of thing."

"You know where you are," said the dragon, "if only you'll search a little harder inside yourself."

"But —"

"You were going to say, 'What about magic?' or some such thing, weren't you?" said the dragon. "Unfortunately, there is no magic anymore — that is the great and final truth that we all must learn."

"I don't agree," I said, though I wasn't at all sure that I meant that. "You can't say there's no magic when here I am, converted into a thing of metal, trapped in an enchanted door, talking to a hunk of sculpted pewter."

"You mean there's other places?"

"Of course," I said. "Like the place I came from. A green place. Very green. Virginia."

"Virginia," said the dragon softly. "Green, you say. I can't, you know, see anything anymore."

But then he couldn't hold on anymore either; the iron rock was ripping; through the tears in the metal I could see and smell the flames of inferno. He gave a great cry — I want to say a great cry but it was more like a kind of desolate wheezing — and sort of dropped away … siphoned out into the musty emptiness that was beyond the door … I watched him whittle into darkness … I did not feel that I had achieved some moment of high apotheosis in the hero's journey … I only felt empty and afraid.

The wind sucked the dragon away; the only sound it made was a peculiar wailing, like Wagner played backwards.

I was trapped in a metal skin in a metal landscape in a metal door. I heard the familiar voice of the woman call me from somewhere within the cavern. I decided to continue on. The only alternative seemed to be leaping off the cliff, and ending up as discarded clockwork.

"Phil," the voice cried.

At least, I thought, I'm not the hero with no name.

But I was still stuck inside the —

Serena Somers:

— doorway of the great ship of fools. Milt's drumming was now a universe away. I don't know what I expected the inside of the ship to look like but where I was was a huge and fleshy place. At first I couldn't see much at all. But I could feel a heartbeat, and I could hear the rush of, like, a great big ocean, the same ocean you hear when you put a conch to your ear. I knew then that the

ocean was the racing of a bloodstream, and that I was
inside some vast organic thing. It wasn't frightening, I
mean this wasn't like some Jonah-in-the-whale deal. I
felt comforted. I felt completely at home. I felt happy.

Serena-in-the-womb.

But whose womb?

I thought I knew the answer. Why wouldn't I know?
Hadn't I once been the goddess? I'd swallowed the goddess once; I guess it was only fair that the goddess had
now swallowed me.

There was the heartbeat, and then, from far away,
that eerie keening that was Chris's music....

A shaft of light ... a warm, red glow that illuminated
what? a staircase? an escalator? I stepped forward. I
could feel the pulsing, hear my own pulse echo it. A tunnel stretched up toward that distant, blood-red height. I
had to be resolute. I had to step into the tunnel. I did.
And then I was caught up in a great wind, a wind that
roared like the ocean that is the conch shell that is the
surging blood. It was a kind of rapture, the thing that the
fundamentalists are always talking about, being swept
up into heaven in the flesh, but there was something kind
of, I mean, lubricious about it too. This scene was definitely pagan. The odor held sex as well as sanctity.

So there I was, being skyrocketed around by a great
big whirlwind inside a twisting tube of flesh. A rollercoaster without seats, without safety belts ... pretty wild,
I guess you'd say.

At last I was deposited on kind of a landing. A woman
sat, with her back to me, working on a massive loom. She
was weaving a tapestry of some kind — weaving with
one hand, and unraveling with the other. I knew that
myth all right — it was the story of Penelope, waiting
endlessly in the Odyssey for her husband to come home.
I watched the woman, whose hair was draped all over
her body ... a sort of Rapunzel type ... in fact, as I became
used to the dimness (she was just beyond the shaft of
radiance that illuminated the tunnel-cum-stairway) I saw

that her hair was the actual thread she was weaving into the tapestry. It wasn't just one myth I was meeting up with ... it was a kind of Cuisinart® version of mythology.

I squinted. I wanted to see the images in the tapestry. They were vivid ... almost too lifelike ... but squeaky-clean, like a computer-generated virtual reality simulation of the world. They seemed to be animated. The thing is, I started to recognize the people, even though they were dressed in kind of ancient Greek clothing ... there was Mr. E., for example, waving some kind of sword and wearing the costume of an ancient hoplite. He seemed to be battling some kind of monster, and there was a woman lashed to a rock with strands of her own hair, though I couldn't see her face. Mr. E. was slashing at the empty air, and the monster was dodging him, but as I watched, he managed to get in a hit, and the monster kind of disintegrated ... or maybe it was just that Penelope managed to unravel the monster at just that moment. Mr. E. looked out from the tapestry with a quizzical expression, straight at me, kind of pointed as if to say — "You? —

Phil Etchison:

— here? in this place?" I said to the woman. She was a young woman, and she was in chains, as they always are in these legends, and she had the kind of floor-length hair that they tend to have in these operations, which more or less draped itself coyly around the naughty bits. Her face was obscured by hair, too. But I knew her. At least, I thought I did.

"Mary?" I said.

She laughed. It was Mary but not quite Mary.

Serena Somers:

I smiled.

Phil Etchison:

She was Serena but not quite Serena.

"Who are you for sure?" I asked.

"You don't know?" She frowned. She was the dragon Katastrofa ... but not quite.

"Aren't you going to cut me loose?" she said. "It's traditional."

I gazed at the treasure piled up in the cavern. Oh, it wasn't your usual rubies and diamonds and gold coins and coronets; instead, there were nothing but blocks. You know, those alphabet blocks that little kids build castles with, only each block had words on it. They were stacked up at random everywhere. Some were textured like wood; others seemed to be cinderblocks; still others were that foam stuff that they use in Hollywood, stunt bricks made to be harmless. All, of course, were really iron, shaded with rust, for I was still inside that metal door, still a semi-flat animated relief; and the woman was all iron, and her hair as harsh and abrasive as steel wool. I still had the sword in hand, of course, but it was not vorpal enough to cut through chains of magical iron. The woman, who was the woman of my dreams and nightmares, moaned; the metal chafed her wrists.

"I don't think," she said, "you're supposed to do it that way."

I looked around me. "How, then?"

"We all have our own gifts," she said, "and you were never a fighter, Phil; you're a dreamer."

"But I killed the dragon, didn't I?"

"The dragon killed itself," said Mary-Serena-Katastrofa. I kissed her, tasted the salt of Mary's suffering, the sweetness of Serena's youth, the bitterness of Katastrofa's rage; I understood then that in a sense, the hero's journey is not nearly as unpredictable or as chaotic as one might think. For you see, it is like a well-worn roller coaster, and provided that you keep you seat belt strapped on tight, you will retread the same dilapidated track that other men have trod; what's different is not the journey, but how you feel about the journey; that's the difference between a hero and a geek; what's all inside oneself.

I looked around me then. The words on the bricks were simple and complicated: short words that held profound meanings like love, home, death, woman, heart; long resounding words like fibrillate, obscurity, insomnia; nonsense words like masticoma, unduleverage, erastomanic, slipslink. I saw now that this was a treasure designed for me alone, the building blocks of poesy.

"So I'm to be like Orpheus," I said. "The super-poet, melting the chains of steel with my honeyed words."

She smiled at me. "Sometimes," she said, "you think too much of yourself, Phil. There's a greater power that's manipulating us all. The road map for this journey was made millennia ago. We're all expendable, in a way. Others could have gone on this adventure. Others could have saved the universe. In the end, it doesn't matter. The universe will be saved whether we want it to be or not. It's the nature of the cosmos to fracture, come apart, heal itself; we're just little pieces of the great plan."

"So it is a mechanistic universe," I said, "and we really are just cogs and spokes." Trapped inside an iron world six inches wide, I felt the most profound despair I had yet felt.

"That's one way of looking at it," said the woman who was the goddess who was my wife.

"You don't sound very encouraging," I said.

"I'm not allowed to encourage you. It's against the rules. You have to find the courage within yourself."

I knelt down to peer at the piles of word-blocks. Antique, antick, antics, attics, antelopes. I lifted one up (they were heavy) placed it on top of another. The clove to each other by some sourceless magnetism. What sentence fragment had I created?

I am

"So I'm to sit here," I said, "and build a toy castle ... an edifice that's also a poem ... and that will set you free?" Oscillate, osculate, osceola, ossia, Austria.

"The pen is mightier than the sword," the woman agreed.

I am a

"But if I do sit here," I said, "and I exercise my imagination ... me, a third-rate poet who teaches in a third-rate college ... won't the poem I create be third-rate too? And won't the quality of your rescue be mediocre, and the healing of the world be imperfect, and —"

"You think too much depends on you!" she said.

"Then who? Whose is that master plan?"

It was then that I heard the music —

Serena Somers:

— echoing in the landing at the top of the stairwell in the shaft of light — and slowly the woman turned to me, and I saw that she was myself. I don't mean a clone of me, I don't mean Serena II — I mean that she had me inside her, this ageless woman from an ancient myth.

Milt's drum still pounded in the world outside. But the spaces between the strokes seemed infinitely long. Lifetimes were passing between each beat of the world's heart. And in the interstices of that slow pulse came the melody that Chris was singing, somewhere aloft; his song was the making of the world, and its unmaking.

I remembered words from one of Mr. E.'s most well-known poems, where he says that

In the blink's breadth between two truths, two truths
Can both be true.

If you slow the world down enough, anyone can be a truthsayer. I think that's what Mr. E. was trying to say, even though he wrote that poem long before he like, knew there was any such thing as truthsayers. People like Theo can grasp all those shifting strands of truth kind of on the fly; they work fast, faster than the speed of light I bet. But a dummy like me, an ordinary human being, even I can see where the strands unstrand, if you run it by me slowly enough. Was that what Milt Stone's dance was trying to do for me, slow reality to a crawl so even an airhead like me could seize it in my hot little hands?

In my own little way, I decided, I too can be like Theo.

So I said to Penelope, "There's another way of doing this."

She turned to me and she's all, "What do you mean?" And I thought: I see clearly now my eyes reflecting in her eyes, see how I carry a piece of Penelope in me, the woman who waits and waits for the right man to show up; I see that she's me, but I don't have to be her.

"How long are you going to weave that thing?" I said to her. "How long are you going to wait for Odysseus?"

"As long as it takes," she said. "It's my destiny." And smiled a wan little smile.

"You must be getting pretty frustrated by now. Did they have dildoes in the Bronze Age?"

"I don't know what you mean. I sit, I weave, I wait."

"This is the 90s, girl," I said. "We women don't sit, weave, wait anymore. We actually do things. Let me show you."

So I kind of leaned over into the tapestry and I stuck my hand into the warp, or the woof, or whatever it's called, I mean right into where her hair was shuttling back and forth on that loom. The hair felt rough, not silky; twenty years of dandruff, I imagined.

I pulled out a big hank of it. It was right in between where Mr. E. was waving his sword around and being very macho and phallic, and the damsel in distress was writhing about against the wall. A big black hole appeared in the midst of Mr. E.'s universe, and his woven image stared woefully down at it.

And Penelope stared at me. I guess she wasn't used to girl fights. I could have punched her out right then and there, but something weird was beginning to happen.

I couldn't pull my hand free.

The strands of hair were kind of twisting and turning around my hand. They were wrapping themselves around my fingers. They were alive somehow. Penelope turned to me and her head was a mass of serpents. It made sense, I guess; Mr. E. would have been able to lecture for half an hour about mother goddesses and snakes and the negative aspect of the earth-mother archetype and so on. But cultural anthropology isn't much of a comfort when snakes are writhing around your hand and coiling and tightening and cutting off your blood flow.

"Thank you for coming at last," she said to me. "Since you feel so strongly about changing the way things are done around here, you might as well take over ... you might as well change things from within."

The snakes pulled me right into the cloth and there I was, right there, inside the tapestry. Everything was virtually two-dimensional. Looked at head-on, Mr. E was a flat line; when I shifted my vision a little he kind of expanded into view until he was fully human to look at. It took some getting used to. I was pretty much 2-D myself, but I think that because I knew about the third dimension, I was able to lift my point of view off the surface of the cloth a little and see the universe for what it really was. I saw him the way a psychic might see me, I guess.

I looked around for a moment, trying to get used to being this flat. I mean, I was fat when I was a kid, and now I had the thickness of a silken thread. The world around me was all fluid and crinkly, just how you'd imagine living on the surface of a piece of fabric might be. The world wavered and billowed. I didn't realize it was so windy outside, but I guess the slightest motion of Penelope's loom was like an earthquake inside these images.

"Mr. E.," I said, "you'd better —"

But you know what? Mr. E. wasn't there anymore. I wasn't looking in on his heroic journey anymore — I had embarked on my own, and the person who was chained to the wall was not some airhead in distress but a man — yeah, he looked something like Mr. E., but a lot more like Oren Karpovsky, president of the United States of Armorica, my lover, my erstwhile sexual harrasser. And behind his eyes, I could see a hint of a third personality. A lost, dead boy. Joshua. I was startled. I called out to him.

"He can't speak to you yet," Oren said. "Not until you free me."

And we weren't inside a dragon's lair at all, but a network of catacombs. Rats ran wild. Bones littered the muddy ground. Half-eaten corpses lay, their wrappings ripped open, their faces missing big chunks, in little niches in the walls.

A stone sarcophagus stood in the center of the chamber. A lone shaft of light shone down from some opening high above us. I looked at myself, felt myself all over, was horrified to find that I had somehow ditched my street clothes and I was dressed as a kind of Amazon woman, brass brassière and all, out of some low-budget adolescent sword-and-sorcery movie. "This isn't me," I said. "This is like, ridiculous."

The coffin lid started to inch open, screeching in the most nervewracking chalk-across-blackboard way.

"Yes it is," said Oren. "Inside every dull, domesticated woman is a wild Amazon struggling to be free."

"I'm not dull! I'm not domesticated!" I shouted.

"Then prove it," he said. "Dare."

"Dare? Dare?"

I couldn't say much more because the lid of the sarcophagus came crashing to the floor and Thorn sat up.

He gazed at me with his slate-colored eyes.

His fangs glistened.

"You're dead," I said. "You were killed, way back, a long time ago, in a different volume of the trilogy. You keep getting killed. What's wrong with you, don't you understand that you can't come back? Why don't you just disappear?"

He started to lift himself from the coffin, carefully brushing the mud from his cloak, which billowed about him as the fabric we were trapped in moved. I looked around for something to kill him with — a pick or a shovel or something — and I ended up going at him with somebody's jawbone. The jawbone splintered.

Thorn laughed. "Very funny," he said. "Jawbone of an ass, I suppose."

Where was a stake when I needed it? Or a phial of holy water? Just as I thought those things, they appeared, one in each hand. Of course they did! This was creative dreaming of a kind.

Thorn said, "You catch on fast."

I said, "I am, after all, the goddess."

I threw the holy water at him. He screamed and melted into a puddle of bubbling effluvium. It couldn't be that easy to get rid of him, surely. Unless he had never been the real enemy. Unless the real enemy had really been inside myself, all this time, and he had only been its corporeal manifestation. Heavy.

The puddle quivered, started to reshape itself into human form —

I rammed the stake right into its ectoplasmic heart.

"Good for you," said Oren. "Now rescue me."

I heard, from overhead, the high-pitched keening —

Phil Etchison:

— that was Chris's song of creation.

I started to pile up the blocks, at random almost, feverishly, words locking into other words, poems jigsawing into a barbarous, crude simulacrum of prosody.

— to be or not, thou still unravished

Bride

of the monster —

I heard, behind Chris's song, the slow heartbeat of the world. In a way, the words of the song no longer mattered; the truth was too deep for words; that was what Chris had come to teach us.

— where Alph, the sacred

river-run, past Eve's and —

Words joined with words, but the blocks ran in all directions. I was building a castle and a poem ran in every direction: famous poems, dirges, threnodies, doggerel, limericks, bathroom scrawls; I was assembling them all, and the poem that was this multidimensional meta-poem was less than a single word, the word that Chris knew, the word that would soon unmake and recreate the cosmos.

The song grew around us, and at long last I forgot that I was creating the poem in order to free the woman, for the woman had long since been freed and was kneeling beside me, gazing at me, bedraggled, in a slow-motion, silent rainfall that I knew to be the first moment I set eyes on Mary, mother of my son, mother of Theo, mother of god; she watched me in wordless wonder as I spun the web of words. For every poem is a spell.

"You are Mary," I said.

"Among other things," she said, and clasped my free hand — the other was assembling another string of words —

I wonder by my troth what thou and I —

lonely as a cloud —

morning's minion,

a mountain wind that shakes the mighty oak-tree —

the still point of

world enough and time.

What did it all mean? All the poetry of the world run through a blender, fresh-squeezed into a killer juice cocktail? Did I care any more? As all true poets know, in the end, poetry writes itself. Was I finally becoming a true poet? No. These were other men's words, mostly, though I detected a few strands in the fabric that were my own.

"Do you want some help?" Mary said at last, after she had looked at me adoringly for long enough.

"I guess so," I said.

She knelt down right next to me and began assembling the bricks along with me. The bricks shot into place, each one locking into the next with a thwup, spinning off more meta-poetry as we went along. It took me a while to realize that Mary was no longer chained up. I don't remember when she had been freed, or which strand of poesy it was that undid her shackles. I had thought that I was building this edifice of words in order to melt down her chains, but I began to realize that the structure was an end in itself. It was a kind of world, internally self-consistent. I don't know how long we were assembling the building blocks, but after a while I began to notice that we were kneeling on a pathway the paving-stones of which were the words we had put together, and that the texture of the world around us was no longer quite as metallic and two-dimensional.

The pathway had railings (each railing, exactly seventeen bricks high, was a haiku, spelled out in Japanese kana, inscrutable to me except that I could count to seventeen) and through the railings came a whispering wind, and in the wind there was moisture.

I crept closer to the edge.

"It's a bridge," I said softly, "we've been building a bridge."

"A bridge of words," Mary said.

"Words," I said, "which are mere airy nothings."

"Where does the bridge lead us?" she asked me.

"I don't know," I said, "but I think, I think —"

We both stood up. The bridge we had been building soared up high over our heads. It broke through the iron world we had been trapped in. In fact, where the bridge

shattered the metal, there were rip marks in the cavern
wall, like a fist that has punched through aluminum foil.
Hand in hand, we followed the pathway. Each paving-
stone I stepped on was a word:

Serendipitous
Huzzah
Calcite
Anaconda
Starstuff

and each word's meaning tingled all through me, as
though the building block was the word itself; and I
thought about the ancient theory of magic that holds that
magic works when things are called by their true names,
which names are known only to mages and wizards; and
I wondered whether each of those words was in fact, the
true name of the building block that bore it. I turned to
Mary and she only smiled, as though she had heard all,
agreed with all of it.

"It almost seems too easy," I said.

"That's because," she said, "what happens in the
world you touch, taste, feel is not necessarily what's
really happening; it's only a blueprint for what happens
in here," she touched my head, "and here," she added,
lightly tapping at my heart with a petite index finger, still
smiling.

We held hands. We started walking toward the rip in
the fabric of the steel universe.

"Where does it lead us?" Mary said, wonderingly;
from beyond the iron door, there came the rushing of a
mighty wind. Like the beating of great wings. I thought
Mary probably knew the answer to that question; wasn't
she, after all, a goddess in this world? Was she just waiting for me to come up with the right answer? Was this
yet another test, another tribulation that lay in the path
of the hero's quest?

At the rip itself, the jagged strips of sheet metal quivering a little in the wind beyond the door, I took her in
my arms and kissed her. Her hair wrapped itself around

us both. I kissed her hungrily, because I had been without her so long; oh, she'd been around, as a hood ornament, as a statue, but as a woman, no. And she was nude beneath her hair, though her hair hissed like a nest of serpents, and hugged me as though it had a life of its own. I parted the hair from between her breasts and that was when I saw what I feared, what I knew I would see: the telltale lesions. This was my wife all right, my real wife from universe number one, my wife was was dying of cancer.

"What happened?" I asked her. "How did you —"

"Become myself again?"

"You were always yourself," I said. "But the very first yourself, the one who came to me in Washington in the rain —"

"The ur-Mary?" she said. And still she smiled, though I now knew she was in terrible agony. "She was always at the heart of me, if you peeled away enough layers."

"But if you're dying, it means —"

"The cosmos is dying? Because I am the world?" One almost expected the strains of that hideous Lionel Ritchie Christmas song to burst into the air, but instead her words were punctuated by Milt's drum, and by the stratospheric coloratura of Chris's voice, from somewhere in the steel vault of heaven.

I understood something profound in this moment, and I said it aloud: "we're seeing each other in our real, original forms, because the the end of the world is finally at hand, isn't it? And this is, as it were, the moment of insight we are all being vouchsafed, this split second of vision ... for a little while, until the cosmos is consumed, we too have become truthsayers, we too can see the way Theo sees, with the eyes of ultimate innocence."

"And what do you think I see?" Mary said softly.

"I don't know," I said. "One can't see oneself. But I would imagine you see the twelfth-rate poetaster that I am, an aging man, a little on the plump side, perhaps, a varicose vein or two, a man who doesn't even know his own son, a man who has achieved remarkably little in his life, considering his talents and social advantages."

"You call this bridge a little achievement?" Mary said.

"But somehow I think I was cheating. It was all so damned easy. And we still don't know where this bridge leads to."

"Let's take another step," she said, "and find out."

I kissed —

Serena Somers:

— Oren Karpovsky on the lips. Hard, wet, as if he were my one true love. And Oren slowly began to dissolve into a mist. The mist was soaking through the tapestry of our universe, and I could see that the walls of the catacombs were getting soggy.

"Where are you, Oren?" I said. I heard a gloppy movement over my shoulder.

When I turned around I saw another Oren, soaked in gore, rising from the puddle that had been Thorn and holy water. This was more of a golem-Oren, because his face and limbs had a muddy, unfinished texture to them. He even had a few qabbalistic signs inscribed on his forehead. "Can you talk?" I asked him.

He shook his head.

Of course he wasn't all formed yet. He had been caged inside the ravening psyche and soma of Thorn for a long time. It's hard to become unpossessed, I guess; it doesn't happen all in one sitting.

But if Oren was inside the Thorn that rose from the coffin, who was inside the Oren that was chained to the wall?

Who was the mist?

"Joshua?" I whispered.

The mist swirled softly around me. I followed the mist, which was almost humanoid, and the golem followed me. The catacombs deepened, narrowed, became mustier; but there was also more light. I think it was from rips in the fabric, places where the thread had worn thin; perhaps Penelope had stopped weaving and was finally contemplating doing what I did — taking matters into her own hands, not waiting around for her husband to come home like an eternal Donna Reed.

Maybe so. The fabric of the world didn't seem to be shifting anymore. The threads were lifeless, motionless. There was a wind of sorts, but it came from like, outside the tapestry, from the world beyond. There was a way out somewhere. I listened. I could hear the rushing of water.

The mist began condensing against the farthest wall. It was eating away the cloth now. It was opening up a ragged exit, wide enough for a single human. The mist wound itself up into a sort of mini-tornado, and thrust itself through the hole. I followed. Behind me lumbered the Oren-golem. We were standing at one end of a bridge.

At one end of a rainbow; and the other end was shrouded in mist. In Joshua, perhaps. He was the gold at the end, perhaps. My one true love, stranded in a world that no longer existed except in memory. I was alone with my mute ex-lover; he had gone from master of the world (or at least some simulacrum of the world) to a brutish zombie, not even all flesh and blood.

The wind was powerful as shit, and freezing, too, even though the sun beat down on us. The bridge had no pavement as such. We were walking on something solid, but we couldn't see what it was. It seemed to hold us up pretty well. The fabric of the rainbow itself was definitely what you'd call gossamer. I mean, you could put your hands right through it and not feel a thing. It was spun out of thinnest air.

The floor of the bridge could have been glass, or some kind of force field, or even —

Philip Etchison:

— yellow bricks, for all I knew. All I could tell is that we were hanging over the most awe-inspiring gorge I had ever seen — dangling on a skein of verbiage — and beneath us the waters were rushing — we were suspended over the confluence of a million rivers, a million worlds.

There were other bridges too, arcing up in the distance; bridges of masonry and steel, of gold and crystal; bridges that were rainbows; precarious bridges that were a single rope lashed to struts of bamboo. And on some of those bridges I could make out tiny figures, human mostly, all making their way toward some unseen nexus.

And below! Whitewater rapids. Geysers and fountains thousands of feet high. This had to be it, the fabled source of the river that runs between the worlds. There were ships down below, too. Shattered against the rocks. I saw the upturned prow of what might have been the Titanic, from which I had recently escaped. I saw triremes and barges, liners and rafts, all dashed in pieces against sheer precipices.

I heard Milt's drum beating behind the roar of the waters.

Where was the shaman? At length I could make him out, a minute figure far ahead of us on the bridge, dancing up a storm.

"Let's go to Milt," I said. "He'll know what to do next."

"As if," said Mary, "you didn't know yourself; you have your mythology pretty much down cold."

I smiled. "You're right," I said. "Let's go, then."

"Yes, let's go."

But for a long moment, we did not move. We merely stood there, almost touching, reveling in the fact that we had come so far and that we now stood on the brink of ... what? A universe was going to end, and another was going to be born. We would be among those fortunate enough to be vouchsafed the privilege of stepping across the line that divided two great cycles of existence. Even though I was still a mediocre poet, and Mary was still a middle-aged mother, dying of cancer, isolated and afraid.

Oren Karpovsky:

I cannot speak.
I can only follow.
I don't know where I am.
The whole world is the sound of water.

Eighteen
The Frodo Syndrome

Theo Etchison:

— and land.

In the confluence of a million rivers, at the place where all bridges cross, there is a pool, a quiet, circular pool, oblivious to the raging of the waters all around. The old mad king lies sleeping on a rock, his scepter cradled in his arms; his scepter is the light that plays in the grotto.   We hear the crash of clashing rivers, and we know it is just beyond the wall of rocks that surrounds us, but somehow it seems infinitely far away.

Ash and I are looking at the king. He's sleeping like a baby, I guess. Like he's not carrying half the tortured souls of the world within the jewel of his scepter.

Ash and I creep up to the edge of the pool.

When I gaze into the water, it's as if all my truth-saying powers have come back to me; it's like I never started to feel the tug of hormones or the pollution of doubt.

"Father says," says Ash, "that the scepter has one last great magic in it. Do you know what that magic is?"

"Yeah," I say, "it's the magic of unmaking. It's the power to unravel the whole cosmos."

"Scary," Ash says.

"As if you didn't know," I say.

"It sounds better," he says, "coming from the lips of a truthsayer. There's a kind of certainty to it."

"I'm not much of a truthsayer anymore," I say.

Then I gaze into the pool again. I see that all the protagonists in this story are slowly coming together, and that we're all going to meet up here, in this little space, to play out the final stages of the drama. I see my dad, striding over the chasm on a bridge of poetry, and my mother with him, shivering in a frayed Navajo blanket, the same blanket she was wrapped in when we were driving to Mexico.

I see Serena Somers hurrying towards us over another bridge. Behind her was a man of clay. Ahead of her was a humanoid mist ... a sort of pre-person I guess; someone who doesn't exist yet, but who will soon exist if everything goes the way it should.

"So what do we do now, truthsayer?" Ash asks me.

"I guess," I say, "we pry away the scepter from your father, and we drop it into the source of the river, and everything returns to square one."

That sounds right. It has that mythic ring to it. But I can't help thinking that it's not that simple, that there's one more piece to the puzzle. What could it be? I gaze into the reflecting pool once more and now I see myself. In some ways I haven't changed that much. I'm still scrawny, I'm still an unkempt, dirty blond kid with scarily clear eyes. Somewhere out there, in one of the many branches of the river, it's still the 90s, the time before the mad millennium, and a dollar will still buy you a coke and a candy bar; somewhere out there I'm still young, so fucking young I still don't know what it's like to be afraid of the all-embracing darkness, I still haven't looked death in the eye, even though I've heard him breathing over my shoulder, and I know his smell too well, the sick-sweet-orange-putrid smell of my mother dying.

But then when you look at me again you see that I've lost my innocence; that the vision I have now is just a temporary flashback to the time before; you see that I have one foot permanently in the real world, the world without magic, the world where truthsaying has no meaning; that's the world where I will end up one day, when the healing's done and the redemption all taken care of. We are all gods, but only for as long as we need to be.

Ash has been trying to loosen the mad king's grip. "This thing weighs a ton," he says. "I just can't get it off him."

That's when I realize what the problem is. It's the Frodo syndrome, of course; the ring gets heavier and heavier the closer you get to the crack of Mt. Doom; just as, no doubt, the cross got heavier and heavier the closer Christ got to Calvary; that's in the nature of redeeming the world.

"Come on," I say, "I'll help you."

The two of us tug at the scepter. To say that it's heavy is an understatement, and it's jammed tight in the mad king's embrace. We pull and push and we can't budge it.

"We're going to have to wake him up," I say, and I start kicking him and pulling at his beard.

The king seems strangely at peace. He hasn't slept much during our long journey, but now, it seems, the weariness of the years has caught up with him all at once. I don't understand it. His eyelids are quivering; he's in a state of REM, I guess; perhaps he's even dreaming the whole world into being, like the Red King in Alice Through the Looking-glass. Perhaps, I think, like in Alice, we will all disappear if he wakes up. Perhaps, I think, that would be just as well in a way. No more terror. No more pain. No more Mrs. Hulan's social studies class, for instance.

"I'm going to have to do it," Ash says softly.

He prods the king lightly on the cheek; when that doesn't work, he kisses him gently on the lips. This time, not as statesmen kiss, not like before; this time he does seem like his father's true son at last. And Strang opens his eyes.

"I didn't die," Strang says.

"No, father, you didn't."

"It's time for me to hurl the thing away."

Strang struggles to get up. But still he's hugging that scepter to his chest, and the jewel glitters, deadly and cold; and you can tell that it weighs him down but he doesn't want to let go.

"Father, father," says Ash, "remember how you answered the sphinx."

"Yes," I tell him, "we have to let go now."

Strang says, "If only you knew ... how many souls are imprisoned in this jewel ... if only you knew how each pinprick death caused me to grow in power until I ... I ... I encircled the whole world, like the river of time...."

"The river of time," I say, "has circled back on itself now, King. We'll help you. Come on, Ash, grab hold of one of his shoulders."

Ash and I heave up the king, a frail thing, yes, a king of shreds and patches as my dad would have called him; and we try to support him, but it's hard because the scepter weighs so fucking much. I keep thinking, Ditch the scepter, ditch the scepter, ditch the scepter, and that inner voice sounds a constant counterpoint to the other music we hear, the music that emanates from the world's heart and from that other truthsayer, the child of my incest.

"Heavy," the king murmurs, "heavy, heavy."

Ditch the scepter! Ditch the scepter!

"You hear it too, don't you," Ash says to me.

"Yeah."

We half pull, half push the king toward the pool. "I don't want to give it up," the king says. "I don't, I don't."

He sounds like a child with a favorite toy. He is, after all, still crazy; that moment of lucidity, in which he and Ash acknowledged each other and their love for each other, was maybe just a flash of lightning in a dark storm that can only deepen.

But the scepter is so heavy we can barely move the king at all, and now we start to hear voices in the scepter itself: they're the voices of lost souls, screaming for release; all of inferno is tesseracted into that scepter, I'm sure of it.

The drumbeat still goes on.

Suddenly, the air above us is full of Thorn's creatures. They hover over us with their gargoyle faces and crimson eyes. I don't know if they're going to attack or not. I don't see their leader, in fact, I thought I saw a vision of him dead, in a puddle of steaming holy water, in some catacomb, when I gazed into the pool. They keep descending, settling on every nook and niche in the wall of rock that surrounds us, until there's like a thousand pairs of demon eyes staring down at us. I can hear their collective breathing, and I can smell their breath, a trace of fetor behind the pure fresh scent of the source.

They don't attack. They only stare.

Then we hear: Ditch the scepter! Ditch the scepter! over and over again, inside our skulls, like a throbbing headache; it's the voices within the scepter, it's the voices of the gargoyles, coming from their minds I guess — you remember in Alice through the Looking Glass Lewis Carroll says that the animals "thought in chorus" — and then what happens next is that King Strang's eyes begin to bleed.

No, no, just his left eye, the one he gave up as the price of all this power. Blood brims up around the iolite crystal, his artificial eye. It oozes down his cheek. And now the sores, the cankers on his face that are the outward symbols of his inner corruption start to erupt. Pus and bile run down his face, his neck, soak into his robe.

He looks like something out of a low-budget monster movie.

He begins to scream in utmost agony. It's hard to bear. I know he wants to get rid of that scepter, but it's like it's glued to his arms. He is the only one who can toss that thing away, because he is the one who originally made the deal to steal the jewel from the river's source.

That's when the demon-creatures start to swoop down.

They come down in twos and threes. They worry at the king with their beaks, try to jab him in the arm. Ash and I try to fend them off, but what can we do? It's like being stuck in that Hitchcock movie, The Birds, you know, where they just keep coming and coming. They screech like banshees, caw like crows, they start pecking at the king's open wounds. Strang screams. He lashes out with the scepter. He bonks one and it sort of disintegrates and gets sucked into the jewel. So even now, it's gathering more souls, more power, becoming heavier.

Ash is doing pretty well at first. He karate-chops a couple of the creatures and they split in half. Why are they even attacking? Don't they know they have no leader anymore?

But I'm wrong. I hear a rumbling. The wall of rock is shaking. Then it suddenly splits, and the prow of the Titanic bursts through; and leaping down from the height, his cloak transforming itself into a leathern parachute as he fell, is Thorn, who has died three or four times during this adventure yet is proving eerily resilient. Behind him, through the shattered rocks, I can see the vista beyond the source: the rushing rivers, the rainbow bridges, the unscalable cliffs and impenetrable mountains, the tiny figures making their inexorable way towards me, the center, the place of their destiny.

"Father," Thorn screams, "give me the scepter now."

The demons circle overhead as Thorn lands beside us. He glances at me only for a moment. "Why do you keep coming back?" I ask him.

"I'm a vampire," he says. "That's what we do. We come back from the dead. You can kill me as often as you like, but it won't do any good."

He turns to his brother. "I'll dispose of you as soon as I get the scepter," he says, and he reaches for it.

King Strang stands firm. But Thorn has a way of getting to him the way I and Ash cannot, because we're not experts at lying; when Thorn tells the truth, the truth hurts his father in a way he can't control, and control is what he knows best. "Father," Thorn says, "do you remember when you divided the kingdom into three, and you gave me all the worlds controlled by Thornstone Slaught? Do you remember what you asked your three children then? To tell you how much we loved you? And do you remember what I said?"

Strang gasps, "You said, 'I love you like the sky. I love you like the earth. I love you like the infinite sea.'"

"What a fool you are, father. I lied."

"You lied?"

"Love was never the issue, father. A vampire does not feel love; he feeds on the love of others; love is something to be sucked out, never given back; that is what I am. Why did you make me a vampire, father?"

"You were born dead," Strang says softly.

I kneel down by the pool and gaze into its depths. I see it all. Vividly, for this is the pool in which all time stands perfectly still, and where every moment of existence is captured in some kind of unbreakable stasis; this pool is the universe's memory bank, the one place where there are no lies.

I see the scene. The palace I recognize from having traveled there inside Ash's consciousness. I see the palace newer now, just after the coming of the firstborn. The king cradling the dead child in his arms, the queen sobbing with grief, the courtiers standing with their eyes downcast, not daring to show any emotion in case the king lashed out at them; the lizard warriors, weapons upright, flanking the walls and staring straight ahead.

I see the dead child's eyes, still open, slate-colored. He's not a baby, even though he has just been born; these are not exactly human beings; perhaps he has been gestating for ten, twelve, fifteen of our years; he's a boy, not an infant. He is being laid in a stone sarcophagus now, and I see the king, inconsolable, speaking to some mage or grand vizier, a man with long black robes embroidered with stars and moons; the mage is whispering back to him, dire secrets about the nature of life and death.

The mourners file past, one by one. The water of the pool ripples and we are no longer in the throne room, but in some dank and foul-smelling catacomb beneath the palace complex. At length, King Strang is alone except for the queen, Thorn's mother, and the body of his son. Then the queen too leaves, dismissed with an angry glance and a harsh command. Strang stands before the body. He is a young king still, his face unlined, his scepter not yet adorned with the jewel that steals men's souls.

He kneels over the dead boy. He whispers words into his ear, words he has heard from the dark mage; and presently he stabs his own wrist, and lets the blood run down his palm, down his index finger, to the dead boy's lips. And he is whispering, "Come back to life, my son, the one I love so much, come back, come back; I don't care if what you are is just a simulacrum of life; I'll accept anything, any shadow, any vestige, any animated imitation of what you might have been, if only you will walk the earth once more and be my son."

The blood drips. The blood of a king is a powerful magic, especially that of a king who rules over not one country, but many worlds. No doubt that's what the mage has been telling him.

The child stirs. I see Strang tremble with anticipation and also a certain fear. The child's eyes open. He looks at his father. Not with affection, but with accusation. Not with respect, but with recrimination. Then Thorn howls, a howl of profound, dark agony, a howl that makes me shiver because I can't ever know what it's like to be undead, always to hunger, to live in a perpetual twilight, an eternal aloneness; I just can't know these things. I'm scared. I look up from the pool, and I see the living Strang, who's been reliving those moments along with me; I see that the agony hasn't stopped for either of them.

"Why, father, why," cries Thorn, "did you bring me back from the grave?"

And Strang says, "Because I loved you, my son."

But they do not look into each other eyes.

Behind Thorn, Cornelius Huang has landed, trumpet in hand. The little Cerberus-creature is yapping at his heels.

"You made it so I can never be swallowed back into the darkness. You made it so I can never know the womb-warmth of the earth; I'm always homeless, always hungry; are you surprised I hate you?"

"I —" says the king. God, how I feel his pain. Sometimes you do hate your parents, sometimes you feel like pummeling them with your fists and shouting I hate you I hate you I hate you but you know that this kind of hatred stems from a kind of love. Thorn's kind of hatred goes a lot deeper. It is perpetual. He can't live and he can't die. He's been killed a million times and still he comes back, breathing himself into fresh clay; he is all hunger, all rapacity.

Only the force of this hate is strong enough to dislodge the scepter from Strang's arms. There it goes. Crashing to the stony floor. A little closer to the source. Thorn dives after it. He can't lift it, though. He tugs at it with all his might but it seems to be soldered to the rock. He screams for reinforcements, and his gargoyle troops dive down in V-formation, each one grasping the tail of the one below; there's a V of demons reaching all the way up to the sun, and the head demon reaches down and clutches the scepter with both fists and all together, hundreds upon hundreds of ruby-eyed monsters, they manage to hoist the scepter up, an inch or two at first, then higher, higher —

Thorn turns to his father. He crows. He laughs the laughter of mad scientists, and, like a comic-book villain, he can't stop himself from lecturing us: "After light, father, there comes shadow; after day comes night; didn't you realize that, glorious and brilliant though your reign was, there had to be an equal and opposite age of darkness? You may think you're saving the world by tossing away the scepter and healing its wounds, but what about us, the creatures of night, who are its wounds, who would be destroyed by the process of healing? You're not saving our world, father, are you? But if I wrest the jewel from you, if I'm the one to plunge the cosmos into a million-year-darkness, won't I be the one to be remembered for redeeming my creatures from the tyranny of light? You see, there's always two sides to everything."

King Strang is too mortified to answer. I watch the scepter slowly rise above our heads. There is nothing I can do. I still hear those voices, though, the ones that cry out, Ditch the scepter, and I know Thorn hears them too, because he's holding his hands over his ears, he's tormented, he's trying to block out the sounds.

"You can't hack it," I tell him. "You can't handle being the adversary, the prince of darkness."

"Of course I can," Thorn says. "I was made for the part. And don't try to bullshit me with some dimestore psychology, kid, because I know you're not a real truthsayer anymore."

"Oh, but I am," I say. "Here, inside this circle, everyone's a truthsayer. So I tell you this: as far as the Great Satan thing is concerned, you're just another wannabe. Inside your black heart there's a frightened little boy, and that boy knows why your father did what he did. He's angry as shit about it, but he always recognizes there's a spark of love behind the selfishness of it. He sees that Strang was desperate when he called you back from the dead; desperate because kings are fated to be unloved, and he wanted something to love him, even if it was only an imitated love; do you understand that?"

"Don't give me that New Age nonsense. I won't be reconciled to my father. I won't forgive him and don't want him to forgive me."

He waves at the V of demons, and Cornelius blows seven quick blasts, and the V jerks upward, and we see the scepter swing back and forth; it's kind of a pendulum effect I guess. The jewel glitters so much that it almost blinds me. They're all undead, all the souls trapped in the jewel; I think if Thorn had it, he could release them all — if you can call it release when you turn a living thing, with free will and all that, into a fucking zombie.

"It's not New Age nonsense," I tell Thorn. "It's the simple truth."

And Thorn knows it, too.

"Never liked truth too much," he mumbles. "Just never liked it."

He waves his arms helplessly at his minions.

With a great flapping of leathern wings, the scepter crashes to the rock once more ... a few feet closer to the pool.

"Father, father," says Thorn. "Maybe I did love you a little bit. But that was a long time ago, before it became too late for love."

He stands, facing his father, his arms outstretched, looking curiously like the crucified Christ somehow.

Strang does manage to lift the scepter up.

"Too late?" Strang says softly. "Too late for love?"

"How do you do that?" Thorn says in wonderment. "You're old and feeble, and that jewel carries the weight of so much death, so much remorse."

I tell him, "You bear your cross, and he will bear his. At least, you see, it's his own."

"You're doing a little too damn well," Thorn says, "in the truthsaying department, you weasel."

I try to smile. But my smile dissolves when Strang does what, I guess, destiny tells him he must do; he thrusts the tip of the scepter into Thorn's chest, cracks through the sternum, penetrates his son's heart.

"You brought me into this world," says the vampire; "I suppose it's only right you should take me out of it."

Blood begins to spurt from the wound with a wet, sick, gloppy sound, like reluctant ketchup. Thorn still has something to say. "Father," he says, "I always thought this was going to really hurt, and you know, it does. But the amazing thing is, I feel it; I really feel it; this pain gives me the illusion of once having been alive."

And little by little, like, frame by frame almost, the prince who once abducted me from the men's room of a Chinese restaurant, who sucked the blood of mermaids, who imprisoned me in a gothic castle and made me navigate his sinking ship, my one time nemesis ... well, he begins to kind of liquefy, like a Salvador Dali clock, and he slowly oozes into oblivion. They are all dissipated into thin air: not just Thorn and Cornelius and the three-headed dog, but also the army of dark spirits hovering in the air; they're all kind of dissolving; the air ripples. Presently, they seem no more threatening than a swarm of flies. In fact, that's what they are. Thorn, distorted and distended now, steps forward. His slate-colored eyes are bleeding; it's not blood exactly, but a purple-green sap; Dad would have said it was ichor, the fluid that runs in the veins of the gods.

King Strang tries to embrace him; it's awkward; even now, at the last minute, he is afraid to love whom he now knows has always loathed him.

Only the scepter remains; and it's even more dazzling now, because it contains the soul of somehow who was truly close to its owner. The jewel of lost souls is as bright as the sun itself.

"Now, King Strang," I tell him. "Throw it into the pool. Before something else happens to slow you down."

The king takes another step toward the source. The scepter is still cradled fast within his arms.

But, at that moment —

Nineteen
This is the Way the Cookie Crumbles

Serena Somers:

I stepped into the circle of rock. Theo was already there, and so was the mad king. They were sort of struggling over the scepter. But amazingly of all, I saw Ash, and he saw me; when I looked at him I was reminded vivdly of all those summer nights, lying alone, thinking wet thoughts, with Ash as my lone imaginary companion.

With the mist that was Joshua spinning above me, and the golem that was Oren behind me, and my dream lover standing at the water's edge, I was surrounded by all the people I had ever had any deep sexual feelings for. Well, there was Mr. E., too, but I guess that had just been a schoolgirl crush.

But I couldn't think about all that right now because there was a final piece of unfinished business I'd been called upon to do.

I could feel myself morphing now, twisting, I could feel the scales push through the skin, the claws protrude through my fingertips and toes. This was the reason I'd been carrying Katastrofa inside me all along ... so she could confront her father for the last time.

My human skin was peeling from me now. Doesn't every woman have a dragon within herself? I felt: I am Katastrofa and she is me.

My scaly self rubbed hard against the underside of my epidermis and yes, I felt pain, such pain, you can't even imagine it; I was giving birth to the dark side of myself. What kind of a dragon was I? The fire scorched my throat as I exhaled. I threw a glance back at the still shiny pool that I knew must be the source of all those rivers. I saw myself; sleek, monstrous, golden-eyed, wreathed in the smoke of my own breath; god I was frightening, and I was beautiful, all at once. I watched myself from a deep safe place inside my mind because the one who controlled the body was now Katastrofa Darkling, not sluglike Serena.

"Father," I said to the old man.

"Katastrofa?" he said. "Aren't you dead? I never brought you back from the dead, never condemned you to an eternity of hunger...."

The Katastrofa in me coiled and uncoiled herself, shook her golden wattles, inclined her head so her scales caught the sunlight and made her all bright and bronze. "But father," I said, "I still never answered your question. I mean, the one about how much I love you."

"Yes," said Strang, "you did. Didn't you? Wasn't that the answer about the sun and the moon and the stars and the planets and the great galaxies that wheel and whirl?" Strang sounded indecisive; he must have known that I was going to disappoint him.

"Oh, father," I said, "I do love you. Let me show you how much."

And so it was that the dragon coiled herself around the old man, and stroked his rubbery flesh with her searing scales, and I realized that Katastrofa's love for her father had been more than filial. It had been that old Electra complex thing.

"Don't tear your eyes out, father," said Katastrofa, seductive and brazen. "Well. you already tore one out, but with the other you still have to be able to look at me. You still have to see that I'm beautiful, I'm your little girl."

With my inner eye I started to catch glimpses of Katastrofa's childhood. She was not always a dragon. She was a little girl indeed, in pigtails, running naked through the palace, chased by the nursemaids, and her father was remote, on his throne, a person who visited her only in dreams or when she saw his stern hologram in the ceiling of the nursery, and always surrounded by those lizard guards, one at each corner of the throne, their weapons perpetually drawn; I overheard a childish thought: He loves those guards more than he loves me.

At night I dreamt of ravishing my father. Only once was I admitted to his bedchamber, and they blindfolded me before they would take me there, and I was escorted by twelve fierce lizards in chrome-colored suits. But my unconscious mind always had a good sense of direction, so every night I flew down those scores of corridors, and each night in my dreams I grew scalier, and my wings sprouted and my fangs began to grow; and one morning I woke up and I was a dragon. The lizard guards had rubbed off on me, because I thought he loved them more than me....

That morning I came to the throneroom. My father's wives fled. The lizards stood firm, knowing what I had become, having, perhaps, some inkling why. The grand vizier, the one who advised my father to make my older brother a vampire, whispered in my father's ear; I stank up the hall with my fetid breath, and melted the gold steps to my father's throne with a single exhalation. And my father looked at me, and I could see all the disappointment in his eyes, because I was no longer little and beautiful; but all he said was, "Is this, Katastrofa, what you really want?"

And I said, "I don't know, father. It just happened, somehow. I think it's because you don't love me enough. I'm not beautiful enough, I'm not your little girl enough, I don't know. Somehow you made this happen." Which wasn't true, not exactly. We had both made it happen. I because of of some dark, lustful emotion no one had ever tried to explain to me, he because he had always neglected me ... now, seeing the broken old man, now I knew he had always loved me ... but I was too angry to want to understand that. I wanted him to love me the way I dreamed about in my childish, hormonally challenged fashion ... and so it was that I was wrapping my limbs and coils around a spent, mad king, and watching him squirm, and becoming strangely, inexorably aroused; even my scales sweated lubricious fluids.

"Get away from me," said Strang, but he couldn't command me anymore. Wasn't I a dragon, and wasn't he a king without a kingdom? In this place, only the truth could be told, and my truth was a shameful truth, but it was so powerful that my dragon frame shuddered with the realization of it.

"Love me, father," I said. "This is the true answer to your question. This is the way I've always loved you. I've been consumed by it, and now I'll consume you too. Fuck me, father, fuck me now."

"Abomination!" Strang said. "You can't really be my daughter."

"Well," said the dragon, "if I'm not, then it's okay to do it, right?"

Strang howls, howls, howls, like the winter wind.

(The I that's Serena watches from deep inside the dragon's mind. I'm alarmed at all this incest. I've taken enough Joseph Campbell in Mythology 101 to know that it's what the gods seem to do best, though when humans do it they tend to pluck their eyes out, as Tom Lehrer says in that song of his about Oedipus Rex, "one by one.")

She wound herself tight around him like a golden boa constrictor. She snarled. She shook herself and sent droplets of flame flying. The old man was horrified, sure, but I could see, through Katastrofa's eyes, that there was something in him a little bit like lust; that was the way

Oren had first looked at me, across the desktop in his congressman's office, predatory and a little jaded; I knew that Strang had feelings for his daughter, long repressed; maybe it was his feelings that had sparked off his daughter's secret feelings, and the secrets had nourished each other through the years, fed on each other until they drove both of them mad.

"You have to consummate this, father," said Katastrofa. "It's the only way this can end for me. I can't completely die, not until I've mated with the god."

"I'm not a god," Strang gasps, "never was, thought I was, perhaps, but never will be now; I am an old man and I have no power."

"Fuck me, father," I said in Katastrofa's metal-tinged voice, "fuck me, give me the scepter."

The flies that had once been demons buzzed about his open sores. He looked pathetic — but, through Katastrofa's eyes, I also saw the magnificent god-king, with his mane of dark hair, astride the world, controller of the gateways between worlds; he was beautiful to her, beautiful even as he was hurting her by his abandonment.

"The scepter! the scepter!" she (and I) screamed. I couldn't tell if it was agony, ecstasy, or something in between.

Nightmarish images flashed through my mind. Strang naked and covered with sores. The dragon thrashing in a crimson sea. The dragon stretching, stretching, elongating herself and tunneling and winding through the thousands of miles of corridors in the king's palace. Meanwhile, the real king writhed in a frenzy of guilt and desire.

At length, I think he must have seen the way out of his dilemma. He lunged forward, scooped up the scepter with a superhuman effort, and raised it high.

"That's it, father," she cried out. "The scepter, the jewel of your manhood, the ultimate power."

And Strang thrust the scepter deep into her — me — oh, God, I felt those thrusts, I felt them penetrate me deep, felt raped and violated, felt my womb become warped and ravaged. He plunged the scepter into me again and again, as relentlessly as a low-budget porno. Katastrofa screamed — I screamed with her — and I knew that this time she would really die. Yes, there was joy in being stabbed to death by father's phallic scepter. I couldn't really understand it, but waves of Katastrofa's twisted love flooded my mind. I couldn't think. I was enveloped in a sea of red. It was the dragon's blood. I was swimming in blood. The blood was fiery and warm. It scorched me, it seared me, but it gave me a strange kind of high, like mainlining heroin or something, not that I've ever done that, but it was totally addictive, totally seductive. Katastrofa was dying in an orgasmic bliss that I couldn't even imagine, but because I shared her mind, I could touch the edge of it and even that was enough to make me jump out of my skin ... well, her skin, actually ... because I found myself, dry and dressed all in white, standing in a pool of dragon ectoplasm.

The scepter gleamed; it was more dazzling than before; it had absorbed not only the essence of Thorn, the lord of the dark places, but also the brilliance of Katastrofa, the dragon who had soared by day and eclipsed the sun with reflected sunlight.

And once again the scepter fell out of King Strang's hands and rolled a little closer toward the pool....

Strang wept in the arms of his one remaining child. Impassively, the Oren golem stood, his eyes shifting from side to side like clockwork.

Theo said to me, "It's almost over, Serena."

My true love's little brother, the truthsayer, still a frail skinny kid; a lot less time had passed in his inner world; we others had all grown old, then grown young again, and Theo hadn't aged at all ... or had he?

"What do we do now?" I asked him.

"Just a few more feet," Theo said. "Then the jewel will be cast back into the waters; then the world will end, and the world will be reborn; then, maybe, we can go home."

"You want me to help you?" I said.   "Throw it in, I mean."

"None of us can. Only Strang."

The old man brushed aside his son and stood. He tottered toward the scepter. "I will do it now," he said. I hadn't been able to touch Katastrofa's lust, and I couldn't comprehend King Strang's sorrow, either; it was the whole world's sorrow.

Then, at that moment, the Oren-golem lurched forward —

"Power," it grunted. "Me, power, me, power, all."

It strode toward the scepter. Lifted it up. Easily. Even though I knew that it had the weight of billions of lost souls. Lifted it over its head. It shone. I had to shield my eyes.

"Me, power, me, power, all," said the man of clay.

"Now what?" I said.

Theo said, "It's time for you to decide who it is you really love."

"But I — but I —"

"No time to waste! Pick sides! The entire universe is going to blow!"

With a line like that, you know you're either imprisoned inside a cheap sci-fi movie, or well like, it's really happening. You start thinking a lot faster. The Joshua mist was spinning next to the source. Who do I really love? It's Joshua, I thought, that's the plain simple truth, totally no contest. I need to bring him back, and I do have the power to, because I've had the goddess inside me, and because of the enduring strength of my love for him. Didn't I once yield up my virginity to save him from the dragon's clutches?

Then I remembered the crumbled fortune cookie.

Way back. Imprisoned in Thornstone Slaught. I'd almost brought him back to life then, hadn't I? It was time to try again. Because now I had many more pieces of the puzzle that was myself, Serena Somers.

In one of my pockets — how many pockets did I have now? hadn't I been transformed into some kind of Amazon lady with a kilt, a sword, and popping boobs, at one stage, before standing here in a virginal, priestessly white? — there should still have been a napkin, and, wrapped up in the napkin, the crumbs with which I had hoped to reconstitute Joshua.

Oren lifted the scepter easily above his head. He wasn't, of course, quite human; I supposed that's why he was able to. In fact, he was becoming less and less human every second. There was an aura that the scepter cast about him, a cold blue light that danced about his clay features, and kind of dug itself in beneath his earthen skin. The dirt was hardening, becoming more glistening, more metallic. It was like he was recapitulating the whole history of robotics — all the way from the ancient Jewish myth of the man of clay — to the chromium androids of the future — and he was becoming more rigid, more powerful.

"That's what you always wanted, isn't it, Oren?" I shouted at him. "You wanted to get rid of the human part of you altogether. You wanted to become a machine."

"True," he said. His voice was hollow and emotionless.

"But what about all your great ideas about saving the world? The Karpovsky health plan? Bringing culture to the proles? Were they just tidbits thrown to the masses on your way to ultimate power?"

King Strang said, very faintly: "Don't do it, man of clay. It isn't worth it."

And Oren swung the scepter, and with each swing more of the wall of rock came tumbling down; you could see past the wall, to the whitewater vista of converging rivers, to the rainbow spaghetti of bridges that spanned the sky. And he said to the king, in a voice of gravel and dirt, "Why shouldn't I do it? You did, didn't you? Look at you now, you desiccated old thing ... don't tell me it wasn't worth it. Don't tell me you wouldn't do it all over again."

And Strang was silent, because, in the end, Oren was right. Power was its own reward.

I found the napkin tucked into my bosom. I pulled it out and there were the pieces of the fortune cookie, and I remembered the words on the slip of paper:

if you build him, he will come

and I thought, there's a double meaning in that, it all boils down to sex again somehow, doesn't it? and that totally confused me. But still, I knelt down on the rock and opened up the napkin and spit into my hand, and then a rolled together the breadcrumbs and started to form them into the shape of a man. I felt embarrassingly domestic for doing it. It was, I mean, not a 90s thing to do at all. But the homunculus started to take shape in my palm.

The mist that swirled around us was Joshua's soul; now I had to make his flesh. I was all goddess and all woman; my personal mystery was the mystery of creation. But how could I make it work?

Theo said to me and Strang, "Everyone has one great piece of magic inside themselves. Everyone does. But after you work that great piece of magic, then you're just a human being again. But you keep going. Because you remember that you had the magic once. And you hope that it will come again. And maybe it will. In the last moments before you die, maybe. At the cusp between worlds, between the unmaking and the unmaking, you know what I mean? There's magic nibbling at the corners of the world. Grab hold of that magic in both fists and reel it in. Dad'll kill me for mixing all these metaphors, but hey, rules are made to be broken, and now's as good a time as any to break them."

I looked at the golem, who was raging up and down, swinging the scepter, striking at the swarms of flies left over from Thorn's army of darkness; I looked at the puddles of viscera that used to be Thorn and Katastrofa, and

I thought to myself, this is a pretty sordid way for the world to end. I'd always heard Mr. E. quote that T.S. Eliot thing about the end of the world, not with a bang but with a whimper, but now I totally saw what he meant by that.

"Come back, Joshua," I whispered.

The mist, which had been whirling around the mirror-still pool, shifted and came to me. It swirled around my face. I could smell him now. I started to cry. I guess my salt tears started to blend with the crisp dry crumbs. Things started to happen. The mist blew over the pile of crumbs. The wetness softened them. There was a little doughboy in the palm of my hand and he was starting to grow.

He was heavy. I was afraid I couldn't hold on. I did for a while, though; I thought of all the times I'd dreamed of Josh, the times I'd looked at him in school; the times I'd wangled a job babysitting Theo on the off-chance I might see him on his way to a game; it's strange to love some-one who doesn't exist, who never existed except in some universe that is, for all intents and purposes, mere fan-tasy, until the moment you turn around, switch paths, and breathe the world back into being....

What can I say? Joshua came to life out of the cookie crumbs (which are made of flour which is made of grain which comes out of the earth and so goes back to the great mother who lived within me) and the mist (which was part of the air which was part of the breath of god which was the sky) and he was more than beautiful; he was the Joshua of my dreams, bigger, better than I ever remembered him; he rode a shining white steed capari-soned in cloth of gold, and he wore armor of solid gold, and he plucked a flaming sword out of the air. He knelt down at my feet and I ripped off a sheer scrap of my bri-dal costume for him to tie to the hilt of his sword. Then he got back on his horse and charged at the golem, and they clashed, just on the other side of the pool of still wa-ter, shrieking at each other in some mediaeval language.

They jousted; Oren unseated Joshua with the scepter, and then they scrambled up and down across the rocks, parrying, thrusting, leaping, dodging.   It was all very swashbuckling I suppose, but I couldn't really get into it. They ran all the way around the pool like cartoon characters and made me dizzy; Josh was quick as lightning, the golem lumbering but full of strength.   They scurried around and around the pool. Sparks flew from the jewel and the flaming sword.   Josh made samurai-like noises, while Oren growled and grunted.

After a decent amount of fighting, Joshua sort of tapped Oren on the head with his flaming sword. Oren shattered into a cloud of clay and metal fragments and landed on the ground in a heap.

"That's it?" I said. "That's the one big magic? Seems kind of lame if you ask me."

Theo laughed. His laughter made me happy because, for the first time since all this began, he sounded like himself, a more-or-less happy teenage boy in more-or-less average circumstances.   Then he smiled a secretive smile, like the kid who comes up to you to shake your hand and he's got a toad stowed up his sleeve, or one of those electric buzzer things. He said, "No, stupid," and laughed again, "that's not it at all. That's just the teaser. The real magic is about to happen ... right ... now."

And here's what happened next:

Strang stood at the edge of the pool. He had managed to lug the scepter all the way there. He paused. You see, Oren was right; power was power, and there is nothing so tempting as power. So finally, Ash went up to him, and very, very gently began to nudge him toward the very edge.

Strang wept.

"You've hurt the world," Ash said, "and now it's up to you to heal it."

Another step.

Another step.

Strang's tears were healing tears. Where they touched his cheeks, his sores were closing up. The pustules on his forehead were smoothing out. The wrinkles were not going away, but they seemed less, well, less wrinkled, somehow. He took another step toward the edge of the source, and now his tears were actually dripping into the pool itself, and the mirror-stillness was shattered. In the rippling, I saw Milt Stone, in the eerie mask and garb of a kachina, banging away at his drum, turning as he pounded so as to face the four corners of the universe. In the rippling, I saw Chris Etchison, eyes closed, lips parted, a wordless melisma streaming from his throat. I saw them reflected, yet they weren't there with us, not yet.

"Father, please," Ash said. He tugged at the scepter. His back was to the water and he was pulling his father in. And still Strang's face was racked with reluctance. "You have to do it," he said.

Strang's cheeks quivered. The weight of the scepter was such that it must have seemed like he was carrying the whole world. But he still couldn't drop it. He continued to weep, and now the tears ran thick. He stood at the very edge and he still wouldn't take that last step, until, until....

"I love you, father," Ash said, "and I know what I have to do."

He flung himself on the point of the scepter and impaled himself through the heart. Strang cried out, one last, heartwrenching howl, and then, as Ash's soul was sucked into the jewel, the scepter attained critical mass; Ash's soul was the last straw, the scruple that tipped the scales. The scepter itself pulled Strang into the water, because he would not let go. Ash held his father in a deadly embrace, pierced by the emblem of his father's power; and the two fell, arm in arm, into the embrace of the waters, and the waters started to churn and froth and slowly, slowly, slowly they sank into its depths.

Only the jewel remained. The waters slowly grew still. A child's hand rose out of the pool and clasped the jewel. The drumbeats pounded louder and louder. The jewel glowed through the clenched fist. Slowly, Chris emerged from the water. He was sitting cross-legged, on a white lotus, and behind him, in a circle of sand, Milt danced and drummed. Chris was haloed with blue light. Chris smiled and his smile outshone the sun. Chris opened his palm, and the jewel was the sun. His other hand held a golden flute, which played of its own accord. His other hand — how many did he have? — held up a marble which contained a map of all the known worlds. His other other hand ... no, two hands ... were playing a spectral piano that hovered in the air behind him. He seemed to have a lot of hands. Another pair was weaving a tapestry, for example, and those reminded me of Penelope's hands. Perhaps all the mythological creatures we had met in this whole adventure had all been aspects of Chris, after all. Mr. E. once harangued me about how if god existed he had to be a solipsist.

Chris's pale blond bangs flapped against one eye in the breeze that played over the lotus. He looked at all of us, including the dead, and said nothing. God, he was beautiful.

"In a few seconds," Theo said to me, "he's going to play the music of unmaking. But if you want, you can make those seconds last for ever...."

And Joshua came to me, his long hair streaming; not a hint of acne; he took me in his arms; he said, "Serena, just say the word, the world doesn't really have to end...."

Twenty
The Last Temptation of Philip Etchison

Oren Karpovsky:

— until this moment, I felt like a man of clay, half-formed, less than human. But now, suddenly, I find myself in the Oval Office, and my finger is hovering over a little red button.

The room is full of men in black suits. Everyone wants to tell me what to do. There's Kissinger, there's Schlesinger, there's MacNamara. I've got the dream team working for me — even dead people — Bill Casey is working the phones at a side desk, even though the top half of his head has been removed, and his carcinoma-riddled brain is showing. And everyone's muttering, trying to avoid my hearing what they're saying, little realizing that the President of the United States of Armorica has ears like a bat. God I'm powerful. This is what I've always striven for. On one wall, dead presidents with electrodes attached to their skulls have been chained up, their heads moving from side to side in approval of all my actions. The decapitated head of Stalin speaks to me from a silver platter.

I look out of the window and see a vista of the whole world, because the White House has been hoisted up on a beanstalk and stands astride the stratosphere. They say I can blow the whole thing up right now.

I am having tea with Marvin the Martian, a little dark creature with a spittoon on his head. He's trying to sell me the rights to his explosive space modulator. I smile, and tell him that there are no arms for hostages deals on the table right now, and hand him the business card of the president of the Acme company, warning him to ignore Wile E. Coyote's lawsuit, even though that infamous consumer advocate is on the cover of Time magazine this week.

"Ja, Mr. President," says Henry Kissinger, fawning over me. "You might as well blow the whole thing away. After all, the universe is going to end in five minutes; why not be the one responsible? Think of the power, the power, the power."

"There's not much real estate left on Planet X," says Marvin the Martian, greedily guzzling his tea, "and they made me check my disintegrator pistol at the gate, so I am unable to blow you away."

A beautiful young girl — one of the congressional pages — is coming in with some document for me to sign. Her name is Serena Somers. She worked on my election campaign once. She smiles at me. So much power! I could make her drop to the ground and give me a blowjob right in front of all these celebrities. Barbra might throw a tantrum, but the press won't even find out. "Mr. President," says the girl, "I'm so proud of you for getting elected. I adore your health plan. Like, you really care about us ordinary people." And I look at her with what passes for compassion in the 90s.

And my finger's still hovering right above the button.

Several of the White House staff look like they're about to cream themselves over this.

At that moment, as I looked out over the earth, misty and blue, I see a child hovering in the window. He's sort of an angel, I suppose. He's playing a golden flute. The melody filters through the window even though there's no sound in space, and one by one all the people here are struck dumb: the military advisors, the dead presidents, the celebs, even the cartoon characters; the only ones who don't seem to be affected are me and Serena.

There is a voice in the music of the flute, and the voice speaks to me, to me alone. And this is what it says: "Oren, Oren, this is what you've always dreamed of; this is the pinnacle of what you can achieve. With your finger hovering perpetually over the button, the cosmos is frozen in the moment before rebirth. You can push the button and be the next great power in the new universe. Or you can walk away."

"And if I do that — ?" I say.

"You will be plain Oren, man of clay," says the angel, his voice emanating from the puff of breath at the head of each pure sweet note that issues from the magic flute.

"I don't know," I tell him. "It's a hard decision...."

Philip Etchison:

And so, at the end of our bridge, we came to a perfect place, a garden. Oh, more than a garden! The source of the river was a waterfall at its center, and we bathed in the sweet clear water and our clothes melted away, and we were as innocent as if we were at the beginning of time.

"Look," I said, "there are signs of a struggle." A smashed scepter lay in the grass. A jewel had been ripped from its mount. There were pieces of clay that seemed to have come from a statue; perhaps the statue had walked once.

"We were late for the final conflict," said Mary, "but not too late to wipe away the last signs of it." Mary scooped up some of the water with the palm of her hand

and sprinkled it over the clay, the scepter ... there were also some pools of blood ... and where the healing water dripped, the things of darkness melted away.

"What place is this?" I said to her.

"I don't know," she said, "but it looks perilously like Eden."

And it was. Because we wandered through it ... having stepped into it, Eden seemed endless. Perhaps it was an infinite garden that was folded back on itself a millionfold through space and time and tied up in a knot for us. There were animals that we did not recognize, and we named them. There were trees and flowers and bushes and ferns, and we named them all; there was a mushroom I named Theo, because Theo means god, because we felt that's what the place needed, a thing called god.

We wandered through the garden. We made love. We ate well, as vegetarians go; it didn't seem right to kill any of the animals, and in any case there was only one pair of every species, and none of them ever seemed to reproduce. Because the world was frozen in its perfection.

I don't know how long we were there for. You don't count the days in a place like this. You laze around and let the warm sun seep into your pores. I rested from my long adventurings. I felt, at last, like the hero returning home from the quest, kicking back in paradise with his woman by his side, not a care in the world; I deserved this; I wanted it to last forever.

But there came a day when we wandered into the apple orchard, and we encountered the angel....

Theo Etchison:

It was the 90s, the time before the mad millennium. A dollar could still by a Coke and a candy bar; I was young, I was puffed up with shiny new epiphanies; I was a truthsayer and I knew everything, and my mother was dying as the station wagon sputtered across the Arizona desert on its way to Mexico and the laetrile clinic.

I'm half asleep in the back, my head propped up on a Stephen King novel, leafing through the book where I've been writing all my dreams, and I'm not really reading it, just catching random words:

In a Chinese restaurant
the recombinant yellow brick road
forest of the night
Caliosper
the darkling wind

and I'm afraid, so fucking afraid, because half the words in here I don't remember putting down, and I think there's other mes out there, other Theo Etchisons driving through other Arizonas, and they're all reaching out to me through this dreambook.

That's when I see the angel, sitting right next to me, a thin little kid in a tattered teeshirt, but like, you can see his wings as they rustle against the worn cotton. The angel doesn't speak exactly; he kind of hums, and I hear voices in my head.

And this is what the voices say to me:

"Theo, Theo, the world sucks, but you can remake it to be any way you want. Your mom doesn't have to be sick, and your brother doesn't have to be an asshole."

"Fucking bullshit," I say, and Dad turns around for a second, but he's not sure if he heard me I guess.

"It's all in the dreambook," says the angel, "just close your eyes, grab the old felt tip out of the backpack, and start editing the past and the future. People do it all the time."

"But, but —" I say.

I do close my eyes. And what do I see? A dragon crossing the face of the sun, her shadow black over a desert landscape. A vampire standing at the prow of a ship. A Chinese restaurant rearing up out of the mist of morning. Fucking Jesus it's weird and I don't know if these are things I've experienced, or if I've dreamed them, or if it's a premonition and I'm going to have to face these things a ways down the road. And I see a mad king, harrowing the ice, dimly, at the eye of a snowstorm.

"Who are all those people?" I ask the angel. "And anyway, who are you?"

The angel only giggles, and then says, "You wouldn't want to know." Then he starts whistling that Tom Lehrer song, one of Dad's favorites:

There once was a man named Oedipus Rex,
You may have heard about his odd complex....

Serena Somers:

He swept me off my feet. And onto the back of the white steed with the gold caparison. Oh, god, I loved him. Why shouldn't I? I had made him out of my own spit and a handful of cookie crumbs. Oh, he was beautiful. His armor glistened in the sunlight. His lance was still adorned with the ripped-up hem of my bridal garment. He took off his helmet and kissed me passionately and rode off with me into the sunset.

When we got to the sunset, though, there was an angel standing there, not smiling, his eyes dead serious, and he said to me, "Serena, Serena, are you sure?"

"What do you mean, am I sure?"

"Is this what you really want?"

"Why wouldn't it be?" I was a princess here, and not a slug. I was dressed all in white. Even my hymen had knit itself back, and a full day of horseback riding hadn't ruptured it either.

"Think, Serena, think," said the angel.

Chris Etchison:

soon I will have to
speak
soon I will have to say it
the word

that will unmake
all I have ever loved
the word
that will lose me
everything

Joshua Etchison:

I am dead. I am floating. It's been an eternity. It's been beautiful. Eternity is a beautiful thing. To lie forever, to rest, to listen to nothing but the slow heartbeat of the universe, to know that nothing matters anymore....

I don't know how much time has passed because there isn't really any time here ... but now I think I'm hearing a voice. Music. Calling me. Telling me I'm not really dead....

Philip Etchison:

... and he was sitting on a tree limb, his legs dangling, dressed in a spangled loincloth, his golden wings fluttering and making a perfumed breeze as we lazed in the afterglow of passion beneath an apple tree.

We looked up. A single apple glistened in the sun. It was golden. I knew what it was right away. I'm not stupid. Just because we had reverted back to the Urzeit didn't make me unaware of mythology. This apple was the querulous quince itself — the fruit of the knowledge of good and evil — it was the thing that would set the world in motion, the catalyst of the Big Bang — the mcguffin, as my Hollywood friends used to call it.

"You don't have to eat the apple," the angel said. Well, he didn't speak exactly. He held a golden flute aloft in one hand, and the flute played of its own accord, and in the interstices of the melody I heard words, or perhaps they were just word-fragments; they were tucked between the phrases of the melody.

"I know," I said.

And Mary looked up and asked the question that needed to be asked: "Why not?"

"The cycle doesn't have to begin all over again," said the angel, "and you have the power to stay here for ever. You don't need the knowledge that's in the apple."

"Why not?" Mary said.

"Because if you were to know it —"

And the angel began to weep.

I said, "Aren't you my son, the one who doesn't speak because what he speaks must be the truth, so he would rather stay silent in front of me because there is a truth that dares not be spoken?"

And the angel wept.

"Is my temptation, then, to stay in Eden, to remain forever ignorant, not to know myself?"

The angel nodded.

"What kind of temptation is that?" I said. I was angry. I felt that my intelligence had been impugned a bit; this didn't agree with Joseph Campbell, not to mention Freud and Jung, at all. Knowledge was to be the temptation, not ignorance.

"But he's right," Mary said, "in a way. We're happy here. We don't have to go anywhere. This world is huge, and we'll never grow tired of exploring it. Can't we just stay here, stay happy?"

I reached up and touched the apple, the

jewel from the source, the

eye of Odin, the

forbidden

fruit

and I felt the jolt of power, and I said softly, "But Mary, how can the world begin without the first little bite of truth?"

And I plucked the apple and the angel began to weep still more, and the thunderclouds gathered and lightning flashed in the distance....

Serena Somers:

... and I said, "You're right; this isn't the real Joshua" — even as Joshua turned his shiny new self away from me — "this is the Joshua that springs only from my fantasies.

And Joshua's weeping as he puts his arms around me and hugs me hard, and he's all metal, sharp and shiny, but underneath the armored skin I can hear the heartbeat of a human being, and —

Theo Etchison:

— but I'm all "Dude," even though he thrusts the felt tip in my hand, "I don't want to be god, I want the story to write itself, doesn't matter how far it goes away from my dreaming," and the angel nods, like a wise old man, even though he's just a kid, and he says to me, softly, "Free will, free will, free will," and in the faintest of all whispers, "You're a good god, Theo, you're the right god for the new world" —

Oren Karpovsky:

— I push the button —

Philip Etchison:

— eat the apple —

Serena Somers:

— rip away the metal cage around my lover's soul —

Theo Etchison:

— throw away the felt tip pen and start ripping up the dream book —

Phil Etchison:

— and Chris, who was once my son, speaks to me for the first time, and says, "Father, father —"

— and I embrace him, knowing that he has just uttered his first lie, and thus unmade the world —

— and Mary says, "You mean, I conceived you in sin?" and Chris sobs, passionately, in her arms and mine; we are not the Holy Family at all, just three lost souls who once forged a brief bond in the midst of the vaster chaos that is the cosmos —

Oren Karpovsky:

— and, as the world blows up in magnificent slow motion from my vantage point in the heavens, the angel —

Theo Etchison:

— begins to dissipate in the flurrying scraps of paper that were once my notebook and —

Serena Somers:

— dissolves into the mist that was once my beloved's breath, and —

Joshua Etchison:

— pulls me out of the womb-warmth of mother darkness into a —

Phil Etchison:

— garden of light that melts into the air and —

Theo Etchison:

— leaves behind a single note of music —

Phil Etchison:

— hanging —

Oren Karpovsky:

— hanging in —

Serena Somers:

— the chill —

Joshua Etchison:

— Arizona night —

Oren Karpovsky:

— Virginia morning —

Theo Etchison:

air.

Phil Etchison:

And so, outside a bizarre and baroque old Chinese restaurant that is already rippling away like a mirage, in the freezing desert night, our family, the four of us, embraces; the memories are already beginning to slip from us; the station wagon is waiting; in a moment, we're going to get in the car, get back on the highway, and head on south to Mexico; it's as though none of this never happened; and yet, yet, yet —

Theo Etchison:

I'm a kid again, puffed up with shiny new epiphanies, but more than a kid, too. Once, in another world that I know is more than a dream; once, I was a —

Serena Somers:

— a goddess, a —

Phil Etchison:

— bard who bridged worlds with mere words, a —

Joshua Etchison:

— hero who faced and conquered Death himself, a —

Oren Karpovsky:

— world-destroyer, a —

Phil Etchison:

— kingmaker, a —

Theo Etchison:

— god.

Phil Etchison:

"I love you," said Mary Etchison, as the moon rose over the bloodstained mountains.

"I love you," I told my two sons, even though they weren't listening to me anymore, because they'd started fighting again. "I love you," I told my wife, "and one day we'll have another child."

Mary said, "How can I? I'm dying."

My two sons stopped fighting. They always do when their mother starts to talk about death. They don't say anything; they just become uncomfortable, withdrawn.

But this time, Theo turned to us and said, "Sometimes death is just a doorway."

And that, I knew, was the truth.

Book Five:

Coda
Fadograph

"a fadograph of a yestern scene"
— *Finnegans Wake*

from a catalogue of an auction to raise money for the Native American Religious Freedom Fund:

On Truth
by
Philip Etchison

Eternal verities....

By now you will all have heard the great news — that I've finally managed to break my writing block, and that, as of last week, I have written over a hundred new poems. Posterity will decide if they're any good, but it means I won't have to give this annual lecture about the nature of truth anymore ... I can actually give poetry readings. But today, let us ask ourselves that imponderable, unanswerable question for the last time: What is truth?

The greatest minds of all time have striven to answer the great question once posed by Pontius Pilate. Well, not all. Jesus Christ, to whom that question was addressed, managed to avoid answering it. And the Lord Buddha managed to skirt the issue by telling us that Truth does not exist.

Let me tell you now — before you cart me away — that the following things are all true. Dragons fly above our skies. Vampires pilot ships of doom through nights of direst gloom. Mad kings rage amid bombastic tempests, and goddesses give birth to planets; and all these things happen every morning of our lives. Lest you think these things are too fantastical, I'll tell you yet more truths. Children comprehend what adults but dimly apprehend. Music cannot lie. My wife is a living incarnation of the triple goddess. I personally have slain a dragon.

I can get away with telling you these things, without being dragged away by the men with the straitjackets, because you believe them to be metaphors. But what is the difference between a simile and a metaphor?

When you use a metaphor, you say that a thing is something else. You say the thing that is not true, elevating it to the status of truth, constraining it into truth, by the transforming magic of poetry.

But I say unto you (do you detect a bit of the messianic madness about me? But you know, they pay me well to occupy this chair of poetry, this utterly useless anachronism in our shiny 90s universe, this lip service tokenism of the human intellect) verily, I say unto you, we stand pereptually at the edges of a cosmic dream. We stand eternally hopeful that the things we call metaphors will one day become concrete, discrete, replete, not to mention paraclete; and if we did not believe (to quote one Samuel R. Delany, semiotician and madman) in the literalization of metaphor, in the ongoing process of becoming one with our metaphoric natures, we would not be entirely human.

I think that now I can proudly stand head to head with George Steiner as far as winning first prize in the impenetrability sweepstakes....

Hey, what I'm really trying to say is:

Who gives a fuck? We know who we are. And sometimes, when we lie awake at night, and it occurs to us that maybe we're really someone else, that outside that familiar bedroom door, closed for the night, a whole different world has suddenly sprung into being, and that world will just as suddenly vanish come morning, when the door flies open once more, and maybe, maybe, maybe, out of the corner of your eye, that glimpse of unreality that you caught could be a little corner of that secret world....

Don't tell me you haven't experienced that. I know you have.

Well, the secret is out now. It's all true. Go home and chew your shrooms and take your peyote enemas, because there

are doors, there are gateways, yes, there
are, I promise you.

— coffee-stained ms. found in a shredder at George Mason University, Fairfax
County, Virginia , along with a prescription for Prozac. In the handwriting of
Philip Etchison, popular lecturer and
poet, and host of the PBS series Reality,
Illusion, and Meta-Reality, which had a
highly successful run before its NEA
grant has canceled by the Helms Com-
mission. It appears that this lecture was
never actually given.

— *offered by an Anonymous Source.*

— *reserve $150*

Twenty-One
Christmas in the White House

Serena Somers:

It was Christmas Eve, and we drove right up to the front gate of the White House, which we were able to do because Oren had congressional license plates, so the guards kind of turned a blind eye.

Nathaniel, the driver, was the soul of discretion. The congressman was getting ready to hit the campaign trail — had a gig in Tucson, and then he was going to bop down to Mexico, to some laetrile clinic, to show his support for alternative medicine. I suppose it was an honor when he asked me to dinner on Christmas Eve, though I kind of suspected there was going to be a bit of the old harrassment thrown in. But what the hell. I'm almost eighteen. I know what I'm doing, and shit, I mean, Congressman Karpovsky, the dream idol of the young, with the MTV spots and the cameo on that Nine Inch Nails video....

And anyways, it was the 90s.

A mad millennium was coming, and we were all getting ready for it in different ways.

So we sat in the limo drinking champagne and watching an outlandish Howard Stern-Rush Limbaugh special — who'd have ever thought it! — and yeah, sharing a joint, I admit it — me and my greatest idol. I had a letter from Joshua Etchison in my purse, you know, postmarked Arizona, and I hadn't opened it in a couple of days. I guess I felt like I was cheating on him. Imagine that! I'd never even gotten past, you know, letting him play with my tits. This was different. Congressman Karpovsky, I mean, you could just feel the power emanating from him, the aura, I mean, he was the bomb.

On television, they said it was midnight.

Christmas had arrived.

The congressman was a little tipsy, I guess. He started telling me the story of his life. He put his arm around me, which was, I guess, okay, and he said, "One day, you know, I might be having Christmas right inside that little ol' mansion. I mean, why not? I've got ambition. Great big fucking ambition."

"I know, congressman," I said.

"Call me Oren."

I giggled.

"I had the weirdest dream," Karpovsky said. "I was in the Oval Office, and I was about to push, you know, The Button, which was weird in itself as you know the Cold War is over. Marvin the Martian was on a state visit, but everyone else was there, too, everyone from Barbra Streisand to the animated corpse of JFK. I was about to destroy the universe. And then, and then —"

"I came into the room, right?"

"Whoa! You a psychic?"

"No, but I have some clue which way this is leading."

"I guess you weren't born yesterday after all, Serena," said the congressman, pouring me another glass of champagne. "So yes, you came into the room, and you were this vision of loveliness, and you see, the world was about to be destroyed, and you were all that stood between — you get the picture."

"You dreamed this, congressman — I mean, Oren? Exactly the way you told me?"

"Well...."

I thought he must have embellished here and there, but, you know, it was a pretty imaginative line of conversation, and not a bad way of turning a young girl's head. But then again, "I've had a dream, too," I told him, "and maybe you won't want to hear it."

"Try me."

"I dreamed it was the eve of the millennium, and you were in the White House, just like you said, and I was there with you ... and you became possessed by a vampire."

"That's kind of morbid," he said. "Look at the Christmas lights." He pointed. A couple of tourists ran by, oohing and aahing, and there was an Indian man sitting on a bench, with a placard in his hand that read End of the World. The congressman held my hand and I didn't rebuff him; probably a mistake.

I went on with my dream. "It was easy for the vampire to get inside your skin," I said, "because you already have this secret desire to be a bloodsucker ... I mean, metaphorically, to drain people, to have total control over them. People like you always have it, even though they may try to deny it."

"You're so serious! And it's Christmas."

"And then, guess what, the vampire finally left you, and what was left behind was a man of clay."

"A golem!" he said. "The first Russian Jew to become president, and you have me turning into a golem — how singularly appropriate!"

Oh, but I laughed. I laughed till the tears started. And then, finally, the moment I'd expected and dreaded happened. The congressman turned to me, and this time he was all predator; his eyes reminded me of another dream I'd had, a dream of a vampire with slate-colored eyes whose father was a mad king and whose sister was a dragon. They were hungry eyes. And he smiled a thin little smile, and said softly, "How about that blowjob now, Serena?"

Our eyes met. For a split second I felt, you know, hunted, I felt how a deer must feel, knowing the rifleman's footfall, the spoor of the cougar, the howl of the wolf. And then I thought of Joshua's letter in my purse, and you know, I decided that it wasn't worth it after all, even though I'd half planned the evening with acquiescence in mind.

"I've got a boyfriend," I said, "and I'm like, saving myself for him. It sounds oldfashioned, but hey, I love him."

For a moment an angel stood between us. I didn't exactly see him. I felt him, I heard a mystical harmony ring in my ears, felt a sudden rush of warmth and love; and you know, Oren was still holding my hand, but the look in his eye was one of regret, of nostalgia; I felt a sorrow in him, and an awful inner turmoil I knew I would never be able to understand.

"Can't blame me for trying," he said at last. "You're a beautiful, beautiful ... oh, shit, jailbait's gonna fuck my career one of these days."

"One of these days," I said, "you might even succeed."

In my dream, he had succeeded after all. And there was something about this dream; god, I think I lived lifetimes in that dream, I think that somehow it was all real.

"What's his name?" asked the congressman.

"Joshua."

"He's very lucky. Where is he now?"

"Arizona ... on his way to Mexico."

"I see ... well, how would you like to meet him there? Give him a cheap thrill, a little surprise? I don't think the PAC is going to miss a couple of extra thousand, one more campaign worker ... you see," he said, "I am not a sore loser."

"Maybe I was wrong about you," I said. "After all —"

"It was just a dream. Is that what you were going to say? Dreams are like the air. But where would we be without them? Or, for that matter, without the air? Let's have a kiss, at least."

And so I kissed him; and in that kiss took back the thousand kisses of my dream, the seven years I'd lived with him, the spats, the petty resentments, even the good times, the laughter, the glamor; I took it all back. The congressman was a good man, in his way; perhaps he'd even make a good president, one of these days.

"You have to have a phone in this car, right?" I said. "I'd like to call Arizona, if you don't mind."

"You're really tempting me to be a sore loser," said Congressman Karpovsky, laughing.

I rooted around in my purse for the letter. It was crumpled, but still unopened. I hoped Josh had had the presence of mind to leave a phone number where I could reach him ... and I hoped Mr. and Mrs. E. would be fast asleep so they wouldn't be able to listen to what we had to say to each other. They always think, because they were in love once, a zillion years ago, that they can understand us. No one can. We can't even understand ourselves.

I reached Josh in a motel on a street named Oracle somewhere in Tucson.

"Merry Christmas," I said. "You'll never believe where I'm calling from."

"I'm dreaming," he said.

"No, you're not," I said. "Dreaming is for dweebs."

"Like my little brother."

"Where is he?"

"Passed out. And he insisted on ordering the Playboy channel...."

"I love you," I said.

"Shit," he said. "You woke me out of the weirdest dream. I dreamed that I was dead...."

"I love you," I said again. Didn't he hear me the first time? But he was doing the teenage macho thing, showing me how tough he was. I probably wouldn't get a response from him today. But tomorrow I'd be in Tucson. I'd be there for him. Everything was going to be all right. I was going to make it all right. Because I'm a woman. Because I'm powerful. Because I've been a goddess, and I know how to tune myself to the heartstrings of the world.

Twenty-Two
In a Laetrile Clinic

Theo Etchison:

— and so we're here, at the laetrile clinic, in a weir-dass Mexican town that's so American it even has a Taco Bell, and me and Josh are sharing a room in an adobe cottage by the sea; the hotel is an extension of the clinic. Today they rushed Mom into some intensive care thing, and Dad has gone with her, and my brother has gone to meet Serena at the border, and I'm all alone, by the sea, looking out at the sunset.

Are the memories really going fade?

Am I really going to get fat and middleaged? I know I see less and less every day. Now it gets so that I have to wait until nightfall and close my eyes, really close them, tell myself I'm not going to wake up unless I see, feel, taste, touch something — the outline of a dark castle, a few flakes of snow, the heat-haze of distant dragon's breath — god, I tell myself, don't let me lose it all, don't tie my feet to this one world, to this one vision of the world.

Did the universe end and start again, and am I the only one who still knows that it happened? And am I too going to forget? Fucking Jesus I hope not; I know I want to be young forever, know I can't be, know there's compensations in being a grownup, wonder if it's fucking going to be worth it; wonder how they can stand it, being so blind, so unfeeling, so empty; and yet, yet, yet, there's got to be more to it than this dark desolation, because out of these grownups comes love; out of them comes the strength that keeps me going; and these things keep coming no matter how much of an asshole I am, no matter how much I rebel, no matter how much I tell the whole world to fuck off.

Today I've started a new dreambook. No, not a dreambook, kind of more of a memory book. I put in a few words here and there so that I can hold on to little pieces of all that happened. Serena came running down from Washington and Joshua's hormones have been thumping ever since, so he's no good for remembering, and anyway, he was dead half the time, or half dead all the time, depending on how you look at it.

These are the words I write down:

vampire
king
dragon
heart
jewel
source
love
death
goddess
life
circle
universe

> forever
> ever

Each word is a key. I wonder how long it will be before they change the locks.

A man is coming up the pathway from the clinic. He is a withered old Indian dude, dressed all in black, like a crow. I know him. When I look at him I hear drums in the back of my mind. It's Milt Stone, I know it is. "Milt," I say, "Milt," thinking, surely he's not going to have forgotten, because he's a shaman, he walks between worlds every morning before breakfast.

"You know my name," he says, and smiles.

It's not, "Hey, how surprising that you know my name," or, "how dare you call me by my name," or anything like that. It's just a statement, him telling me that he knows I know he knows.

"What are you doing here?" I ask him.

"They called me in from the reservation," he says, "because there's a lady here who has visions. She sees a clear, cool spring, and a crow hovering over the water, and the crow's flying in circles around her head, and with each circle that he flies, she becomes more and more herself, more and more whole."

"I see," I say, laughing a little, "that's ... out there all right. One step beyond even laetrile." Because I know that these miracle cures don't do a goddamn thing, I know she's really only coming here to die.

"But you see," says Milt, "I too have been having visions. And in my vision, I am that crow, and the woman is mother to the world."

My heart almost stops beating.

"What is the woman's name?" I ask him.

"You've been old," he says, "but soon you will be young again."

"What the hell is that supposed to mean?"

"You've been lost," he says, "but soon you will find yourself."

"I don't get it."

"Come back to the clinic with me," he says. "They sent me to fetch you."

Mom is sitting up in a highbacked wooden chair, and she's completely wrapped in a Navajo blanket. Dad sits on the bed, and he gazes, uncomprehending, at a bank of monitors and oscilloscopes. It's all very hospital-like, even though this place is kind of bogus as far as hospitals go; they don't even have real doctors here.

Mom's eyes are closed. She's sleeping, I guess. She's breathing evenly, which doesn't happen much anymore; so I know she's not feeling too much pain. Maybe she's all doped up though, and can't feel anything at all. That would be okay. I don't want her to hurt anymore. I think maybe the doctor's going to come in and say, Dudes, that's it, say your last goodbyes now.

Milt walks over to my mother; Dad holds up a hand as if to say no, no, not yet. "We're still waiting for Joshua," he says.

And Joshua shows up, in a rush, with Serena in tow; their hair is all mussed up and I wonder what they've been doing. Josh says, "I don't know why I'm here, we were all parked by the side of the highway and suddenly, I don't know, I get this feeling —"

"Good," Milt says. "Trust your feelings."

Then he crosses the room and places one hand over my mother's brow, and softly he begins to sing to her. His voice is all quavery and whistly, like a bird, and I hear another voice too, a melody from another world; I don't know if it comes from the pinging of the oscilloscopes or the thrum of some life-support unit, but it blends in with Milt's eerie wheezing and it all comes together, like a an ancient car engine cranking itself back to life.

"What's going on?" says Josh. "Who is this Indian dude?"

"Wait," I say. "Wait. In a moment, you'll remember...."

"Oh, wait a minute, yeah," he says. "You're a crow."

Milt begins to spin, very slowly. When he spins clockwise he's a man, and when he spins counterclockwise she's a woman, but the transformations are so complete that you can't even believe they ever occurred. Back and forth and back and forth, and he's still singing, and there's a drumbeat too, but maybe it's my own heart pounding, can't understand why it seems to keep perfect time with the music.

Soon he's whipping around so dizzyingly that I can barely see him at all, and then, for a split second, I see someone else — someone who looks a little bit like my mom, and a little bit like an angel, and a little bit like me — but he's just a flash in the blur, and then he's out of sight, and then Milt is back with us, only this time he's wearing a white labcoat, has on a pair of hornrimmed glasses, and is making furious notes on a clipboard, shaking his head.

"Mrs. Etchison," he announces to all of us, "has inexplicably gone into remission."

My mother opens her eyes.

"I've had," she says, "such a strange, bewildering —"

"Dream," we all finish for her in chorus.

"We went to the very ends of the earth," Dad says, "and you bathed in the redeeming blood of the Holy Grail."

Josh says, "We fought monsters. We defeated wicked wizards and horrible dragons. I don't know where all the treasure went. I guess it kind of vanished into thin air."

"Yeah, Mrs. E.," says Serena, "it was cool I got to go along for the ride. I mean, even though you guys aren't really my family." She looks shyly up at Joshua. "Yet."

Then it's my turn. I think we're taking turns. I say, "We didn't dream any of it. It was all true."

And that is the last statement I shall ever make as truthsayer; it's the last pure shining truth that will ever fall from my lips; because from now on I'm going to be just plain Theo, human being, loving son and brother. I won't know what it's like to see the one true stream that's clearer than all the others. The river will be as muddy for me as it is for everyone else, and you know what? I don't care. Maybe we did redeem the universe, but for me it's not about that. It's about getting my family back. It's about starting again. It's about me and Mom and Dad and Joshua and maybe, a little bit, Serena, because I can tell she's going to be one of us. Fucking Jesus, I can barely believe it worked, and I can barely grasp how we moved heaven and earth, literally, to make it happen, but it did work, and we're home now, home again at last.

Milt, who has become Mom's doctor in this new version of reality, explains, patiently, how remission doesn't necessarily mean a complete cure, but how one might lead a productive, healthy life for months or even years without any sign of the cancer returning; he tells us to savor each moment, to make each little thing count, because nothing is certain. It's a speech that doctors have been making since time began, and Milt's totally good at it; he sounds so reassuring, so soothing, it doesn't really matter what he says because the bottom line is that we've all come back from the edge of the abyss.

So, like that night, we celebrate our asses off, because it's coming up to New Year's anyway and we never really did Christmas because we were so full of pain. Dad gets so drunk we have to put him to bed in the hotel with a trashcan beside his pillow in case he pukes. I guess that's good; I never saw him be that way before.

Serena tells stories about Congressman Karpovsky — how in his dreams he hobnobs with Marvin the Martian and Wile E. Coyote. She makes us laugh till we practically piss our pants.

Then she decides to give Joshua a tour of Karpovsky headquarters, on the other side of the border, and I'm left alone with my mother, sharing a marshmallow and a cup of hot chocolate, watching someone else's fireworks beyond the cliffs in the clear Mexican night.

"Mom," I say softly to her — and I haven't hugged her yet, haven't even touched her yet, because, you know, of the thing we did, back in the other universe, and I'm still scared to be close to her — "Mom," I say, "how much do you remember?"

Her eyes sparkle. Maybe it's the reflection of fireworks. Or starlight. Or the crescent moon. She says, "I remember as much as you want me to remember."

And she kisses me, gently, on the cheek, and I know that she knows everything. "But," she cautions me, "we'll never speak of it. Or we'll end up in that horrible old asylum together, you and me, having cold pointy thermometers shoved up our butts by nasty old pschyoanalysts."

"They really did that to you there?" I say.

"As I recall," she says.

"You really do recall," I say.

"I love you, Theo," she says to me, "but don't get fresh. Remember, we are human now, and I am your mother."

And so, after I kiss her goodnight and she goes in to my drunken snoring father, I go to my room and turn on the television; I debate whether I should order up Playboy; Josh, I know, won't come back tonight.

I get a Coke and a candy bar from the in-room refrigerator. I munch the candy bar and sip the Coke and watch the TV until the station goes off the air and then I watch the snow for a long long time ... once in a while, I think I see the angel hovering above the million flecks of white and gray ... I think I see the mad king raging and the jewel glittering ... I think I see my son, the once, the future, the never-present ... the truthsayer who might have been.

I close my eyes, and —

Strang! Thorn! Katastrofa!

A whole universe died and was reborn so my family could start to heal itself. What a strange and amazing truth. What a thing for a young boy like me to know. How long will I know it for, how long, how long? How long until I just come to think that I have too much imagination, too much, too much? Oh, fucking Jesus, it's a huge burden to bear, this truth, and maybe I should just slough it off, emerge a born-again innocent, a shiny new dragon from the river of time ... maybe I should let go ... but not just yet, please, not just yet ... I still want to stand in the twilight edges of the dream country ... I still want to look back at the burning citadel of my childhood.

Katastrofa! Ash!

There is a cure for what ravaged my mom's body, and for the sickness that still gnaws away at the world's dark heart.

Chris

(oh my heart aches the most for him)

Yes. We have found the cure. We harrowed hell for it. We racked the four corners of the universe. God we fought hard, and now we hold it in our hands. But we can't quite identify it.

We're not sure what it's called, this magic herb that can seal up our wounds, renew the world, turn back the clock to rub out our mistakes.

Maybe the cure is laetrile.

Or maybe it's love.

Bangkok, Los Angeles, 1994-6

About the Author

Once referred to by the *International Herald Tribune* as "the most well-known expatriate Thai in the world," Somtow Sucharitkul is no longer an expatriate, since he has returned to Thailand after five decades of wandering the world. He is best known as an award-winning novelist and a composer of operas.

Born in Bangkok, Somtow grew up in Europe and was educated at Eton and Cambridge. His first career was in music and in the 1970s he acquired a reputation as a revolutionary composer, the first to combine Thai and Western instruments in radical new sonorities. Conditions in the arts in the region at the time proved so traumatic for the young composer that he suffered a major burnout, emigrated to the United States, and re-invented himself as a novelist.

His earliest novels were in the science fiction field but he soon began to cross into other genres. In his 1984 novel Vampire Junction, he injected a new literary inventiveness into the horror genre, in the words of Robert Bloch, author of Psycho, "skillfully combining the styles of Stephen King, William Burroughs, and the author of the Revelation to John." Vampire Junction was voted one of the forty all-time greatest horror books by the Horror Writers' Association, joining established classics like Frankenstein and Dracula.

In the 1990s Somtow became increasingly identified as a uniquely Asian writer with novels such as the semi-autobiographical Jasmine Nights. He won the

World Fantasy Award, the highest accolade given in the world of fantastic literature, for his novella The Bird Catcher. His fifty-three books have sold about two million copies world-wide.

After becoming a Buddhist monk for a period in 2001, Somtow decided to refocus his attention on the country of his birth, founding Bangkok's first international opera company and returning to music, where he again reinvented himself, this time as a neo-Asian neo-Romantic composer. The Norwegian government commissioned his song cycle Songs Before Dawn for the 100th Anniversary of the Nobel Peace Prize, and he composed at the request of the government of Thailand his Requiem: In Memoriam 9/11 which was dedicated to the victims of the 9/11 tragedy.

According to London's Opera magazine, "in just five years, Somtow has made Bangkok into the operatic hub of Southeast Asia." His operas on Thai themes, Madana, Mae Naak, and Ayodhya, have been well received by international critics. His most recent opera, The Silent Prince, was premiered in 2010 in Houston, and a fifth opera, Dan no Ura, will premiere in Thailand in the 2013 season. His sixth opera, Midsummer, will premiere in the UK in 2014.

He is increasingly in demand as a conductor specializing in opera and in the late-romantic composers like Mahler. His repertoire runs the entire gamut from Monteverdi to Wagner. His work has been especially lauded for its stylistic authenticity and its lyricism. The orchestra he founded in Bangkok, the Siam Philharmonic, is mounting the first complete Mahler cycle in the region.

He is the first recipient of Thailand's "Distinguished Silpathorn" award, given for an artist who has made and continues to make a major impact on the region's culture, from Thailand's Ministry of Culture.